WEDDING *war*

Romance in Rehoboth
5

K.L. MONTGOMERY

great to
meet you!

KL Montgomery

Mountains Wanted Publishing
P.O. Box 1014
Georgetown, DE 19947
www.mountainswanted.com

ISBN: 978-1-949394-91-7

Cover Design by Teresa Conner of Wolfsparrow
Publishing

To my dad, who taught me everything I know about running a business.

CONTENTS

The Ultimate Wedding Playlist

Shut up and Dance - Walk the Moon

The Way You Look Tonight - Frank Sinatra

I Wanna Dance with Somebody - Whitney Houston

All of Me - John Legend

Unchained Melody - Righteous Brothers

Wonderful Tonight - Eric Clapton

At Last - Etta James

What a Wonderful World - Louis Armstrong

Your Song - Elton John

Marry You - Bruno Mars

Everything I Do - Bryan Adams

A Thousand Years - Christina Perri

ONE

Hannah

In Rehoboth Beach, no one makes a Hatfield and McCoy's reference to describe two feuding families. They say, "It's like the Fridays and the Robinsons" instead.

The problem with being the youngest member of the Robinson clan is that I seem to be the only one who doesn't know why we are feuding with the Fridays. This has been going on almost my entire life, and I have no idea what it's all about. Every time I bring it up to my mother or my grandmother, they both shoot daggers out of their eyes. Not even my daddy will tell me, and his lips are kind of loose after he's had a couple of gin and tonics.

I hadn't actually thought about the Fridays for a

long time until I arrived back in Rehoboth Beach with my freshly minted Masters in Business Administration to find my parents in a tizzy about something. I hadn't even unloaded my car that was weighted down with the contents of my apartment in Durham when I heard my daddy shout to my mama, "Liz, come read this paper! Then you better get us both a drink. Make 'em doubles!"

I rush into the living room where I find my father in his favorite leather recliner, his legs extended and the *Cape Gazette* spread across his body. He's a short man, so it's basically only his sock-covered feet poking out one end and his shiny bald head poking out the top. My mother dashes in right behind me, only she's not carrying anything, least of all drinks. She's obviously been doing dishes, though, because she wipes her hands on her apron.

Yes, she wears an apron. She hasn't gotten the message that we're in a whole new millennium now and there are dishwashers and other modern conveniences. She washes the dishes by hand. But that's another story. She is seriously old school. Both my parents are.

"This is going to be the end of us!" my father barks as he looks up to meet her worried eyes. "This is going to be the end of Delmarva Beach Brides!"

"What?" My mother's voice is extra-shrieky today. "What are you talking about, Morris?"

He lays the paper down in his lap and points a stubby finger at a bright, full-color ad that takes up the entire page. "Über Brides is coming to Rehoboth Beach."

My mother instantly gasps and clutches at her neck as if she's having trouble getting air into her lungs. From the looks on their faces, you would think the paper just announced we were about to undergo an invasion of alien body-snatchers.

"What's Über Brides?" I think it's a valid question. I mean, if they're both going to suffer massive heart attacks, I kind of need to know what to tell the paramedics when they arrive.

They both turn and look at me with a definite glare in their eyes. It looks an awful lot like parental disappointment, which is something I've spent my entire life trying to avoid. I was banking on that brand spankin' new MBA being a source of pride for a good while, but apparently it wore off fast!

"Über Brides is only the biggest wedding superstore in the country," my father says in that patronizing tone he's been using to explain things to me since I was a little girl. "Didn't you learn anything in your graduate classes about business? About competition? About market share?" He shakes his head with continued, maybe even *refreshed* disappointment. "I can't believe you spent all that time and effort to get a master's degree and you don't even know the biggest company in our industry!"

Ugh. Okay, Daddy, thanks for making me feel like a total idiot.

"Oh, *that* Über Brides." I give him a sheepish smile. "They're opening a store in Rehoboth Beach?"

He nods. "Yes, and somehow they're doing it next week. I don't know how the hell a—"

"Morris, language!" my mother snaps. She throws her hands to her apron-covered hips in exasperation.

"I guess when you're a billion-dollar company you can hire a hundred people to get your store set up lightning fast." He shakes his head again. "I wonder what ol' Friday is going to think about this."

My eyebrows shoot up. "Why? Who cares what he

3

thinks?" If I play along, maybe he will spill the beans on what this longstanding feud is about.

"It might even hit them harder than it does us!" my father continues as if I didn't just ask a question.

"It doesn't matter," my mother jumps in on the action. She lays a hand on my dad's shoulder and squeezes. "We've weathered recessions and internet stores and Lord knows what else in the past thirty years. I'm sure we'll be able to weather this storm too."

"So what are you going to do?" I glance up at my parents, who still have their eyes locked lovingly on each other. These two are like a Hallmark movie that never ends, so in love with each other that sometimes I consider jumping up and down to get their attention and remind them I'm still here. When we were younger, my brothers and sister and I were always telling them to "get a room!"

"Well, you're the one who just got your MBA," my mother states, finally shifting her gaze to me. "Why don't you put that degree to good use and come up with a plan?"

"Excellent idea, my love!" My dad reaches up to pat her hand. "Why don't you come up with a proposal and present it to the board on Friday?"

Proposal? Board? The Board is made up of two of my brothers, my sister and her husband, my parents, and my grandmother. That's the Board.

"Friday? But it's already Monday night, and I literally just drove six hours!" I protest.

Mama closes the distance between us in two long strides before reaching up to pat my springy blonde-tipped curls. "It's a dog-eat-dog world out there, Hannah. That's just how business works. You better get used to it!"

Later that night when I'm unpacking everything I brought home from my grad school apartment, part of my brain is busy developing a marketing plan to demolish our new competition. Another part is dedicated to thinking about Jason Friday.

The Fridays have four children in their family who approximately align in age with the five children in my family. Like me, Jason is the youngest, and we were in the same grade in school. Wondering what he looks like now, I pull out a box from my closet where I store memorabilia from elementary and high school. I should really be putting stuff away, not dragging it out, but I don't seem able to stop myself from digging through the ancient, dilapidated box for my senior yearbook. It's hard to believe it's been ten years since I graduated. I spent four years in undergrad, four years working in New York City, and then two more years in grad school. Ten long years...and I'm finally ready to start officially adulting.

I happen to flip right to our class's photos, probably because I've scoured row after row of my classmates' pictures so many times before. I turn a few pages, and there he is: Jason Taylor Friday. He was tall and lanky in high school, a basketball player. In the photo he's wearing a tux, just like all the boys in our class. He has a little smirk etched on his face like he isn't quite taking the whole senior picture thing seriously. He was cute, funny, and popular, but I kept my distance from him.

If I brought him up at home, my mother would shake her head and say, "Those Fridays. They're all bad news. You stay away from that boy, Hannah!"

"But why?" I always asked, just wanting to understand what could be so bad about him. Our peers clearly liked him. He'd never done anything mean to me, though he'd never really spoken to me either.

"The whole family is bad news. Just trust me on that!" my father would murmur his agreement, as would my grandmother if she was around. And then someone would promptly change the subject.

I run my finger over the glossy yearbook page, wondering if Jason is still in the area. If he works for his family business like I'm about to do. I wonder if he is also trying to figure out how to keep Über Brides from destroying everything his family has worked so hard to build.

My drive home from work is not a pleasant one, and for once, it's not because of traffic, though that too is out of control. It's because when I passed the property where they just built yet another Royal Farms and put in that new fancy-schmancy organic grocery store, I saw a new sign at the abandoned department store next door—a huge, colorful banner that reads *Über Brides*.

I shake my head at first, wondering if I'm just hallucinating. Maybe it's a bad trip from that horrible gas station burrito I scarfed down at lunch (cut me some slack, I only had a few minutes to eat). I squeeze my eyes tightly shut, then pop them open hoping to see something—anything—but Über Brides.

Fucking Über Brides.

It's literally the worst company on the planet. It's the wedding equivalent of that online retail giant named after a race of female warriors. They do bridal gowns, bridesmaids, tuxes, cakes, flowers, photography, invitations, reception décor, catering. They even have an entire aisle of crap you can buy for your wedding guests to throw at you when you leave the reception: fake rice, confetti, birdseed, glitter, bubbles, sparklers, bottle rockets. Okay, not bottle rockets. I made that one up.

My parents are going to shit a brick when I get home and tell them of this development. The huge banner reads "Coming Soon!" in bold fuchsia letters. My father has already been having health issues. This isn't going to bode well for him at all.

Maybe I shouldn't tell him. My brother and I have pretty much been running the show since my father's health began to deteriorate a few months ago. Maybe Russ and I should come up with a plan to keep our parents from ever finding out.

Instead of driving home, I end up going straight to my brother Russ's house. His wife Jen answers the door with my three-month-old niece strapped to her in some sort of sling contraption. "What's wrong? Weren't you guys just at work together?"

Apparently she can already see the panic on my face. *Awesome.* "Uh, sorry, Jen. Is Russ home? Am I interrupting dinner?"

"You know, if you wanted to come over for dinner, you could have just asked," Russ says, appearing behind his wife seconds later with a big goofy grin making his dimples pop out.

"I guess I can go make another salad." Jen's face twists with a little annoyance, but she shrugs as she shoots my brother a glare and heads back into the kitchen, the baby still clinging to her like a tiny orangutan. I should definitely *not* use that analogy out loud, even though the baby does have bright, carrot-orange hair and chubby cheeks. It would probably not go over too well with my sister-in-law.

"What's wrong?" Russ narrows his dark eyes at me as he scans my face. He too can sense something is up.

"We need to talk, man." I huff out a breath as I step over the threshold into his house, which smells a little like his daughter just had a dirty diaper changed. *Yuck.* He leads me into the living room where I sink into the deep sofa cushions, pulling out a baby toy that somehow ended up under my butt. It's some sort of cat that squeaks when you press its stomach. Of course, now I can't seem to stop making it squeak. Why are baby toys so entertaining?

My brother shoots me a glare until I put the toy down. "What's going on? We were just at work, and things were fine." Russ sits down on the loveseat opposite of me and leans forward with his elbows on his knees. His unruly curls are bouncing on top of his head with each breath he takes.

"I know we just got the books straightened out and

got back in the black—and we've been having a strong second quarter so far, but—"

"Just spit it out, dude!" he chides me. "You're freaking me out! Dad's okay, right?"

"Yeah, yeah, Dad's fine." I swallow the lump that's been growing in my throat and blurt it out: "Über Brides is setting up shop on Route 1...in the old VonMart."

This is how I know it's bad: my older brother, who is never at a loss for words, doesn't say a damn thing. He's completely speechless.

"Say something, Russ," I prod him. "Come on."

He shakes his head and looks up at me with a deep crease between his brows. He looks just like our dad when he makes that face. "This is not good."

"I know." I stand up and walk toward the window. My fingers slide through my dark hair as I grip my scalp, like I'm trying to stimulate my brain into coming up with a way to keep this from happening. Like I can stop the powerful, sweeping force that is Über Brides.

"I've been following this company's story for a long time," Russ says, standing up as well. "They started in some guy's basement back in the 80s. Mail order at first. Then he opened his first brick and mortar store in 1993. Every city they've infiltrated has killed the small, independent businesses there. Every single one: Orlando, Houston, Albuquerque, Minneapolis, Annapolis, Indianapolis—all the 'apolises!"

I blow out another breath as Jen pokes her head into the living room, sans baby. "I just fed Jemma. If we want to eat, now is the time."

"I don't know if I can," Russ says, clutching his stomach.

I walk over and sling my arm around him. My

brother hates it that I'm younger but was blessed with about three more inches of height than he was. "We'll figure something out. We have to."

We both walk to the dining room where I can smell homemade lasagna. My bro did good by marrying a nice Italian girl. Russ may not be hungry, but fortunately I have learned to compartmentalize my appetite so that business stuff never affects it. I plan on leaving here quite stuffed and with horrible garlic breath.

"Well, what are all the other mom and pop stores in town going to do?" Russ asks as he fills his plate with salad, bread and hot, steaming lasagna.

I really wish we weren't so embroiled in this horrible Über Brides controversy so we could just have a moment of silence for the masterpiece that is Jen's lasagna. I lift my hand, silently begging him to give me a second to appreciate this delicious aroma and mouthwatering mozzarella with all the reverence it deserves.

"Like the florist on the corner? Or the bakery down on the avenue?" he continues, completely ignoring me. "What about the Robinsons?"

My eyes automatically shoot over to him like they're missile-guided. I'm so shocked he said the R Word, I'm rendered speechless, which he'll tell you is also a pretty rare phenomenon for the younger Friday brother.

"This affects all of us." Russ glances over to his wife as she bounces their daughter on her knee.

"Are you guys going to tell me what's going on?" She hasn't even touched her lasagna. Of course, I don't know how she's supposed to eat with a baby on her lap. Moms must have superhero powers or something.

"Über Brides is setting up shop in Rehoboth Beach," I fill her in. Her face instantly pales, that beautiful olive complexion turning stark white in a single heartbeat. "Don't worry, we'll be okay. Friday's Formalwear has been around for decades. We're not going anywhere."

Russ fires a look that hits me square in the jaw. I've never seen my brother look so panicked before, not even when Jen's pregnancy test came back positive. Well, I'm not going to let my parents or my brother and his family down. I'm going to keep the family business intact—if it's the last thing I do.

"Who are the Robinsons?" She lifts the baby up in the air and puts her nose directly to her butt. "Oh god, not again, Jemma!"

We both just stare at her to see if she is going to attend to her daughter's dirty diaper or press the issue about our family's most epic rival. She swivels her head toward her husband and gives him a look. Now, I'm not married, and I've had very few serious girlfriends, but every man on the planet knows what that look means. It means *spill it and spill it now*.

"They're a rival formalwear shop," Russ explains. "Our parents and the owners of Delmarva Beach Brides had a falling out like twenty years ago, and we still pretty much hate each other. We weren't allowed to associate with any of their kids when we were in school."

"Wow." That is her one-word response. Then Jemma begins to cry, and that is the end of that. Jen excuses herself from the table, shooting her husband another look. If I'm not mistaken, it is the message that he is responsible for doing the dishes.

It's easy to pretend like Armageddon isn't breathing down on us when the shop is so busy. It's the end of prom season and the cusp of wedding season, and we are as busy as busy can be. There is one more local prom this weekend, and most of the customers coming in are awkward, pimple-faced teen boys, alone or with their girlfriends or mothers, to pick up their rentals. Ah, I remember that age. I was crowned Senior Prom King. It's hard to believe it's already been ten years. Those were the days.

The phone rings from the counter, but I'm clear across the store helping a groom choose a vest and bowtie for his special day. After four rings it becomes apparent that my assistant isn't going to answer it, so I politely excuse myself and leap over a display of dress shoes to get to the phone before it stops ringing. It's not like it has a cord. It's a cell phone, but can I remember to carry it around with me? No, apparently I cannot.

"Friday's Formalwear," I manage, only slightly out of breath.

There's a pause at first, and I think it's going to be one of those super-annoying telemarketers when a smooth voice finally asks, "Jason?"

"Yes, ma'am. How can I help you?"

I hear the sound of a throat clearing and then, "Hi, Jason, this is Hannah Robinson."

I try to swallow the gasp that threatens to escape. *Hannah Robinson? Now there's another blast from the past.* Naturally, I didn't know her well, being verboten and all, but I don't have any trouble remembering her doe brown eyes and bright white smile. She was a good student, was involved in drama club and choir, and had a ton of friends. Okay, if I'm honest, I also have to admit to admiring her curvy figure and the way she filled out a pair of jeans.

"Hey, Hannah. What can I do for you?" *Won't hurt to be polite, right?* I don't know why, but just the sound of her voice is making my heart pound against my ribcage.

"Well, I'm sure you're surprised to hear from someone in my family, but I'm assuming you've seen that Über Brides is about to open up a shop here?" came that silky voice again.

"Uh, yeah, I haven't been living under a rock. Why?" I glance over to where the groom I was working with is milling around. I guess he has made his selection, so I better wrap this up fast. *Where the hell did Tiffany go?*

She wastes no time giving it to me straight: "I'm sure you're as concerned about it as my family is, and I wondered if you'd like to get together to, you know, strategize?"

I wave to the groom and lift a finger up to let him know I'll be just one moment. His fiancée looks rather perturbed by the delay.

"Oh, you know, I'm sure we'll manage. I have a customer waiting on me." *See?* I don't need to strategize. I've got this business thing completely mastered.

Her voice turns sickeningly sweet. "I did some research, and within a year of Über Brides opening in a city, eight percent of their competition closes up shop."

"Wow, okay," I stumble out, wondering how she

did that kind of research. Maybe she's making it up? The Robinsons have always been prone to exaggeration. "I'm sorry, but I've really got to go. We have lots of customers today."

"Meet me today at 4 PM at that coffee shop on the corner of Route 1 and Rehoboth Avenue." It doesn't sound like a question. It's more like a demand. I had no idea she was so bossy! "If you care about your family and your business, you'll be there. I've got a few ideas."

I sigh. I can't let anyone know I'm going to be seen in public with a Robinson. That really would make my dad's heart explode. "Can we go somewhere else? Somewhere less...conspicuous?"

"Don't want to be seen in public with me?" she fires back. "Wow, you really are as big of a jerk as I imagined you'd be." She lets out a long, drawn out puff of air.

I doubt any of my family or friends would be in the park at four in the afternoon. "Fine, meet me at Cape Henlopen—by the observation tower across from Fort Miles."

She blows out yet another exasperated breath. She seems to have an endless supply of them. "See you then."

I don't know what I was more nervous about: saving the family business or seeing Hannah Robinson again for the first time since high school graduation?

TWO

Hannah

It's such a warm spring afternoon that I toss off my pink cardigan, leaving it in the passenger seat of my car. The sun beating down on my tawny brown shoulders feels amazing as I adjust my sunglasses and head over to a bench at the bottom of the tower. These observation towers dot this section of coastal Delaware, left over from World War II when they were used to scout for approaching German boats in the Atlantic. I sure hope Jason doesn't want me to climb the tower in these shoes. I glance down at my platform wedge espadrilles, pink to match my cardigan. I'll never make it up all those steps in these darn things!

There aren't as many people around as I anticipated on such a nice day. A few families with children are scattered about, and I hear the kids' laughter echoing down the tower and out into the May sunshine. A herd of serious power walkers is heading toward the entrance of Fort Miles, and a cute middle-aged couple is setting up a picnic at a wooden table several yards away. I don't see anyone I know. Heaven forbid someone catches me fraternizing with the enemy!

A newer model shiny black pick-up pulls up in the lot across from the tower, and I watch Jason Friday curl out of the cab and press his key fob to lock it up. He's wearing khaki pants and a hunter green polo shirt— nothing too fancy. As he approaches me, his eyes darting left and right to survey our surroundings, the Friday's Formalwear logo with its black bowtie comes into view on his shirt.

I give him a coy wave when his eyes meet mine. I've never forgotten their unusual color. They look like the Atlantic on a stormy day, a steel grayish-blue. His dark hair still looks as thick as it did in high school, and it's still cut in the same boyish style, a little long on top and spiked up a bit at the front. He's already sporting a golden tan, and a five o'clock shadow is beginning to crop up along his sharp-cut jawline. He's filled out a bit since I knew him; the bands of his polo shirt are tight around his sculpted biceps, proving he's spent more than a little time in the gym since graduation. His khaki pants are slung low on his hips with a brown leather belt holding them up.

I didn't know what to expect, but the tall, lanky basketball player I knew in high school has grown into quite a piece of man candy. A sudden burst of heat rockets through my body upon this realization, and I'm glad I left my sweater in the car. Adding more fuel to the fire, his entire face lights up when his eyes rake up and down my body.

"Well, if it isn't Hannah Robinson," are the first

words out of his mouth. "Long time no see!" He extends his hand to shake.

I fight the urge to launch myself forward with my arms spread wide for a welcoming hug. I come from a big family of huggers. But then I remember everyone's warnings about the Fridays being downright evil. I think my grandmama even said they are "heathens," which is code for *they don't go to church.*

I settle on the handshake, not expecting his hand to be so warm, his grip so firm. "Hi, Jason. Thanks for coming."

His brows lift as he withdraws his hand from mine and levels his gaze on me. "So, do we need to go have our meeting up there so we can avoid starting any rumors about a truce between our families?" He points up to the top of the tower.

A scoff hurtles out of my mouth. I mentioned the whole shoe incompatibility thing, right? "You're the one who didn't want to meet at the coffee shop."

"Oh, you know how the coffee shop is," he argued. "It's like the headquarters of the Rehoboth Gossip League. There's probably what—two degrees of separation between any of our mutual acquaintances? And like a seventy percent chance one of them would be in the coffee shop this afternoon? I don't see how that would end well."

I'm not able to suppress my eye roll. I have a feeling it won't be the last eye roll of the afternoon. "So this bench, then? Is that reasonably safe, or they've recently restored the underground bunker over there in Fort Miles."

He chuckles. "Actually, there is a good spot over there at the fort. Come on." He reaches his hand out to me like I'm supposed to take it. And like an idiot, I do.

He's just one of those naturally gregarious people you don't question. He can immediately put folks at ease. The girls were always clamoring for his attention when we were growing up; guess that's how he got to be prom king back in the day. Of course, it didn't hurt that he was wearing the nicest tux money could buy thanks to his family's business.

My hand in his feels strangely comfortable. I can't even remember the last time I held hands with a guy. I was so focused on getting my MBA the last two years, I didn't have time to date. I did have a boyfriend most of the time I lived in Manhattan, but he wanted a lady who was content to get married, pop out kids and stay home to raise them. He seemed a bit intimidated by a woman who wanted to rule the world. *Or at least the bridal gown industry.*

When Jason squeezes my hand in his, I feel a bolt of lightning shoot up my spine. It's so disarming, I nearly trip over my own two feet, but somehow I manage to catch myself just prior to making a devastating faceplant on the sandy soil.

"Watch out, there's a root there," he offers, glancing back at me as he pulls me along toward the Fort Miles sign.

I haven't actually been to Fort Miles since we visited on a high school field trip with my US History class. Jason tugs me toward a huge gun mounted on a circular concrete pad. I can't believe we're going to sit on a bench and stare at such a massive weapon during our whole conversation, but here we are. I spread out my floral skirt around me, and Jason settles in on the wooden bench.

"It's actually pretty appropriate that we're here, you know," he says as he stares off toward the Atlantic, which is sending its rolling foam-crested waves to crash upon the dune-lined beach.

"It is?" My eyebrows arch as I study his face, which is suddenly very serious.

"Yeah. Über Brides is the enemy. 'Über' is German. The Nazis were German. Fort Miles was constructed by the good guys—us—to fight the Nazis. Duh!" He smirks at me, seemingly waiting for me to shower him with praise for his oh-so-profound analogy.

Instead, I offer up that second eye roll I predicted earlier. "Yeah, good one. So...what are we going to do? What's the game plan?"

He laughs at me. I think he's perfectly encapsulating what my grad school roommate described as a "tool."

"'Game plan,' huh? You really like to cut to the chase, don't you?"

"Look," I retort, wanting to grab him by the collar of his green polo shirt and jerk that stupid smirk right off his face, but I somehow manage to control myself. "My family's business is the most important thing in my life right now. It's my future. I just finished up my MBA with the understanding that someday I'll be taking over when my dad retires. And I had to prove I was the right person for the job even though I'm the youngest of my siblings. I'm the only one who went to college and grad school and actually built their entire education around being at the helm someday. This is my future—and I don't want some horrible, nefarious megacorporation coming in here and destroying it!"

"Okay, okay!" He shakes his head like he's trying to brush off my frustration. "They're opening next week. I've been thinking about this ever since I saw their sign a couple days ago, and I wondered if maybe we could infiltrate the enemy camp...you know, send in a spy?"

Clearly he is still stuck on this WWII thing. I hate to admit this, but it is kind of like a war. Über Brides marched into coastal Delaware, setting up camp in *our* territory, and they're going to try to blow us up—maybe not directly, or even on purpose, but that's the effect of their generic, mass-market products and bargain basement prices.

"So, basically, you think we need to go on the offensive, not the defensive." I'm trying to wrap my head around this war metaphor now. I need to think like a General, not just a businesswoman.

"Yes, that's exactly what I'm saying." He nods and stands up. The way he's positioned himself, his body is bisecting the massive weapon in front of us so the base of the gun is extending from his right side and the barrel from his left. With the late afternoon sun silhouetting him, it looks like it's going right through him.

"Just beefing up our own advertising and running sales isn't going to work," he determines. "We need to get on the inside. Cut off the head of the beast. There has to be a way—"

I'm more of a details person than the creative type. I'm racking my brain, but nothing is happening. Unfortunately, when he turns toward the sound of a gull crying as it flaps toward the ocean, I get distracted by the eye candy that is his backside. *Damn, he has a fine derriere!* And I don't curse. *It's so fine that he made me curse, the jerk!*

"I got it!" He whips around. "Their banner says they're hiring. What if you went and applied for a job?"

My eyes widen. "Why me? I have an MBA. Do you think they'd actually hire me for an entry-level position?"

"That's the beauty of it," he explains, reaching out to me, and once again I don't hesitate to take his hand. He pulls me up and twirls me around, the wind catching the skirt of my dress. I'm pretty sure I just flashed him my own backside and my lacy lavender panties as well. He doesn't seem to notice, thank goodness.

"You go in there all gung-ho—tell them you just got your masters and your dream is to work in the wedding industry. You may get a low-paying job, but you'll be so capable, they'll trust you with a lot of stuff. And you'll be able to sneak around and get insider info, you know?"

I purse my lips, skeptical about whether or not his idea could work. "You make it sound too easy—"

His eyes light up, a flash of blue infiltrating the stormy gray. "You're charming, well-spoken, obviously a people-person. You can do this, Hannah."

I wish I wasn't so flattered by his compliments, but the way he's looking at me with an undeniably gorgeous smile on his full flips, it's exceedingly hard to ignore how freaking attractive he is. I had no idea when I called him up to strategize and potentially unite against our common enemy that he'd turn out to be so handsome.

"So why do our families hate each other, anyway?" I question, trying to break free of his enrapturing spell.

He scoffs then runs his fingers through his dark hair. "I don't really know the whole story—but it's in the past. Maybe it's time we bury the hatchet and work together to defeat our common enemy."

"So we're like the US and Russia, then?" *See?* He's not the only one who can make historical references.

"You were always a nerd in high school, weren't you?" He laughs at me, but in a way that I can tell it's a compliment and not an insult.

"Proud nerd," I correct him. "And I still am."

"I'm glad you called me," he changes the subject. "I really think we can do this. I believe we can drive Über Brides out of business if we put our heads together. And even if we don't drive them out of Rehoboth Beach, at least we can figure out a way to save our family businesses."

"Perhaps." I like his positive attitude, but I also think he's underestimating the threat. I don't know if we really have the power to go up against a giant like Über Brides. They've been crushing their competition for years. And we're just two twenty-something third-generation mom and pop shop employees. "But we can't tell our families what is going on. Not yet, anyway."

He nods. "I agree. My dad is in poor health, and I'm keeping the whole Über Brides thing from him as long as I possibly can."

"I'm sorry to hear that." I notice his eyes have turned back to the stormy gray again, like a hurricane is moving in. Another gull squawks as it swoops down then immediately launches itself back into the sky. The breeze picks up, making goosebumps prick my bronze skin as the sun slips behind a cloud.

"You know, my family warned me never to have any contact with you," he shares, his gaze once again piercing into me.

"As did mine. But I still don't understand why. No one would ever tell me the whole story." I can't disguise the disappointment in my voice. Lord knows I've asked enough times. I don't know why we need all the secrecy.

"Me either." He shrugs. "But who cares? From what I understand, it goes back a long way. But it's in the past as far as I'm concerned."

I nod. "Okay. We will call a truce for now. And maybe if we can pull this off, our families will finally let bygones be bygones."

"You never know. Miracles can happen." He winks at me as he gestures toward the main road out of the fort.

"I think we're going to need a miracle—or two."

"So how'd you manage to get out of the house?" I look my brother up and down, finding it strange to see him outside of work *and* outside of his home. I'm pretty sure it's been months since we've gone out to grab a beer together. Pre-baby days for sure.

"Let's just say I'm on diaper duty for the next three days." Russ sighs and chugs the rest of his beer. "But it's totally worth it; I can already say that without a doubt."

I chuckle. "Good. You deserve a break every now and then." I take a sip of my own beer then steeple my hands in front of me. "I hate to ruin your night with business talk, but before the band starts playing and it gets super loud, I do have something I need to talk to you about."

"Oh?" My brother's eyebrows shoot up. "Speaking of this band, are they any good?"

He is clearly in no hurry to shift the topic back to

Friday's Formalwear, which is something we both eat, sleep and breathe fifty to sixty hours a week, especially since our father's heart issues kept him convalescing at home. I'm relieved Russ and I have both been able to step up to steer the ship during our father's recovery— if he is ever able to work fulltime again. Our two sisters both married and moved far away, and they stay completely out of the loop as far as the family business is concerned. In other words, this whole thing is riding on me and Russ—which is why I want to come clean about conspiring with the enemy. I know we agreed not to tell our families, but I tell Russ everything. Besides, he won't tell our parents, and that's what really matters.

"Jase...the band?" Russ slams his empty mug down on the table, hoping to catch the attention of our server.

"Oh, right. It's my buddy Pete's band, him and this girl he's shacked up with and her brother. And some other dude on drums." I roll my eyes. "He texts me like every other day to invite me to a gig, so tonight's the night I finally succumbed. If it's bad, at least I have you here for company."

"Wow, well, thanks for choosing me." My brother grins as the waitress delivers another frosty mug to the table. I'm still only halfway on mine.

"I figure if I have to suffer, you should have to suffer too. That's the way brotherhood works, right?" I watch him clear the head off the beer in one gulp, then I decide it's now or never to drop the bombshell on him. Pete and his buddies are setting up, carrying in instruments and arranging cords and amps all over the stage area. I better get this off my chest.

"So, what is it you wanted to talk about?" Russ seems to read my mind.

I take a deep, fortifying breath. "So I met up with

Hannah Robinson today."

He almost drops the heavy glass mug on the table as his jaw falls open. "You did what now?"

"Remember Hannah Robinson? She was in my class...two classes behind you..."

"You met up with a *Robinson*?" he repeats, the shock still evident on his face. Shock may be too mild of a word because it's almost like he's forgotten there's a beer in front of him.

I gulp down the rest of mine, hoping to give him a moment to adjust to the idea, then I signal for the waitress to bring me another. This is going to be a multi-beer night, after all. Alcohol is definitely required to get through this talk, plus the buddy's band thing.

"She called me up yesterday at the shop and asked me to meet with her to discuss the whole Über Brides thing..."

"And?" His brows are still elevated, but he seems to have remembered the beer, and he chugs down a long swallow.

"Well, we're joining forces. We're going to try to infiltrate the enemy ranks." It sounds even more awesome when I say it out loud. It's some real special ops kind of shit.

My brother scoffs at me. "You're going to what?" He studies me like some alien lifeform has taken over my body, and he doesn't believe it's really me in here.

"Hannah is going to apply for a job there. She'll be our spy, find out what makes them tick, get the lay of the land. Then we are going to systematically dismantle their empire." I smile at the waitress when she delivers my fresh mug. "Well, at least the Rehoboth Beach branch of their empire."

"That sounds ambitious. What makes you think it's going to work?" It's not the first time my older brother has been condescending about one of my stellar ideas.

I can't seem to wipe the grin off my face, I'm so anxious to get started on this. "Simple, really. Hannah is very smart and convincing. I think together we're going to—"

"Wow...." My brother's eyes narrow as he stabs his gaze into mine.

"What do you mean 'wow'? I'm trying to—"

He laughs at me, a deep, rumbling chuckle that starts low in his gut and bubbles up his chest. "You're into her, aren't you?"

"What?" I protest, glancing around the bar like someone might have overheard his accusation. "No, I just think we're going to make a good team—"

"Is she still hot?" he presses. "I seem to remember she was pretty cute. So was her older sister in my class, if I remember correctly."

"Forbidden fruit is always tempting," I tell him. "But that's not what's going on here. It's strictly professional."

Though she did look pretty amazing in that pink sundress she was wearing...the way the top fit perfectly over the curves of her breasts, the way her shapely legs were crossed when I first approached her sitting on the bench. She has the most beautiful eyes, too...

"Uh huh." My brother is still laughing at me as he finishes his second beer. The band is tuning up, and my buddy Pete is testing the microphone. I may be saved by the start of the show.

"Well, Mom and Dad can't know we're conspiring with the enemy." I'm finally able to force a serious expression onto my face.

"No, no...that would probably make Dad's heart explode right out of his chest," Russ agreed.

"Helloooooo, Rehoboth Beach!" Pete shouts into the microphone, followed immediately by an ear-piercing squeal of feedback.

"Holy crap, this is not starting out well!" Russ's hands fly up to cover his ears as the bassist, who must be the girlfriend's brother, adjusts an amp behind them.

"Sorry about that, guys!" Pete uses his pick to pluck a few guitar strings, and they adjust the sound yet again. "Just want to thank you all for coming out tonight. I'm Pete Bacon, and this is Wendy Torr on vocals. Wade Torr is on bass, and Eddie Donahue is on drums."

The crowd musters up a smattering of applause. I'm just glad to have a second beer. As they start up their first song, which is, incidentally, pretty goddamn awful, I see a flash of dark skin and pink across the bar. My head involuntarily swivels in that direction. When my heart starts to beat a little faster, I realize it's because I am still thinking of Hannah Robinson. And then it sinks a bit deeper into my chest when I'm disappointed it isn't her.

THREE

"Are you going to be ready for your presentation tomorrow?" my father questions just when I'm about to leave the house for my interview at Über Brides.

I whip around to face him wearing my most sophisticated tailored suit, the one I wore every time I had to give a presentation in grad school. It dawned on me that I should have saved the suit for the presentation, and it's probably way overkill for the entry-level job I'm applying for over at the enemy camp.

"Oh, sure, Daddy. I just have to track down a bit more data first." I give him a reassuring smile, which doesn't budge the worried look on his face.

"Where are you going now?" He furrows his brows as if he suspects I'm up to no good. I recognize the look from when I was younger, and I was going out to do something he wouldn't approve of and concocted an elaborate ruse to cover it up.

"Oh, I—" *Darn it, why am I not a better liar?* I need to get with the program if I'm going to pull off this whole spy thing at Über Brides. "I'm going to get my nails done." I flutter my fingers in the air. "So I'll look nice tomorrow. You know how I have a tendency to talk with my hands."

"You're awfully dressed up for that, but whatever you say, Sugarbunz..." His voice trails off as if he's still not convinced.

"Well, you know what they say: dress for the job you want, not the job you have!" I lean in and plant a kiss on his cheek before swiftly sliding out the door—not giving him any chance to reply.

My hands are trembling as I steer my car toward Über Brides, practicing in my head the entire time what I've planned to say. I have to give my real name. They are going to want to see an ID, social security card, and all that when I fill out my employment paperwork. There's really no way to get around that. I'm just glad that Robinson isn't a particularly unusual last name, and our business isn't named after us. It's Delmarva Beach Brides. So I'm hoping they won't make the connection.

Only about half of the lights in the main showroom are working when I push the tinted glass door open and step inside. There are boxes everywhere, though they've already installed a long rack on the far right side and it's been filled with bridal gowns still in their plastic bags. It looks like a mess – all the whites, ivories, champagnes, blush pinks mixed together, along with the laces and satins.

No one unpacking the boxes even looks up at me,

despite the fact I'm making a racket with my heels clicking across the tile floor. "Hello?" I call toward the back, behind where the main counter is stacked with even more boxes and plastic-wrapped items. A hallway extends toward a back door, and it's fully illuminated as if they used all their light bulbs on it instead of on the showroom.

A short woman pops out seemingly from nowhere a moment later. She's a little chubby with mouse-like facial features and ruddy skin, and she's wearing a flowy white and black zebra-print blouse over a pair of black capri pants. "May I help you?"

"Hello, I'm Hannah Robinson. I have an interview? I'm a few minutes early." I give her my best, most competent smile, making sure my shoulders are pushed back and I'm standing tall and straight, just like my mama taught me to do when making a first impression.

"Oh, hello. Can you give me just a moment?" She seems less than impressed, like I'm putting her out.

"Sure, of course." I watch her disappear down the hallway. A young man with blondish hair is unpacking more gowns over by the long metal rack, just tossing them onto the ground. I rush over there as fast as my high heels will carry me.

"Oh, please don't do that!" I scold him, though I'm trying to make my tone as pleasant as possible. "I bet some of those gowns are worth thousands of dollars!"

He shoots me a glare and then steps back. He looks almost too young to be working, like he doesn't look a day over fourteen. Maybe he just has a baby face.

"Here, let me help you," I offer, picking up a couple of the hangers. I carry them over to the rack and part the sea of mismatched colors and styles. "So, these are both Layla Mills Couture designs...and this one is a HEA

Bridal. And these are white…whereas these are ivory. So you want to keep the white gowns on one side, probably first since that's what you'll have the most of—"

"Wow, you really know your stuff, don't you?" The short redheaded lady is back, armed with a clipboard and a pair of reading glasses on a gold chain around her neck.

"I've worked in the industry for a while," I explain. "My family used to own a shop." I don't mean to over-enunciate the word "used," but I'm afraid it came out that way.

"Well, I could use someone to help me get this floor set up," she says, stepping toward me. "I'm sorry I didn't get a chance to introduce myself, but I'm Patsy Laroche. Corporate was supposed to be sending me someone, but who the hell knows—"

"Wow, well, I'd be more than happy to help you set up!" This was way easier than I thought it would be. *Wait until Jason hears how disorganized they are!*

"Great, when can you start?" I almost see a smile on her face, but it's more like a pinched-up smirk. She doesn't appear to be a very happy woman, though maybe if I can work my magic on her showroom, she'll sing a different tune?

"As soon as you need me!"

"Great, come by tomorrow at eight, then!" she says, reaching out to shake my hand. "You're hired! And feel free to wear something more casual tomorrow since you'll be doing a lot of physical stuff."

I'm so surprised and happy that I don't remember till I'm walking out the door that I'm supposed to make my presentation to the Beach Brides' board tomorrow at the same exact time.

I'm the one watching the shop tonight while Russ spends some much-needed time with his family. It's been nonstop busy until one hour before closing. I've been waiting to hear from Hannah to see how her spy mission went, but she never answered my text.

"Jason, honey, why don't you let me finish up here so you can go home?" my mother calls from the office in the back. I hear her voice getting closer and closer to me until finally she's leaning against the counter with her elbows on top.

"Oh, Mom, you should be the one to leave. I'm sure Dad is wondering if you're ever coming home at this point." She's been at the shop a lot in the past few weeks. I think she's gotten tired of taking care of Dad, to be honest. Coming into work is a break. Well, my father can be a bit of a pain sometimes.

She gives me a sheepish smile. "Did I tell you I hired a nurse to stop by every afternoon for a couple hours?"

"Wow, really?" My eyes widen as I search her face for any signs she's joking. Not that my mother is known for having a jokester side. She's actually a pretty serious lady, a take-charge kind of gal.

"Do you think I'm an awful person for doing that? She's a real cute, sweet young thing..."

As soon as she says those last few words, I have a

sinking feeling about what's going to come out of her mouth next.

"...and I was hoping maybe tomorrow night you'd like to come over and have dinner with us so you can meet her? She's just a few years younger than you. Her name is Brittany..."

My mother is always trying to set me up. Always. It's not good enough that three of her four children are happily married and have already popped out a few grandchildren between them. She's got a seventy-five percent success rate in getting her offspring married off, but that's apparently not good enough for her.

"Mom, we talked about this—"

She flashes me a pleading smile. "I know, Jason, but you're not getting any younger. You're going to be thirty before you know it, and you've hardly even had any girlfriends!"

She doesn't know that I've had *plenty* of girlfriends, just not any serious enough that I wanted to subject them to my family. I mean, my parents own a formalwear store. Every time my mom mentions a tuxedo, she laments that she wants to see me wearing one. It would only take one or two casual mentions of this in front of a serious girlfriend for the two of them to start conspiring to plan a wedding I have no desire to be part of.

It has been a while since I've dated anyone, though. Now that I'm so far removed from high school, it seems like most of the kids I grew up with have moved away. Maybe that's why I've been a bit nostalgic since Hannah contacted me a few days ago. She's one of the few people from our class who is still around, and apparently she was away at school for a long time collecting all those fancy degrees she was bragging about.

"Jason, you don't do anything but work! When was the last time you went on a date? Or even went out with friends?!" she presses, now agitated enough to have moved her hands to her hips, like she always does when she wants to emphasize a point.

"I went out with Russ for a few beers last night," I fire back.

"To talk about work, no doubt!"

"We also listened to my friend's band!" I counter. *They were horrible, but hey, we were there.*

"When was the last time you went out with people you aren't related to?" She gives me a victorious look like she's sure she's won the argument now.

I don't think she would be too happy if I told her about my secret rendezvous with Hannah Robinson at Fort Miles a couple days ago. As desperate as she is to marry me off, she would be extremely displeased—*no, furious*—if she knew I was cavorting with a Robinson girl.

"I hung out with my buddy Meric and our friends Shark and Ryan last weekend," I suddenly remember. *Who's the winner of this argument now, Mom?!* I want to add but refrain.

She just shakes her head at me. "What kind of name is Shark, anyway?"

And just like that, she's off on some other tangent. That's when I notice my phone lighting up. I put Hannah's number in as HR, so now it looks like the Human Resources department is calling me. Which we don't have. Our little family business isn't big enough for that. I'm basically the HR department.

Of course, my mother sees it, and her brows immediately fly up into her hairline. "HR? Who is calling you, Jason?"

My heart begins to race, and I don't know if it's because I've tripped my mother's maternal suspicion sensors or because Hannah is finally calling me. "Oh, it's nothing, Mom. I have Meric in my phone as HR."

"Why?" she continues to harass me as I move over to grab my cell phone off the desk behind the counter. I hold up a finger to ask her for a moment, but she's still ranting away.

"Hello?" I try to pretend like I'm talking to my buddy Meric. "Just a moment, okay?"

"Why would Meric be HR?" She's exasperated now. Yep, the hands are back on the hips.

"I've gotta step outside for a moment, Mom. Meric's having some girl problems," I lie.

She dismisses me with a wave. "I wish you had a girl to have problems with..." she begins to rant again, but I miss the last part of it when I walk toward the back of the building with the cell phone pressed against my ear.

"I'm sorry about that..." I whisper. "What's up?"

"Do you want the good news or the bad news?" she questions, her silky voice streaming down the line.

"Uh...I only want good news." *And that's the truth.*

"Well, the good news is I got the job," she tells me. "The bad news is that I'm supposed to start tomorrow morning, which is the same time I'm supposed to be making a presentation to my family about how we are going to ward off the competition."

"Oh..." I'm pretty sure I still hear my mom mumbling, but then I hear a chime, and she's either left or someone has just arrived. *Please let it be a customer,* I beg whatever higher power might be listening.

"So, yeah. Not sure what to do about that." She lets out a soft sigh.

"You'll think of something," I assure her. "You could pretend to be sick. Let your parents know you need more time."

"I'm a terrible liar." She groans in frustration, but it sounds sexy when she does it, so I lose my train of thought for a moment. "I think I used up all my deception already today when I had my interview."

"Look, you're going to have to figure it out, okay? You need to get in there and start taking notes. And we're going to have to meet up to strategize soon. Like maybe this weekend…"

She takes a deep breath. "Okay. I will figure it out."

I almost say, "That a girl," but I have a feeling she'd reach through the phone and strangle me if I was that patronizing. "So you *do* want to meet up this weekend?"

She laughs. "Someone seems anxious to get together again…"

"Oh, I—" I scramble for words when I realize how much my last question sounded like I was asking her out. "I've just been brainstorming a bunch of ideas is all." I actually have, that's not a lie. "I'm *anxious* to get to work," I explain, using the same word she did.

"You almost sound like you've done this before." There's more than just a twinge of suspicion in her voice.

"Well, I did execute a pretty flawless dog-napping campaign last summer—you can ask my friends Meric and Lindy about that," I tell her, fondly remembering the late-night mission with Meric's girlfriend and company.

"Uh, okay, that's weird." She sounds totally neutral

and not the least bit interested in my canine rescue heroics. "Well, you'll be pleased to know their store is a mess. Boxes everywhere, half the lightbulbs are missing. I have no idea how they're opening next week. A bridal miracle is going to have to happen to pull it off. I can't believe I've been hired to help the enemy set up."

"They're never gonna know what hit them," I promise her as a sly grin spreads across my lips. "Make sure to take notes."

"I will. Don't worry."

I head back out to the floor where my mother is gathering up her things to leave. "I guess you're right. I probably should go take care of your father. Did you get things straightened out with your...accountant?"

Just the way she says the word leads me to believe she's not buying that was my accountant on the phone for a minute. "Yep, all's well."

"Didn't you file your taxes in April? It's May now. Don't you have a while before you have to worry about next year?" my mother presses. She just can't let it go. Our whole family is like that. No wonder we're still in a feud with the Robinsons for over twenty years, and no one even remembers why at this point.

"Yes, Mom. Just planning ahead. Oh, and Meric may be popping the question soon to his girlfriend, Lindy," I tell her. I totally made up that last part, but anything to get her off my back.

"Oh, that's nice. Well, you can give him and his groomsmen the family discount, of course." She smiles. "I'll tell your father you'll be over for Sunday dinner."

Sunday is the only day our shop is closed, so family tradition is to have a big afternoon meal. Well, my sisters don't come, of course, because they are long gone. But me, Russ and his family, and my parents are all there. And every single week, my mother laments about how she is looking forward to the day I bring a girl over for Sunday dinner.

Can you imagine what she'd think if I brought Hannah with me?

I scrub the thought from my wild imagination when my mother walks over to me and presses a kiss against my cheek. "See you tomorrow," she says, and just like that, the shop is empty again. She must have helped the last customer when I was on the phone with Hannah. And now it's time to lock up.

I glance at my phone, realizing it is flashing with a text message. For some reason, I expect it to be Hannah, telling me she's come up with a plan for starting her first day at Über Brides and handling the presentation she's expected to give at her family's business, but instead it's Pete.

Hey, buddy, what did you think of the band? We're playing again this weekend in Dewey. We'd love to see you there. No pressure, of course.

Ugh. I roll my eyes as I quickly close out of the message. Even thinking about that horrible music is making my head pound. I'd rather have my toenails forcibly pried off than be forced to listen to that crap ever again.

FOUR

Hannah

I glance around the shop and see no one. Where are all the legions of workers sent by corporate to set this floor up? The kid I saw yesterday when I was here to interview is gone, and I don't even see my boss—Patsy, I think her name was?

"Hello?" I call toward the back. Approaching the counter, I look down to see tons of plastic and hangers littering the store. There are also metal shelving units, screws, power tools, and god knows what. It's like they started to work, but then everyone just vanished and didn't bother to pick anything up.

"Oh, you're here! Thank goodness!" Patsy calls, her voice getting louder as she approaches from the back. "I hope you can work in that." Her eyes trail up and down my body.

I'm wearing a pair of stretchy black pants and a sleeveless blouse with a tangerine-colored cardigan over the top. I really struggled to figure out what to wear this morning. First of all, I feigned illness so I could get out of my presentation at Beach Brides, and that didn't leave me much time to get ready. Secondly, I wanted to strike a balance between looking presentable on my first day of work and being comfortable enough to move around and lift things if needed. This was the result. I don't know what she was expecting, yoga pants? My parents would flip out if I ever wore pants to work. This place already seems way more casual.

"Oh, I'll be fine if I just take off my heels and my sweater," I assure her. "I'm ready to roll up my sleeves and get to work!"

"God bless you, child," Patsy says as she walks toward me with a clipboard. There's a schematic attached that shows how the floor is supposed to be set up. It is very precise, with exact measurements between displays. There's the bridal gown section along one side with several carousel racks of bridesmaid, flower girl, and mother-of-the-bride dresses. The other side is flanked with the menswear department. In between are displays and aisles full of every wedding-related thing you can think of: cake toppers, invitations, floral doodads, centerpieces, favors, guest books, aisle runners.

"Where is everyone else?" I look at her and then scan the premises, counting each box I see in my head. It takes some degree of mathing, but I can see over one hundred, and there may be even more in the back.

"Oh, it's just you and me until later this afternoon when Jeremy comes back in." She shrugs. "Sorry, they only give us a skeleton crew to start off. How else would they make so much money?" She covers up what was probably a completely true statement with a witchy cackle.

Her voice trails off, and I start to wonder if Jeremy is the barely-teenage boy who was ruining the bridal gowns yesterday. "So let me get this straight: corporate wants all of this done by Monday with only three— excuse me, two and a half-people?"

She lets out a heavy sigh. "That's right, so you better get busy. I've got some phone calls to make to set up more interviews." She starts to head back to her office. "Good luck!"

If I cursed, I'd be silently mouthing a nice, long juicy string of expletives about right now. I was going to feel sorry for Patsy, but it sounds like she has only dumped all of her work onto me. She left her clipboard on the half-constructed shelving unit for me to consult. I'm not too good with power tools, but I am somehow going to wrangle all these pieces into submission.

I grit my teeth and pick up the cordless drill. This is the way Über Brides treats their employees? Severe understaffing, I already know the pay sucks, and absolutely zero training? Oh, yeah, I can't wait to take these *bleep* *bleep *motherbleepers* down!

I feel a little like Ferris Bueller in that scene where he's trying to beat his parents home from work so they don't find out he faked being sick. I feel awful for doing that—I am not the type to deceive anyone, especially not my parents, but I just didn't see any other way around this. If they knew how badly I want to save our family business, I'm sure they'd forgive me!

I can't wait to get my own place, but right now, it's just not feasible. And now that my entire future is in jeopardy with Über Brides looming over the family business, I don't want to put down a deposit on a place or sign a lease until I'm pretty certain I'm going to be employed steadily—hopefully at Delmarva Beach Brides and *not* at Über Brides. So for now, shacking up with Mama and Daddy it is.

My entire body is going to ache tomorrow; I can just feel it. I slip out of my casual clothes and stash them in the bottom of my closet. My high school yearbook is still prominently displayed on my shelf, just where I left it when I first got the idea to call Jason Friday. Speaking of which, I need to check in with him and let him know how understaffed Über Brides is. Patsy told me before I left that she'd be interviewing all day tomorrow, so hopefully I will have help soon. She seemed moderately pleased with what I accomplished today. I felt like one of the slaves building the Egyptian pyramids today. The only things missing were the blazing sun beating down on me and wearing nothing but a loincloth.

I throw on my pajamas and collapse onto my bed, hoping I look convincingly under the weather. As tired as I feel, I am fairly confident I can pull off this ruse. I just know my mother is going to come in and check on me as soon as she gets home, but I want to call Jason before she does, just so I can avoid him calling while my parents are around.

Ringing...ringing...

"Hello?" comes his deep, smooth voice.

"Hey, it's Hannah," I tell him, though surely he has me in his phone. Or maybe he doesn't. I have him listed under J. Sounds so mysterious, doesn't it?

"So...how did it go?" I hear some static and some fumbling like he's trying to get to a safe place to talk.

"Oh, boy, you're not going to believe all this," I begin. "They have like zero help. She's only hired two people! I don't know how in the world she plans to open up on Monday. It's like mass chaos in there, though I managed to wrangle some of it into submission—"

"I bet you did," he interjects slyly.

"Haha, so funny. I had to give her a primer on bridal gowns," I share. "My boss knows nothing! I was all like: well, these have a ballgown shape, and these are mermaid or trumpet, and these are sheath, et cetera. It's like this company doesn't do—"

"Hannah? Are you home, honey?" I hear my mother's voice call at the same time her footsteps begin to sound on the stairs.

I don't even have time to finish my sentence before her dark head pops through my cracked door. "Hannah?"

"Oh, shit, is that your mom?" I hear Jason's voice on the other end.

I have never felt more like a deer trapped in the proverbial headlights than I do in this exact moment. I'm completely frozen in panic, my lips unable to move.

"Hannah? What's wrong, sweetheart?" My mama's voice is full of concern. "Who are you talking to?"

"Is my Sugarbunz okay?" *Oh, no.* That was my father's voice. He pops his head through the doorway right beside my mother's. "Who are you talking to, Sugarbunz?"

"Sugarbunz?" Jason repeats. "What the hell kind of nickname is that?"

At this very moment, I truly do feel like I am about to be sick.

"Is it a *boy*?" my mother mouths.

"Mom! I'm twenty-eight years old!" Okay, her comment managed to nip that nausea I was feeling right in the bud. "Can you guys give me a moment? It's a friend from grad school, okay? I'll be right down."

"Alright, Sugarbunz, sorry to disturb you," Daddy apologizes. He gives my mother a knowing look, like there's no way I could possibly be talking to someone from grad school.

"See you downstairs, darling," my mother says, her mouth still moving like she's silently enunciating the words like she did her earlier question about boys.

I huff out a long, exasperated breath of air. "I'm sorry about that."

"Look, we need to strategize," Jason says, choosing to ignore the very fertile ground for teasing we're standing upon. I didn't know he had that kind of maturity in him. "I am assuming you need to work tomorrow, and so do I. Can we get together after work?"

"Yes," I automatically answer. "I need to come up with something to tell my parents too. I'm thinking of telling them I've infiltrated Über Brides as a spy. I won't mention you, of course."

"Are you sure that's a good idea?"

"No, but I have to tell them something." I roll my eyes. There he goes questioning my judgment again after he told me I was going to rock this whole assignment. That attitude is not exactly inspiring a lot of confidence in myself. "Look, just tell me when and where to meet you."

"Well, Fort Miles again?"

All this eye rolling is starting to give me a headache. "Really?"

"Well, do you have a better idea?" He sounds as frustrated as me.

Maybe the reason our families hate each other is because the Fridays are jerks. "I would invite you to my place, but I'm living with my parents right now after grad school—till I get on my feet. Which I'm not going to be able to do if I'm not able to save the business."

"Well, you could just keep working at Über Brides," he suggests, and it actually sounds like he's serious, which spawns a rush of anger to boil up from some deep, dark, primal place inside me. "I mean, it already sounds like you know more than your boss."

I try to swallow down some of my rage so I don't blow up at him for making such an asinine comment. "Doesn't that make you even angrier? That they are understaffed, underpaid, and undertrained, yet they sell their crap so cheaply, their customers don't even care? And *no one* gives a crap about the small local businesses they are hurting—"

"Which is exactly why we need to think even more broadly than just our two shops," he states. "We could talk to the local florists, caterers, bakers and everybody else affected by Über Brides and get them on board too. Maybe we could do a social media campaign about buying local?"

"Yeah, well, we can't plan that very well at Fort Miles. We need a computer and a place to take notes." I'm struggling to brainstorm a way for us to get some privacy when the crazy notion of a hotel room comes to mind.

Where in the world did that come from? Can you even imagine how awkward that would be? It's preposterous!

"Just come to my house," he finally concedes. "There's no way my parents will be coming over, not with my dad in the condition he's been in with his heart issues. And I live far enough away from them that word probably won't get back to them."

"And your neighbors? They won't snitch?"

"Look, if you can infiltrate Über Brides, surely you can sneak into my house, alright?" He takes a deep breath and blows it out so loudly, it nearly tickles my ear.

"Hannah? Are you coming down for dinner?" my mother's voice calls from downstairs.

"I've got to go. Can you text me your address? Say seven o'clock?" I'm a little panicked one of my parents is going to come back upstairs.

"Sure thing, Sugarbunz."

I start to groan at him overhearing my father's nickname for me, but he's already hung up.

I'm not sure why I'm so nervous.

I'm only having a female who is not related to me in the house for the first time in probably six months. *Okay, nine months, but who's counting?* I broke up with the last girl I was *kind of seeing* in August. *Kind of seeing* is the relationship status I'd use to characterize most of my relationships, to be honest.

I keep thinking about what my parents would say if they walked in and saw Hannah Robinson on my sofa. Would they even recognize her? She looks an awful lot like her mom, from what I remember seeing on their commercials. Yes, Delmarva Beach Brides has television commercials on our local cable channels, and I have been known to watch them from time to time. You keep your friends close...and your enemies closer. Isn't that how the saying goes?

I guess that will be my excuse if my parents were to somehow randomly show up. But they won't. Nah. That would be totally out of character for them. They go to bed at like eight o'clock anyway.

I'm still trying to straighten the pillows on the sofa and make sure the place doesn't smell bad when the doorbell rings. My little cavapoo lets out her high-pitched bark that sounds just about the total opposite of menacing. "Shhh, Tank, we have company. And you better be on your best behavior!" I glance down at her fuzzy little caramel-colored head that tilts when she looks up at me with her curious brown eyes. She is too damn cute and gets away with too damn much because of it.

"Hey, come on in." I open the door to reveal Hannah. This time I don't even notice what she's wearing—all I can focus on is the huge grin on her face when my dog starts to jump up and repeatedly try to lick her.

"Oh my gosh! Look at this cutie!" She reaches down and picks the little furry beast up. Normally Tank is somewhat standoffish with strangers, but her tiny body is wriggling so fast I think she's going to take flight.

"What's her name?"

"That's Tank. She was my sister-in-law's dog, but when she and Russ had their baby, the dog was acting out and being a royal pain, so somehow I ended up with her. Don't let her fool you, she's a spoiled brat."

"Oh, that can't be true. Look how adorable you are, you sweet little thing!" She sets the wiggly dog down, and Tank proceeds to race circles around her.

"Wait." She stops admiring the dog and snaps her eyes to mine. "Did you say this precious fuzzball's name is *Tank*?"

I shrug. "Yeah, because she's obstinate and stubborn. Like a tank."

"You can't call such an adorably floofy snugglebug 'Tank!' It's like calling a perfectly iced cupcake a can of sardines!" She narrows her eyes at me like I'm a hopelessly horrible person for inflicting such a moniker on a tiny innocent creature.

I huff out a little exasperated breath. "Well, her name was Dolly when Russ and Jen had her, but I couldn't exactly go around calling her that, could I?"

"Why not?" Her hands fly to her hips as she leans forward, challenging me.

"It's not very manly, is it? I mean...it's kind of...effeminate for a guy to have a dog named Dolly," I argue.

"Says the man who fits other men in tuxes all day!" A crystalline giggle erupts from her full, raspberry-colored lips as she throws her head back in amusement.

Okay, now that pisses me off. I do get hit on by a fair number of gay patrons, and I'm not homophobic by any means. To say my job is "effeminate" is as much an insult to women as it is to anyone else. I want to fire back some dig about her job, but I can't quite get any words out. I'm too busy noticing how beautiful she is when she laughs. Why do I get the feeling I'm in big trouble? And not because she doesn't like my dog's name.

"So how did today go?" I change the subject, ushering her into my living room. My house is humble, but it is only a few blocks from the beach. I'm not going to lie, it was a pretty big investment, as beachfront property in Rehoboth is not cheap. My buddy Meric lives a few blocks away, and we're always talking about how great of a location it is. We can walk down to the boardwalk and have our pick of any number of bars and restaurants. And the Atlantic is so close, we can smell the ocean breezes from our porches. So no regrets here. I just hope this damn Über Brides business won't make me lose my house.

I barely finish gesturing toward the loveseat when she collapses onto it with a whoosh. She slings her arm over her eyes and groans. "Remind me again why I have to be the spy?"

There's a moment I can't speak as my eyes sweep up and down her curvy figure sprawled across my sofa cushions. Her breasts are heaving with her exhausted breaths, and her normally bouncy curls are looking a bit smooshed. A pang of guilt rushes through me, though I worked all day too. At least I wasn't doing manual labor. All I can think of to say is, "Can I get you something to drink?"

"I'm not much of a drinker," she says, sitting up, "but I'll take whatever ya got. My head is killing me. My shoulders are all knotted up, and my thighs are burning from the four million squats I did today when I was emptying out boxes and setting up merchandise."

"Wine?" She doesn't even look at me, her head thrown back against the cushions, face pointed toward the ceiling. *I hope I even have wine. I think I do...*

I pour some Moscato as fast as wine has ever been poured and return to my living room in a flash. I have to keep her motivated. She has no idea what a brilliantly strategic position she's in right now. She knows more than her boss. We can use this to our advantage!

I hand her the glass, and she takes a sip. "Wow, this is really good! And I'm not even a wine girl." A few sips later, and her whole glass is empty. "More please!" she says, handing it back to me.

I smile and return to the kitchen to grab the bottle. I top off my glass and refill hers, then sit down next to her. I wouldn't ordinarily sit so close, but I've got my laptop on the coffee table with some ideas I've written up for how we can work her position with Über Brides to our advantage.

She settles down with her fresh glass of wine and doesn't seem the least bit uncomfortable with me in such close proximity. That's when I realize she smells absolutely divine. I catch a hint of vanilla...and possibly gardenia wafting off her body like she's just applied lotion. Glancing down at the sleek sienna skin on her chest and her arms, I can't help but wonder if it's as soft and smooth as it looks.

"So?" she interrupts my thoughts. "Did you have something to show me?"

I almost burst into laughter, immediately taking her question to a place located somewhere in the vicinity of the gutter. "The laptop!" I exclaim. "Yes, yes, I do, as a matter of fact." She gives me a puzzled look as I pull the computer onto my lap and angle the screen so we can both see it.

"So these are your ideas?" She tilts the screen down a bit so she can read more easily.

I can't help but watch her wide honey-brown eyes dance over the words. I wish I could read her full expression, but I do detect a tiny smile, the edges of her lips just barely curled up.

"So, the name of the game is sabotage," I tell her, anxious for her reaction. She glances up from the screen, but her expression is still too hard to read. "We want to ruin their reputation, make them get a ton of horrible Yelp reviews...you know, keep customers from coming in. People don't want to screw up their weddings, so they're not going to risk that just to save a couple of bucks—"

"Well, that's the problem I see with some of these ideas," she says, the edges of her lips now curling down instead of up. "Some of these stunts could ruin weddings—" She looks back at the computer. "We want to ruin Über Brides' reputation, but we don't want to ruin actual customers' weddings. I mean, these are real people we're talking about, and they didn't ask for trouble."

Her frown is contagious. Reviewing some of the ideas I came up with, I can see her point. There still has to be a way to pull this off, though. There has to be.

"We can do some stuff that's a little more subtle," she suggests. "Like, what if I order the wrong stuff for a customer? Then, you know, they still have enough time to order the right thing, but it reflects poorly—"

"And you can give really bad customer service," I agree, running with her idea. "Act like it's their fault instead of yours."

She sighs. "Yeah. Ugh, that will go against every fiber of my being!"

"You're playing a role, Hannah. All's fair in love and war...and this is war."

"I know." She reaches for the wine glass she'd set on the end table and drains it. "I think I'm gonna need more wine."

I fill her glass as some more ideas start to dawn on me. "What if we recruited some friends to pose as customers? Then we could mess things up for Über Brides and not hurt any real customers—"

"I don't see how that would help, though?" She takes a sip of her third glass of wine.

I scramble to collect my thoughts. "So, it will be documented, right? Whatever the mix-up is, it will be clear Über Brides is at fault. When customers complain in their online reviews and call up corporate to try to get their money back, eventually they are going to send someone down to see what the hell is going on in Rehoboth Beach, right?"

"Yeah?"

"Then we're another step closer to getting them shut down. And we all know word of mouth around here is everything, right? We just have to put as many kinks in the armor as we can."

"I think you mean 'chinks,'" she says dryly as she finishes her third glass of wine.

"Oh..." I look at her, and though there's not a smile on her lips, there is amusement in her eyes again, just like when she was teasing me about the dog's name. "What did I say?"

"Uh, 'kinks,'" she says, now unable to stifle her laugh. When I say *unable*, I don't mean she lets out a delicate little giggle. No, not this woman, this member of my family's archnemesis clan. She bursts out with a downright brutal chuckle that rattles my bones with its intensity.

"I thought it was 'kinks,' though?" I stare at her, absolutely floored that she thinks that was so funny. *Oh, wait...*

She had three glasses of wine. *And I said "kinks."*

"I am pretty sure the expression is *chinks in the armor*, but if you want to talk about *kinks* instead, we can certainly do that!" She's still laughing so hard, I can't be certain that's exactly what she said, but it's what I was able to make out.

The springy curls on top of her head are shaking with her unrestrained giggling, and I can't stop myself from reaching out to push them out of her eyes. She instantly freezes, looking at me with such awe that my breath catches in my throat. I wonder if that means she felt the same bolt of electricity race through her that just raced through me.

I want to kiss her so damn bad. I'm nearly as impulsive with my lips as I was with my touch, but something stops me. Our family situation. Trying to be professional. *My dog suddenly bounding into my lap.*

Next thing I know, Tank is the one doing the kissing, and she's taking turns between the two of us, leaping back and forth from my face to Hannah's. "Tank, no!" I shout, but it's too late, we're both laughing, which is only making Tank more excitable and affectionate.

Later that night when I walk Hannah out to her car, us still chattering away about the next stages of Operation Wedding War and how she is going to tell her parents she can't come into work for the next few weeks, I can't help but wonder what might have happened if Tank hadn't jumped on the loveseat when she did. I have a feeling my lips and tongue would have been the ones on Hannah instead of my dog's.

FIVE

Hannah

Stores should not have their Grand Openings on Mondays. It's bad enough that I'm distracted by two extremely divergent trains of thoughts, but the incompetence of the "staff"—and I use that word loosely—that Patsy has hired is probably going to give me gray hair and an ulcer before the day is done. And where is she? She's in her office supposedly trying to wrangle more money from corporate to hire a few more people. Who is left to train this ragtag group of weirdos she apparently found in some dark alley or under a big, moss-covered rock? Me. Me, that's who.

"Oh, Stacy, can you please put all the invitation design books on the counter over there?" I point to the back where we have our special consultant area. This is where we hook brides up with florists, photographers, cake designers, DJs, limo services, etc. Every wedding vendor you can think of, Über Brides has a preferred (*read: discount*) partner. Not all of our services are in place quite yet because we're waiting on corporate to tell us who these mystical people are. But apparently we do have a vendor for invitations. I am pretty sure it's some weird guy in his mom's basement printing them out on a circa early-2000s laser printer.

Stacy looks at me, flustered. "What?" she questions with a dazed look on her face.

That's when I realize she's wearing earbuds. First day on the job, and she has earbuds in her ears, listening to god-knows-what. What the heck is wrong with people?

"Take out the earbuds. You shouldn't be wearing those to work," I admonish her. She gives me a sheepish giggle. "Put the invitation design books on the counter in the back please."

So, problem #1 nagging at me is the discussion I had with my parents last night about my plan to save Delmarva Beach Brides from being bulldozed by the competition. It went a little something like this:

Me: Hey, Mama, Daddy, I need to talk to you about something.

Mama: Honey, you're not still feeling sick, are you?

Daddy: Should you go to the doctor, Sugarbunz? We can't have you sick at work!

Me: Well, actually, it's about that. See, I wasn't actually sick the other day.

Daddy: You lied to us?

Mama: Oh, Morris, surely she wouldn't lie to us! You didn't lie to us, did you, Hannah?

Me: *facepalm*

Also me: It's actually the good type of lie. I was doing something to help our family business.

Mama: What is it?

Daddy: Yeah, what are you up to, Sugarbunz?

Me: I needed to go interview over at Über Brides so I could get a job there.

Mama and Daddy: ...

I think they are about to collapse from simultaneous heart attacks.

Me: Mama? Daddy? Are you okay?

Daddy: How can you jump ship like that? After everything we've done for you!

*Mama: You might as well have gotten a job at Friday's Formalwear! *clutches at neck* Morris, I think she's trying to kill us. Honey, are you trying to kill us?*

*Me: No, I'm being all strategic and stuff. I'm going to sabotage Über Brides working from the inside. You know, like a spy. Except I'll do stuff to bring them down. *flexes arm muscles all tough-like**

*Mama and Daddy: *look at each other, bewildered**

Me: It's going to be great!

Daddy: You thought of this all by yourself?

*Me: *lies* Uh, yep!*

Mama: Oh, I don't know, Morris, it sounds like a terrible idea to me!

Daddy: Liz, this is pure genius! Our daughter is a certifiable genius!

*Me: Really? Well, I... *blushes**

Mama: Are you sure about this, darling?

*Me: Yeah, I start on Monday. *decides not to tell*

*them I've already worked there two days**

*Daddy: *rubs hands together* This is going to be epic! Did I use that word right?*

Me: Yes, Daddy.

Daddy: I'm so proud of you, Sugarbunz!

So, now that my parents know what I'm up to, I'm feeling even more pressure to make my efforts pay off. But I can't let them know I'm working with Jason. Somehow I have to make them think I'm doing this all on my own.

"Hey, Dave, what are you doing? You can't leave those boxes there!" I shout across the floor to another new recruit. I probably shouldn't have done that with customers on the floor. *Ugh.* Fortunately, Patsy didn't see me. *Because she's totally MIA at this point.*

"Can you go help that chick over at the counter?" Stacy asks as she approaches from the wedding décor aisle.

I feel like she's probably as well-trained as I am to handle whatever this customer wants, but this may give me a chance to work some Operation Wedding War magic. I start trying to get into the right frame of mind as I walk toward the counter. I swear in the back of my head "Eye of the Tiger" starts to play, and I begin to get into *What Would Jason Do?* Mode. I really do have to psyche myself up to be an unhelpful biatch. *Gosh, I can't even say the real word in my head!*

The bride-to-be is fingering the invitation designs, and it appears to be her mother standing next to her. They look identical except the mom is older (obviously) and a tiny bit shorter. I strain myself trying to wipe my normal "customer service smile" off my face. "Can I help you?" I ask as gruffly as I can. *Still comes out a little on the sweet side.*

They don't even seem fazed by my fake rudeness. "Can we order these?" the bride asks, pointing to a selection about midway through the book.

I pull out the keyboard to the desktop computer perched on the counter. "Sure thing." I take down her name, address, and phone number first. "What's the item number?" I poise my fingers over the keys as I await her response.

"It's 19987423," she says, enunciating one digit at a time.

I read it back to her as I type, but instead of a three at the end, I type an eight.

And so it begins.

Lunch affords me a whopping fifteen minutes to think about the other issue that's claimed real estate in my brain. I cram a turkey sandwich and some baby carrots down my throat while flashbacks of sitting next to Jason on his loveseat the other night filter through my mind.

I don't know if it was the wine or—

Okay, we're going with the wine here, alright?

Is it just me or was he sitting very close? And when I teased him about the whole "chinks" versus "kinks" thing, and he touched my hair... Well, I probably should have slapped his hand away, but that wine made my reflexes unnaturally slow. And I'm sure that *also* explains why I was hoping he was going to lean in and kiss me.

I can't believe I just said that!

It had to have been the wine.

Still, he was so cute sitting there in his casual t-shirt and shorts. He reminded me a lot of the Jason Friday I knew in high school, the one who was off-limits, who I couldn't even bring myself to talk to. If I was in a class with him, the other students would separate us. "Oh, I bet Hannah doesn't want to sit that close to Jason. Come sit back here, Hannah!" I remember one of my friends saying. I even remember a teacher asking me if it was okay for us to be in the same class!

That's what I mean about this arch nemesis thing. I've never understood it. I never really had anything against the Fridays, but I was told my entire life that they were cheats, swindlers...and I think my grandfather even said they were racist.

I really, really hope the issues between our families don't have anything to do with the fact that my family is black and his is white. I refuse to believe it, in fact.

Before I can head down that path too far, I notice my phone buzzing on the table next to me. I glance down to see it's a text from "J." *Speaking of the devil...*

How's work treating you? he asks.

Me: It's hell on earth. Thanks for asking.

Jason: Let me buy you a drink tonight.

*Me: Whaaaaat? *surprised face emoji* And be seen in public together?*

Jason: What if it was out of state? Ocean City?

Me: That might be safe. Why OC?

Jason: My friend's band is playing, and just warning

you, they're terrible, but they have a couple people they want to impress coming tonight so they want some bodies there to make them look...you know...more popular.

Me: You make it sound so enticing. *bored face emoji*

Jason: Well, the drinks on me are supposed to be the enticing part.

Me: I told you I'm not much of a drinker, right?

Jason: That's what you said, but that's not what happened the other night. *wine glass emoji* *drunk face emoji*

Me: Fine. *tongue sticking out emoji* Name the time and place.

And just like that, I've agreed to go to Ocean City, Maryland, to meet Jason tonight.

"Are you sure this is a good idea?" Russ asks me as we stake out a corner table as far away from the band as we can get but still look like we're there to see them.

"I'm never sure any of my ideas are good, but I think it's time you meet Hannah and help us with our plan. We can't expect her to do all the work," I explain. "Plus, I promised Pete I would drag you along."

"Oh, shit, are you kidding me? That's the band we're here to see?" He shakes his head. "That's low, bro, even for you. These guys suck."

I flash him my best victory smile. I feel like I've gotten him back for some prank he probably pulled on me when we were younger. As my next oldest sibling, he was always razzing me about something.

"Is that her?" He gestures his head toward the entrance clear across the room.

Hannah must have gone home and changed because that is not what I imagine she wore to work today. She's wearing a stunning black dress that hugs her curves in all the right places. I struggle to keep my jaw from hitting the table as she sashays her way toward us in her strappy fire engine red heels. She looks like she's on fire, with red lips to match her shoes.

She shoots me a dagger-filled look when she notices my brother sitting with me. I'm sure she remembers him from high school—you almost always remember the upperclassmen jocks, right? My brother was our star quarterback, so everyone knew him.

"Hannah Robinson, you look amazing," Russ says, standing up to greet her. He starts to shake her hand, but she pulls him into a hug.

I don't know why, but this rubs me the wrong way immediately. I didn't get a hug when we met. I still haven't gotten a hug, not even last night when we were both liquored up.

But before I can take my complaint any further, she turns to face me with her arms outstretched. "Come on, we're out of state. That means I can give you a hug!"

"I had no idea our family feud was confined to Delaware," I joke, but my words are immediately lost when I feel her ample breasts pressing into my firm chest. I squeeze her to my body, probably a little too hard, taking in another deep whiff of her vanilla floral scent that I noticed last night.

She pulls away and immediately gestures for the server, who gives her a nod before starting to approach our table. "What was it we had the other night...the wine?"

"Moscato," I fill in.

As soon as she says "the other night," my brother's eyes grow to the size of saucers. He kicks me under the table as if to ask, *what about the other night?!*

"Do you have that?" she asks the server, and he smiles with a nod.

"Nothing happened," I mouth to Russ. Just then I hear the familiar nails-on-a-chalkboard screeching, the telltale sign that Pete and his crew are taking the stage.

"So this job is probably going to be the death of me," she announces as she settles in the chair beside me. "But I did manage to kick Operation Wedding War off...at least I hope."

"Oh, yeah? What did you do?" I lean forward, gazing into her warm brown eyes. The lighting is dim in the bar, but something about it is creating little sparkles in her pupils that seem to be drawing me in like magnets.

"I changed the item number on some invitations a bride wanted to order. So when they come in, they'll be the wrong thing. Plus, you'll be proud of me for this, Jason, I was as rude and unhelpful as I could possibly be." She crosses her arms over her ample chest and gives a proud nod, making her burnished curls dance around her face.

"Wow, 'as rude and unhelpful as you could possibly be'! Sugarbunz, I'm so proud of you!" I gush, watching her expression instantly morph into one of fluster.

"Don't call me that," she says coolly. "That's my father's nickname for me. And it is sacred."

"Oh, so some taunts are off-limits, I see," I volley back. "Guess that means you can't make fun of me for measuring men's crotches all day long."

Russ is cracking up beside me. Oh, sure, I bet this is really entertaining for him. But before we can get any further in our war of words, Pete steps up to the screechy mic, which is still sending some feedback out into the crowd. A few people near the front are covering their ears with their hands. I'm just shaking my head. They have a lot to learn.

He introduces himself and his bandmates just like last time, and they ease into a cover of some Eagles song. I'm pretty sure Glenn Frey is rolling over in his grave, and if they keep playing, Don Henley will be soon as well. Fortunately for Hannah, the waiter returns with her wine, and she gulps it down like it's a handful of painkillers. It's about two seconds later that I signal the server to bring us all another round. We're going to need it to get through this torture.

I guess that's just what kind of friend I am. I am willing to put myself through actual physical pain to support you.

We make it about three songs before Russ says he has to get home to Jen and Jemma. "It was really nice to see you again, Hannah. Maybe next time we get together, we'll actually come up with some good business ideas?"

"I hope so too. This music makes it too hard to concentrate!" she manages, cringing at a flat note the lead singer just hit.

"Take care, bro," Russ says, clapping me on the back.

"Yikes, this is really...wow," she settles on, as if she doesn't want to offend me. She moves closer to me so I can hear her over the cacophony.

I lower my head so I can speak directly into her ear. "I told you they were terrible," I defend myself. "It's not like I forced you to come."

"I was under the impression the drinks would compensate for the terribleness," she sighs as she downs her second glass of Moscato. "But I think I'd need something more powerful than wine to achieve that!"

"Well, that could be arranged." My eyebrows wiggle up and down, making her smile.

Is it bad that I have absolutely no desire to talk about this business stuff? I mean, we're in the thick of this thing, and I care about my family's livelihood and all, but I'm back to wondering what her lips would taste like.

She pulls me back down to her so she can shout into my ear, "I do have to drive home, you know. And since we're in Maryland and all..." Her breath fanning my neck sends a sizzling hot burst of heat right down my body.

She turns her head so she can hear my response: "And it's Monday night. Guess if I'm going to get you liquored up, I should probably at least do it in Delaware...and when you don't have to drive home. And on a weekend."

Oh. I probably should not have said that.

Her eyebrows immediately fly up into those bouncy golden-tipped curls, and she pulls back, her hands gripping the table in surprise. "Is that what you were trying to do the other night?"

"What?! No...I...." *Crap, how do I go about explaining this?* I beckon her back down so I can have her ear again. "I actually did want to come up with some ideas for the sabotage...and we did. But I enjoyed the other parts too."

"The other parts?" she questions, those perfectly arched brows still hovering over their natural resting place. She bites her succulent-looking lips as she awaits my answer.

I've only had two beers, so I'm not sure I can blame them for suddenly fumbling my words. "Oh, you know, the joking around...the witty banter..."

She rolls her eyes as if that wasn't what she was expecting to hear, and she's a little disappointed. Or I could just be reading into it...

Her face softens. "I guess it was kinda fun. And you are pretty witty...for a Friday..." She playfully bats at my arm with her fist.

"Hey, what's that supposed to mean?"

She's now turned toward me, and my arm is resting on her chair. If I moved my arm forward a few inches, I'd have it directly around her shoulders. When she laughs and tilts back, her curls brush against the hairs on my forearm, making them stand on end when goosebumps spring up from my wrist to my elbow. I'm metal, and she's a lightning bolt. Next time she strikes, those hairs might get singed.

Still laughing, she pulls me toward her again by the shirt. "Oh, you know, the family feud. Though no one will ever explain what caused it."

"Maybe it's over?" I haven't heard my parents mention it in a while, and Russ didn't seem to say much about it after he got over his initial shock that I was conspiring with a Robinson.

"It'll never be over as far as my parents are concerned," she laments, and there is definitely disappointment in her voice this time. I know I'm not imagining it.

"You wanna get out of here?" I shoot the words directly into her ear. I know I'm shouting, but it feels intimate, like we're whispering our secrets to each other.

She nods. I've already paid the tab, so we both stand up and head for the door. I do a quick sweep of the bar to make sure I don't see anyone I recognize.

It's a cool spring night, and this close to the ocean there's a chilly breeze that envelops us as soon as we step outside. When she shivers, I automatically pull her close to me, wrapping my arm around her. There's a full moon, and a gauzy cloud has draped itself over its lower half like it just stepped out of the shower and is wearing a towel around its waist.

"Thank you," she says, and this time her voice is so soft, it is almost a whisper. I barely hear it over the sound of the band still pushing its way beyond the doors and windows of the bar like an evil force.

"Where's your car?"

"It's around the block. There wasn't any more parking," she explains, still shivering.

"You should have brought a coat!" I tease her. "I'll walk you over there."

I feel like she's about to say something else, but she ends settling on a nod before she angles us down the sidewalk toward her car. The air has sobered me up immensely. Inside, while we were cocooned in that god-awful racket and buffered by sweet, boozy elixirs, I felt my judgment was a little clouded, a little askew. Like if an opening had presented itself, I might have tried to kiss her for real this time. And there was no annoying little cavapoo to interrupt my advances.

"This is me," she says, stopping abruptly beside a navy blue sedan. It isn't exactly what I imagined she'd drive, but then again, she's a classy, old-school kind of girl. I think that might be something I like about her. If I'm being honest, there's a lot to like about Hannah Robinson.

Which is why she makes a natural ally for this mission, I remind myself. It's not like she could ever be anything more than that.

I always imagined if I ever *did* settle down—not that I have any intentions whatsoever of doing so—it would be with someone like her. Someone real. Someone who had no trouble being themselves. Not one of those women who wrapped themselves in twenty layers of fake every day: fake boobs, fake tans, fake smiles, fake eyelashes, weird fake contouring makeup jobs. I have no interest in the plasticky perfection society tries to sell as beauty. That's not beauty to me.

Her headlights flashing when she unlocks her car break me out of my internal soliloquy. "You okay?" she asks as she leans down to open her door.

"Here, allow me." She steps aside so I can have the honor of swinging open her car door for her. "Your chariot awaits, madame," I say in my best formal voice.

A smile creeps onto her face. "Why, thank you, Mr. Friday. And thank you for the drinks. If I keep having days like today, I think I'm going to have to take up drinking wine every night. So thank you for introducing me to my new friend Mocsato..."

"Moscato," I correct her, finding her mispronunciation absolutely adorable. "You sure you're okay to drive home?"

She laughs. "Sorry, no, I'm not drunk. I'm just a wine noob. My family doesn't drink much, and I didn't indulge much in college—either time around. I'm kind of a nerdy bookworm, if you didn't already notice." She slips off her heels and throws them into the passenger seat.

"I did notice," I assure her. "And I think it's quite becoming, really."

"Becoming, huh?" she eggs me on. "1958 called. It wants its word back." She gives me a wink.

I chuckle and shake my head. She is classy and sassy all at the same time. "Do I get another hug?" I bravely ask.

"Sure, why not? We're still out of state..." She reaches up to sling her arms around my neck.

She doesn't give the type of hugs some girls give where you feel like you're hugging a feather, and if you squeeze them at all, they might be crushed. She actually squeezes her arms around me and presses her face into my shoulder. I'd almost forgotten how short she is without heels.

I breathe in another whiff of her scent. She probably has no idea how delicious she smells. "You're a very good hugger," I compliment her, and when my words hit her ears, I feel her shiver in my embrace.

"Thanks. You're not bad either...for a Friday." She laughs and pulls back.

I fight the urge to pull her back toward me again, but I can see she's cold...and it's getting late. It's not like we won't be having many more business meetings. I'm sure I will see her again soon. And I can have this fight with myself about why I shouldn't kiss her—even though I so desperately want to—all over again.

Hannah

I start up my car and watch Jason start down the block toward the parking lot where his truck is. My fingers are trembling as I place them on the steering wheel, and it's not solely because I'm cold. If I'm being honest, I'm not really cold at all. That hug flooded my entire body with enough heat to get me through a long, frigid winter.

I'm 99% sure he's feeling something here too. And once again, I really thought he was going to kiss me. I would probably let him, too...I just need to figure out what really happened between our families first. If it was something really horrible...well, then I might need to call this whole alliance off. I mean, I'm mostly doing Operation Wedding War by myself anyway. Maybe I could go it alone.

Or maybe I will find out it was some silly misunderstanding, and not only can we continue to unite forces...but we can unite some other body parts as well...

SIX

Hannah

"I want you to train Stacy on how to order products today," Patsy instructs as soon as I set my purse down in the little cubby in the back room. "Not gowns or anything, but something small. We need to order something for a new display we're doing for bridal showers and bachelorette parties."

"I'm not sure I fully understand how the ordering system works myself, to tell you the truth. Is there any way you can show us both?" I flash my boss my brightest smile. Every morning she gives me some impossible task, and I just have to grin and bear it. *Fake it till ya make it*, like my mama always says.

She hands me a big blue binder she's holding. "The instructions are in here. Sometimes the teacher learns as much as the pupil, you know?"

I squint at her, wondering if she's actually for real right now. I try to freeze my eyeballs to keep them from rolling, but I think they force themselves into a half-roll much to my dismay. Fortunately, Patsy has already left me standing there holding the heavy binder. I let out a frustrated sigh as I venture out to the floor to see if I can find Stacy.

I spot the dishwater blonde across the floor, putting back some gowns that were tried on the day before. That really should have been done yesterday—instead of leaving them hanging around. Sometimes I wonder if anyone in this place has any respect for the thousand-dollar price tag on some of this merchandise. Sure, they don't sell anything here nearly as nice as what we sell at Delmarva Beach Brides, but seriously, a little care goes a long way!

"Stacy, can you come here for a moment?" I use the sweetest voice I can muster then carefully switch the blue binder to the other side. If I'm going to build muscle carrying around this lead weight, I might as well build it evenly on each side, right?

She gives me the other half of the eye roll I just gave to Patsy before throwing the remainder of the gowns she is carrying over a chair and heading in my direction. I can't help but bury my face in my palms. "Careful with the gowns!"

"Oh, sorry." But she doesn't bother to fix them.

I have her follow me behind the sales counter at the back of the store. Setting the binder down on the counter, I tell her to get behind the keyboard. I am going to walk her through exactly what to do. After she logs in, the catalog of Über Brides products is displayed. We go to the party supplies and favors section and begin to scroll down the thumbnail images.

"So what are we ordering?" she asks as she scans the photos. "Oh, this is cute." It's one of those cheap garter sets with white lace and blue satin: one to wear and one to toss.

I nod absentmindedly as I glance over the instructions in the binder. Whoever wrote these blasted things tried to find the most complicated language in the universe to explain even the simplest steps. Once I get past that, I see it's really not that hard.

"Okay, you simply click on the images, put in the quantity, hit the order button, and it goes into the cart. Just like any online shopping system I've ever used," I surmise.

She looks up at me with a smile. "This is kind of fun!"

"Yeah, isn't it?" I flip through the book to see if it gives any idea on quantities to order, or if there's some sort of protocol about how to choose products.

"Oh, check this out!" She giggles as she moves the cursor to an image of tiny penis-shaped soaps.

"Oh, well, we have to have some of those!" I blurt out without a second thought. Jason would be laughing his butt off if he were here right now.

"Nice! How many?" She looks at me with questioning eyes. It's such a serious expression considering the subject matter.

"Um...one hundred?" I shrug.

"Okay." She punches in 1-0-0, then returns to the main screen, where she laughs again. "Oh, look, they have little chocolates, straws, whistles, confetti—I've never seen so many penises in my life!"

I'm cracking up by this point in time, and a customer over in the cake topper area is eyeing me suspiciously. "Well, let's get one hundred of each, then!"

"Alrighty!" She begins clicking on each item and typing in 1-0-0, then adding it to our cart. "We'll be well-stocked with tiny dicks!"

"We most certainly will!"

The customer who was eyeing us approaches the counter, and I lay a hand on Stacy's arm. "Hey, go help her, and I'm going to get his order submitted, alright?"

"Okay," she agrees and slips out from behind the counter.

I fill in our store number, and under the associate name, I type in *Stacy*. Then I choose three of the items randomly and add a zero to the quantity. We're getting one thousand chocolates, confetti packs, and soaps. It's going to be a veritable army of tiny penises up in here!

Well, you remember what Jason said: *all's fair in love and war*!

"So, how was work today, honey?" Mama asks as she sets the pot roast on the table. The fragrant aroma of the meat, potatoes, carrots and onions is wafting up to my nostrils, reminding me of how I've always imagined heaven smelling.

"Oh, you know, the usual: trying to bring down the evil empire." I dab my napkin to my lips, hoping to sop up any drool that has inadvertently pooled there.

"That's my girl!" my father raves. He takes a helping of green beans, then passes the dish toward me.

"It's nice having you here, Hannah." She never uses my real name unless she is being very serious, so I reach out to squeeze her hand to show her I understand what she means by it.

"This meal looks amazing, Liz! You've outdone yourself," my father praises. Mama leans down and gives him a kiss on the cheek before she takes her seat next to him. Next thing I know, we're joining hands around the dinner table while Daddy blesses the meal.

"Amen," Mama and I both echo him, and when my eyes pop open, I notice a little card sitting by my plate. She must have slipped it there while we were praying.

"What's this?" I eye the envelope and turn my gaze first to my mother, then to my father.

"Oh, it's just a little something—a graduation gift," Daddy says, his lips spreading into a grin. The chandelier over the dining table is reflecting off his bald head, making him look like he has a halo. I almost giggle at that before my mother pipes up.

"I know you said not to get you anything, but we're so proud of you, Hannah. We are really looking forward to showing you all the ins and outs of Delmarva Beach Brides and hopefully learning a lot from you too. We have the thirty years of experience, and you have the master's degree. Together, we are really going places, I just know it!"

I bite my lip, trying to keep the tears stinging my eyes at bay. I knew my parents were proud of me; they didn't need to give me anything to prove it.

"Well, go on, open it," Daddy says.

With trembling fingers, I break the seal on the envelope and pull out a glittery gold and silver card. *Great, that stuff is definitely going to be clinging to me for days!* I read the sentiment on the outside and open it up to read the sweet note my mother has inscribed. A check slides out and falls onto the table. I don't mean to look at it, but it is hard to get past that many zeroes. I pick it up to make sure I read it correctly.

"Oh my gosh, Mama, Daddy! I can't accept this kind of money from you!" I drop it like it's a hot potato.

"Of course you can," my father assures me. "We want you to have some money to get started on your own: an apartment, maybe a down payment on a house, if you'd like. A new car. We've been saving it for quite some time—since you were a little girl, really. We were going to use it for your college, but you were so smart and got so many scholarships, you didn't even need it. It's been drawing interest for a while now."

"Honey," my mother says, placing her hand on top of mine, "the Lord has been good to your father and me. He has provided us with a thriving business and children and grandchildren we are so proud of. We want you to have the same blessings in your life that we have enjoyed while running the business we've lovingly built from the foundations your father's parents established thirty years ago. Our whole family is in agreement that you will be the one at the helm of our ship."

Tears are rolling down my cheeks now; I'm so touched by their generous gesture and kind words. "I don't even know what to say."

"You don't have to say anything right now!" he assures me. "Just keep working hard to keep our business safe, and all will be well. We are so proud of you for taking the bull by the horns, and we have been praying about this—God is going to do great things through you; we both know it!"

My mother's smile fades, and her eyes take on a

piercing, almost biblical look. I soon find out why when she quotes: "'The LORD shall cause thine enemies that rise up against thee to be smitten before thy face: they shall come out against thee one way, and flee before thee seven ways.' Deuteronomy 28:7."

Oh boy, Mama is dragging out the King James Version. That means she's super serious.

"'Flee before thee seven ways,'" I say with a giggle. "I'd be happy if Über Brides flees one way."

Daddy wrinkles his nose and purses his lips. "I hope if anything, they make the Fridays go out of business, not us!"

"Oh, Morris," Mama says, shooting my father a glare. "Do not bring up the Fridays at our dinner table! How many times have we been through this? This is a No-Friday Zone!"

An idea suddenly flashes into my head. They aren't going to like this at all, but I have to try. "Okay, so I will take the money from you under one condition..."

Both pairs of their eyes snap to me so fast I'm afraid they just got whiplash. "What's that, Sugarbunz?"

"You have to tell me why we're in a feud with the Fridays," I demand. "Or I'm ripping up this check."

My mother's mouth falls open in a perfectly shaped O. "Hannah Grace Robinson, you cannot threaten your parents like that!"

"I'm twenty-eight years old, and I've known about this family rivalry my entire life. No one has ever given me straight answers about it, and I want to know once and for all what it's about!"

They both just stare at me, dumbfounded. I have never really disrespected their authority like this before, not even when I was a teen. Like I said, I was a total nerd.

Still am. But something about taking on the role of General Robinson in Operation Wedding War has emboldened me, and I'm tired of being blown off.

"Is it actually a business thing?" I question. "Or a personal thing?"

They look at each other, and Mama closes her eyes briefly as if she's praying for the right words to tell me. I don't know if God is going to help *her*, but *God help me* if I don't get the answers right now! I'm tired of being in the dark about this. And I refuse to go any farther in my alliance with Jason until I know whether or not his family is really as deplorable as my family has made them out to be.

"Why are you so interested in knowing about this, Hannah? You've been hounding us about it since you got home from school. Why the sudden interest?" my mother questions.

I love how she is deflecting, don't you? I huff out a breath of exasperation. "I've been asking my whole life—except when I was away at school. Now I'm back, and I'm an adult, so I figure it's time for me to finally understand. If it's a business thing, I'd like to know so I don't make enemies of my own someday."

My father glances down at his folded hands resting on the table. He's pushed away his plate. I guess I've ruined his appetite, and I do feel bad about that, but I also feel like if they'd just tell me, then I wouldn't have to keep nagging them.

"It's not something...racist, is it?" I whisper the word "racist" like it's a curse word.

My mother shakes her head. "No, Hannah. I don't think the Fridays are racist—"

Whew, well that is a relief. I never got any vibe like

that from Jason...

"It's a long story," Daddy begins, his voice low. "It has probably lost its impact through the years. If you knew how it all started, you'd think, how can two families actually become enemies over something like that?"

He looks at me like he's said too much already. "Go on..." I encourage him.

"It's just, something happens to spark an initial issue, and then more and more negativity gets dumped on top...and then it creates an entire mountain of issues, right?"

"Like making a mountain out of a molehill, got it." I try to smile, but his face is so serious. He's looking off into the distance like it's painful for him to dredge up these memories. Maybe I shouldn't be pressing the issue.

"I knew there was a saying about that," he says, shaking his head. "It's just the way things are now, you know?"

"I've imagined so many things throughout my whole life," I tell them. "Horrible things. Like maybe Jason's grandfather was in the KKK, or maybe they spread a bunch of rumors about our business and everyone boycotted it. Or maybe his grandfather and my grandfather were both fighting over the same woman—"

When I blurt out that last thing, Daddy's back straightens.

"What?" my eyebrows fly up as I study every slight change in expression, the tilt of his lips, the angle of his brows.

"Maybe you should talk to your grandmother," he

tells me with a sigh that sounds like defeat.

My eyes bulge out at the idea. *There was some sort of romantic entanglement?*

"Come on, Daddy...you can't leave me hanging like that..."

"I really don't even know all the details myself," my father admits.

"And neither do I," my mother adds.

"What? Are you serious? All this time—and you guys don't even know the whole story either?"

"Talk to your grandmother," my mother says. "But really, we need to eat. Dinner is getting cold, and I don't want the Fridays to ruin it. They've ruined enough stuff through the years without ruining dinner!"

I'm waiting for Tank to finish doing her business when my phone rings. *Ugh, answer the phone or scoop up poop? Such a dilemma.* I go with answering the phone.

"Hey, Jason?" comes a sweet, feminine voice I immediately recognize as Hannah's.

"Yes? How was your day?" Tank finishes and turns around to look at me as if to say, *it's your turn now, buddy. Get busy!*

"Do you know anything about our grandparents'

relationships, back around the time they first opened up their shops?" Her voice is full of suspicion and intrigue and immediately piques my interest.

I swallow hard and try to stay calm. "I know Friday's has been in business longer." I take care of Tank's droppings and continue down the sidewalk. It's a beautiful spring evening. I can smell the ocean on the wind, and the boardwalk still has plenty of people milling about. Might be an ice cream night. Tank would love that!

"Yeah, I was wondering if there was ever a time when our families got along. Did your parents and my parents go to school together like we did? How did our families know each other?"

"I don't know." I shrug even though she can't see me. "Why are you so interested in this? We have bigger fish to fry, Hannah. Were you able to accomplish any sabotage today?" Tank is pulling me toward the ice cream parlor like she read my mind.

Her sigh fills my ear, but she doesn't say anything.

"What's wrong?"

"I don't know, I'm just—"

"Do you like ice cream?" I stop at the bench right outside Tank's favorite ice cream shop.

"Duh," she retorts. "Why?"

"You wanna come grab ice cream with me and Tank?"

"Do you mean Dolly?"

"Of course I do, *Sugarbunz*," I tease her.

"Where are you?" She doesn't even dignify my taunt. *That's no fun!*

"On the boardwalk. Come on, it's still early. Come

hang out, and we'll talk about the next step of Operation Wedding War."

I know it hasn't been that long since I saw her, but my fluttering heart when I heard her voice proves I'm anxious to see her again. I'd been thinking about calling her all evening, but I was really hoping I would hear from her first. It feels like victory to me—almost as sweet as the ice cream I just asked her to come share with me. Now that I have her on the phone, just talking to her doesn't seem to be curing my Sugarbunz craving. I still have lingering regrets for not kissing her when I saw her in Ocean City...

...lingering regrets that I haven't been able to admit to myself until just now.

Her honey-laced tone suddenly becomes the voice of reason. I don't know anything unsexier than the voice of reason. "You want to meet on the boardwalk? Like the most crowded place in Rehoboth Beach?"

Unsexier isn't a word, is it? Alas, I press on: "Well...I don't think anyone from my family is down here this late on a weeknight. And it's crowded. Can't we blend in?"

"Says the guy who hasn't wanted to meet in a crowded place unless we are in another state." I have a feeling she's going to be throwing that in my face for an eternity. "I don't think it's a good idea," she concludes.

"Fine. My house? I'll just buy a quart and bring it back there."

"First you want to buy me drinks, and now it's ice cream," she says. "I guess I shouldn't look a gift horse in the mouth. That's what my grandmother always says. And, by the way, I'm going to be talking to her about the sworn enemies thing soon, and I want to go in armed with as much knowledge as I can..."

It seems like only a few minutes elapse before Hannah is sitting on my loveseat. Tank is so worn out from the walk and her ice cream, she's curled up on the armchair, which means Hannah and I are forced to sit right next to each other again. *Drat the luck, eh?*

"So I ordered a thousand bridal shower favors with little...uh...male genitals on them," she tells me like it's an ice breaker.

I very nearly choke on my bite of ice cream. "Uh...you mean like penises?"

If her skin wasn't so dark, I swear she'd be glowing red right about now. She hides her smile and a mouth full of ice cream behind her hand as she tries to keep herself from laughing. Then: "Yep. I taught one of the new girls how to place orders today."

"Well done! Have you gotten any complaints about the wrong invitations yet?"

"No...that's the problem, you know? We're not moving fast enough. Something really tragic has to happen so customers will call and complain. But somehow I have to keep from getting fired—"

"Will the bridal shower favors order come back to you?"

"No," she tells me, her face brightening. "Like I said, I've been put in charge of training people—when I have just about zero training myself. My boss sits in her office all day doing who knows what. So I put the girl I was training's name on the order."

"Smart! Well, we pretty much knew they'd take advantage of your awesomeness," I praise her. "Okay, here's an idea that came to me this morning."

She leans in. "What?"

"You guys have any tuxes going out this weekend, or is it too early for that? I know your store just opened." My head has been spinning with this brilliance all damn day. When I wasn't thinking about her, of course.

"We do! Some folks from the Philly area are getting married down here and had the order for their wedding transferred down to us now that we're open. It's a huge party too: the groom, six groomsmen, a ring bearer, and father of the bride, all getting tuxes."

I stop to look at her, taken with the sparkle in her eyes, such a rich color, almost a cinnamon brown. She has beautifully sculpted cheekbones and long, thick eyelashes. Her full lips are painted that bold raspberry again, and I find myself watching them open and close, forming the words she's speaking without any of them actually registering in my brain.

"Jason?" Her brows draw together as she shoots me a confused look. "Is there a problem?"

Oh, shit. Caught in the act. I straighten up and take a deep breath. "No...I just was thinking about my evil plan." I tap my hands together à la Mr. Burns in *The Simpsons* when he says "*Excellent!*"

"So are you going to tell me or leave me in suspense?" Her eyes rake over me, and from the sass in her voice, I can't tell if she's teasing me about the plan, or if she is busting me for staring at her.

"You've got a seam ripper, right?" Her eyebrows arch in interest before she nods. "Take the seam ripper and loosen all the seams in the tux pants, the ones that go down the butt."

"What?!" Her face fills with such glittering amusement, I'm afraid she's going to spit ice cream out all over me. "How in the world do you think of these things?"

"How did you think of ordering a thousand tiny penises?" I fire back, equally amused.

We both spend the next few minutes cracking up—and then silence. We stop abruptly as our eyes, watery with tears from our laughter, meet. She ever so subtly slips her bottom lip underneath her top teeth and bites down.

That's all it takes. I have to kiss her. I've been fighting this urge the last I don't know how many times I've seen her, and I can't fight it anymore. I lean in toward her, expecting her to jerk away in a mixture of surprise, revolt and disgust, but I get the shock of my life when she leans toward me as well.

My lips tentatively brush against hers, and the very first sound I hear escape is a tiny moan. *Oh, wow.* I've never heard anything sexier in my life. I deepen our kiss, teasing her lips open with my tongue, expecting her to come to her senses at any moment and push me away, but instead, her arms wrap around me. My hand comes up to gently grasp her face, angling so I can explore her mouth. A shiver races through me when her hands tickle the back of my neck, then her fingers weave through my hair as she pulls me closer to her.

This is happening. This is really happening.

Hannah Robinson—the youngest member of the clan of my family's mortal enemies—is not only sitting on my loveseat, but my tongue just happens to be shoved down her throat at the moment.

And it feels more right than any other kiss I've ever experienced in my entire life—

SEVEN

Hannah

"I—uh...I shouldn't be doing this!" I gasp out, breaking our kiss and leaping to my feet. "I'm so sorry, Jason...but I think we should keep this professional..."

He stands up beside me, his face awash with a combination of disappointment and confusion. "I'm sorry, I didn't want you to feel uncomfortable, I just—"

"It's fine; it's fine." I think I'm reassuring myself as much as I am him. My heart is beating so fast, I'm surprised there's enough leftover energy in my body to make my mouth work.

"Hannah, please don't go." He is helplessly watching me gather up my purse and my ice cream bowl, which I walk over to the counter between the living room and the kitchen.

I whip around to face him, still desperately trying to get my heart to calm down. "I will try to complete the next task for our mission tomorrow." Even though I'm aiming to make my voice as even as possible, with the remnants of our kiss still buzzing on my lips, it's an exercise in futility.

"Can we please talk about this?" His stormy gray-blue eyes search mine as he steps closer to me, positioning himself between me and the door. Dolly leaps off her perch on the chair and rushes over to him, jumping up his legs and begging for attention.

"Maybe next time, Jason... It looks like your dog needs her daddy. I'll check in tomorrow," I tell him, forcing a stiff smile across my lips.

He flashes a look of defeat as he scoops the small dog up off the floor. She wriggles in his arms, tongue out, hoping to give him kisses. After watching her lick his mouth, I am about 300% less interested in kissing him again. *Good.* I need some sort of antidote to the power he has over me. I can't believe I let down my guard long enough to—

"Night, Jason." I take advantage of his distraction with the dog and brush past him, letting myself out the door and into the muggy night. Fortunately a little breeze whips past me, blowing my curls about my head as I throw myself into the driver's seat of my car.

This night has been too much. First the thing with my parents and their money and their refusal to answer my questions...then this. I couldn't wait to finish grad school, but if I'd known things were going to be so messy and complicated when I came back home, I would have gone on for my PhD. Showing up at class, taking the tests and writing the papers is easy compared to this.

Real life is an exam I didn't adequately prepare for.

With my trusty seam rippers in hand, I sneak into the back area where we store the tuxes we are going to rent out until they are picked up. Filling my lungs with a fortifying gulp of air, I lift the plastic and fumble for the seam I want to loosen. *Pluck, pluck, pluck.* I imagine I'm playing an instrument, a guitar, I guess, plucking out a cute little folksy melody as I do my dirty work.

I am probably the least vindictive person ever. No wonder the family rivalry—as well as Operation Wedding War—seems so out of my wheelhouse. I don't like hating people. I'm a lover, not a fighter. Turn the other cheek and all that, isn't that what Jesus says?

What really gets me is how my grandmother and my parents, who are about as godly as you can get, are the first ones to ask *What Would Jesus Do?* But yet they still hate the Fridays. I mean, what could Granddaddy Friday have done that was so terrible?

I make quick work of the groomsmen's tuxes. I don't feel nearly as bad about sabotaging those as I do the groom's and the father of the bride's. I grit my teeth and clench my jaw, working up the moxie to just *git 'er done. Just do it*. Whatever motivational propaganda might help push me over the edge.

"Hannah? What are you doing back here?" comes Patsy's shrill voice from behind me. I freeze in place but somehow manage to dump my seam ripper in the pocket of the groom's tux. Oh no! It has my fingerprints all over it. Why didn't I wear gloves? I'm so dumb. I can practically hear the police sirens and see the flashing red and blue lights...

"Hannah?"

"Oh, hi, Patsy. Just checking to make sure these tuxes are in order for pick up later today." I flash her the most genuine smile I can muster, and her hard features finally soften just a smidge. Kind of like when you try to melt butter in the microwave, but it's still hard as a rock except along the edges, which cave in a little, losing their sharpness.

"Okay. Hey, I got a voicemail on the main customer line about some wrong invitations that were ordered. Do you know anything about that?"

"Uh...I don't think so?" I shrug as nonchalantly as possible and breeze past her, hoping she doesn't notice any vestiges of the guilt I'm trying to wipe off my face.

"They're coming in later to rectify the situation. Can you help them with that? I think Marcus or Stacy must have typed the item number wrong." She glances down at her clipboard with a frown twisting her mouth.

"Oh, sure, of course." I turn back around to face her. "Anything else?"

"Yes, can you make sure Marcus and Jeremy unload the truck when it arrives? Oh, and how are you with social media? I need someone to start posting on our Facebook page."

My eyebrows fly up at the mention of their Facebook page. Facebook business pages can collect customer reviews. It's yet another way for me to rock the boat...

She mumbles something about how there's no way corporate is going to give her any more help, not even seasonal, as she trudges back to her office and shuts the door firmly. Not really a slam, but not a gentle shut either. I take out my phone to update Jason on the situation, and all I can think about is our kiss the night before. Just thinking about it causes a wave of heat to crash over my body.

I've already decided I'm going to talk to my grandmother after work.

Most grandparents' houses are so stereotypical: you know, lace doilies, plastic on the furniture, ugly floral wallpaper and knickknacks everywhere. Not my Grandmama. Actually, she doesn't even want to be called Grandmama. She asked me when I was about twelve to call her Rose, her given name, but I've never quite been able to wrap my head around it.

She's barely five feet tall, and she is the most stylish seventy-eight-year-old you have ever seen. Her nails are always perfectly manicured, and she has approximately four million pairs of shoes, each pair matching an impeccably tailored outfit. And her house is so sleek and modern, you'd think she hired a decorator from one of those HGTV shows. But nope, she picked out everything herself. Stainless steel, spotless bright white trim, immaculate tile and carpets everywhere.

She retired about ten years ago, around the time I graduated from high school, though she still sits on the Beach Brides' board. I remember when I was younger, she told me she planned to see the world. She and my grandfather did indeed go on several cruises; then, about five or six years ago, my grandfather suffered declining health, which meant she was unable to travel while she was taking care of him. He passed away a few years ago, and now she's making up for lost time. If she can't find a girlfriend to accompany her on her adventures, she has no issues going alone. She's even told my parents a few times not to be surprised if she brings home an exotic younger man she collects as a memento of her travels.

"Grandmama?" I call out as I knock on her door. She left the front door wide open, and the screened storm door is letting the fresh May breeze into her house.

"Is that my Hannahbunz?" she calls back, her own version of the nickname my father gave me when I was a baby.

"Yes, Grandmama, can I come in?"

"Well, of course! Don't let any bugs in, though," she warns me. I find her sitting in her cozy reading chair with her feet propped up on the matching ottoman. She isn't reading a physical book, no. She's too high-tech for that and uses an e-reader. She devours books like they're air. "If I'm not on an actual trip, you better believe my mind is on a trip!" she always says.

I present myself in front of her, hoping my retro-styled floral dress and peach-colored cotton shrug meets with her approval. She has never hesitated to tell me if my wardrobe is not up to par.

"Well, don't you look mighty adorable!" she coos. "Like a fresh-picked daisy! Come have a seat, child. Would you like some tea?"

"No, ma'am, I'm fine. I just came from work. How are you doing this week?" My eyes sweep up and down her tiny, compact body, which is looking rather spry in a pair of aqua-colored capri pants and a white eyelet blouse with tiny aqua flowers. She's wearing a white, aqua and coral scarf with a swirling pattern and large coral earrings that dangle from her drooping earlobes. Not a single hair is out of place. She's had the same hairstyle since 1987. It almost looks like it's frozen into a helmet that she places on her head every morning.

"This week? You haven't visited me since you returned from school. I haven't seen you since Christmas!" she fires back with an eyeroll.

"I'm sorry, Grandmama. It's been busy—" I don't want to tell her about Über Brides, and I hope to God she hasn't seen it in the paper.

"Does that have something to do with that whole Über Brides mess I saw in the papers? You and your father better be putting your heads together to figure that out!" She wags her finger at me.

"I'm trying, Grandmama." I take a deep breath and arrange the skirt of my dress around me on the sofa opposite her chair. I probably do need tea to make it through this conversation. Now that Jason has introduced me to the idea of soothing my frayed nerves with alcohol, I think a Long Island Iced Tea would do just fine. I obviously didn't catch my grandmother in the greatest of moods.

"Quit calling me that! Call me Rose, child! How many times do I have to tell you?"

How am I going to ask her about the feud if she's going to yell about all this other stuff? My hands are trembling as I play with the fringe on the pillow propped up on the cushion next to me.

"Oh, Hannahbunz, please don't get upset," she finally says, noticing I've gone silent. I'm not very good about disguising my expressions, so no doubt I have some hurt splashed across my face. "I'm just bitter it's

93

taken you this long to come visit your grandmother, child. Now, I can only assume there is a purpose to your visit. I don't get the impression you just happened to amble by my house."

It's true; she does live a little out of the way. And it's true that I should have come to visit before I'd been home for a couple of weeks.

I suck in a sharp breath and lean forward, placing my folded hands in my lap. As meekly as possible, I eke out: "I was wondering if you could tell me a little bit about the Fridays."

Just like that, her e-reader slipped to the floor, hitting the rug with a soft thud.

"Rose?" I choke out. Her face has paled, and the wrinkle between her brows keeps getting deeper and deeper, but her mouth is set in a thin, straight line. "Please? I want to know what happened?"

She shakes her head and glances at the electronic device which is face-down on the chevron-patterned rug. I leap up and grab it to hand it to her. I don't mean to look down, but the screen flashes on, and the first thing I see is a word I never ever wanted to imagine my grandmother reading or knowing. *Where's the brain bleach when you need it?*

Yet, I am somewhat emboldened. Because if she can read the type of thing I think she's reading, then she should be able to suck it up and tell me what the heck happened with the Fridays.

"I'm not leaving till you tell me," I say as I resume my position on the sofa. "Mama and Daddy told me to ask you, so here I am."

"Well, child, it was a long time ago now. More'n twenty years ago..." Her voice trailed off as her gaze wandered somewhere above my head, as if she had just taken a little trip in her mind to an undisclosed location.

"I know that." I sigh, hoping to snap her out of her daze. "So does that mean it's water under the bridge now? Is the feud over?"

Her eyes widen as they snap back to mine. "Why? Are you thinking about teaming up with the Fridays to run Über Brides out of town?"

My whole body freezes again. *How in the world could she have guessed that?* "No...I..." Stammering, I force my shoulders to slide back down from their position near my ears. "Well...what if I *was* thinking of doing that?"

"Child, this is not my story to tell, and it's not my feud to decide if it's over and done with," she states and then intertwines her fingers as if that is her final word on the matter.

"Why did they tell me to ask you, then?" Now I'm even more confused. I wasn't supposed to leave here with more confusion—I was supposed to get some stuff cleared up. *For once.*

"You'll need to talk to your brother," she announces, then looks around as if she can't believe she let that secret slip out of her mouth.

"My brother?" My brows furrow. "Which brother?" *I have three.*

"Why, Morris the Third," she states matter-of-factly. "It's really up to him to decide if it's time to call a truce."

"Hey, I wasn't expecting you." And despite that, my lips are curved into a smile as my eyes sweep down Hannah's vintage-looking dress. She always looks so beautiful. Tank is leaping up and down, anxious for me to open the door so she can jump all over our company.

"Sorry," she apologizes as she brushes by me and prepares herself for the canine onslaught. Sure enough, Tank is all over her, hoping for lots of kisses. "Hi, Dolly! How's my sweet girl tonight?" She doesn't even look up as she begins to address me, "I wasn't going to drop by tonight, but I wanted to ask you something."

My heart skips a beat wondering if it has something to do with our kiss.

"Do you have any old yearbooks?" She straightens her spine until she's completely upright, her eyes pinned on me curiously, awaiting my response.

"Old yearbooks?" I shake my head. "Oh, there was something I was just getting ready to text you!" I hand her my phone, open to a review of Über Brides-Rehoboth Beach on Facebook.

Her face lights up with a grin as her eyes scan the one-star review: "I ordered our wedding invitations last week, and the ones that came in were completely different than what we ordered. Then when I came into the store to take care of it, the girl who helped me was a real bitch. Terrible customer service! We'll be ordering our invitations someplace else, TYVM!"

"Are you the bitch?" I question, my eyes bouncing between hers.

"That I am," she admits, laughing. "It was so hard, too! It went against every fiber of my being to be like that to the poor lady!" Her laughter fades as she situates herself on my loveseat.

"Can I get you something?" I'm standing between the living room and kitchen. "I'm going to grab a beer."

"Do you have any more Moscato?" She jumps up and follows me into the kitchen. Tank is right behind her. "So, yearbooks. Do you have any? How about your brother? What year did your oldest sister graduate?"

"Whoa, slow down!" I lean over to take a bottle of Dogfish Head and an unopened bottle of Moscato I bought last week, hoping she'd come over and drink it, out of the fridge. "Where is all this coming from?"

"I went to see my grandmother today," she explains.

After pouring her a glass of wine, I usher her back into the living room and claim a cushion on the loveseat, waiting to see if she will take the cushion next to me or put some distance between us by sitting in the chair Tank has not, as of yet, commandeered. Moments later, I feel the warmth radiating off her skin when she slides in next to me. This shouldn't thrill me so much, but it does.

"And?"

"Well, first my parents said to talk to her, and then she said to talk to my brother! I'm getting really tired of everyone giving me the run-around. I know something happened around twenty years ago, and if it involved my brother, then it would have been when he was in high school. I don't have any yearbooks from that time period—do you?"

"Oh." And here I thought we were either going to talk about Operation Wedding War or my undeniable infatuation with her. Okay, so I'm a bit relieved it's not the latter, though I'm feeling rather unrequited at the moment.

"Oh?" She purses her lips at me. "Was your oldest sister in school at the same time as my brother Mo?"

"I don't know, what do I look like, the family historian?"

She huffs out a breath of air. "Don't you want to understand this? If it's something silly, we can put it behind us and help our families reconcile—then we can get them to help us with our mission to destroy Über Brides. It's not working with just you and me—we aren't moving fast enough!"

"Well, we got a bad review. And your tiny penises are coming in soon...and you completed Tactical Exercise #4, otherwise known as Busta Seam. Right? I know this is going to take a little time..."

She buries her face in her palms, and it's all I can do not to wrap my arm around her. "Look...on my lunch hour today I went through some reports for Delmarva Beach Brides. I know it's only been two weeks, but sales are down for us. And this should be one of our busiest months. Next summer's brides are starting to come in, and winter brides are finalizing their selections before the summer rush."

"Wow, you're doing work for your dad during your lunch hour at Über Brides? That's—"

"That's hard work, Jason. It's dedication. It's every bit of tenacity and determination my parents have instilled in me and their parents before them." She shakes her head as she stands, smoothing out the skirt of her dress with her hands. When she crosses the room, Tank follows her, looking perplexed as to where Hannah is going. My little doggo is as perplexed as I am. I don't know how to convince her everything's going to be okay.

"You don't think my parents and grandparents instilled the same values in me?" I stand up to join her, folding my arms across my chest. I don't like what she's implying, that I don't care as much as she does. "Like you said, it's only been two weeks. Yes, we are going to have to recruit some help, but it doesn't have to be our families—and it shouldn't be. I haven't even told my parents yet. My dad is still convalescing..."

"Then who? I just moved back here. I don't even have any friends around here anymore." The sad tinge to her voice leads me to believe her lament goes further than not having friends we can recruit into our Wedding War army.

"I have friends," I assure her. "I have Meric and Lindy—I've already told you about them. And I have a friend named Shark, and one named Ryan. And Meric's friends, Drew and Chris and Jack. Hell, Drew owns an entertainment venue we could even use for a fake wedding if we wanted to stage one—and he even has a band—"

"Better than your friend Pete's band, I hope!" she retorts, trying to suppress a giggle but failing miserably.

"Oh, yeah, The Gallant Misfits is way better!"

"Oh, The Gallant Misfits is on Über Brides' list of partners," she shares. "I remember seeing their name."

"Anyway, my point is, I know some people, okay? And hey, my friend Meric, his girlfriend and most of those other people are all theater geeks. They put on a production last summer called *Yo Ho Rehoboth*, which his friends Jack and Claire wrote—it was amazing. I am sure they'd be able to play any roles we asked of them: bridezillas, drunk officiants—whatever we need!"

"Really?" Her eyes widen as they travel up and down my body, taking in my Friday's Formalwear polo shirt and my ubiquitous khaki pants. Now I'm really wishing I would have gotten a chance to change clothes after work before she stopped by.

I want to walk over, lift her chin with my finger and fix her gaze on mine as I promise her everything is going to be okay. I want to wrap my arms around her and pull her close to my chest, assuring her I'm going to do everything in my power to save both of our family businesses.

"I know you have no reason to trust me," I tell her instead. "I guess that's the real reason you want to know about the feud so bad..."

"Ding ding ding!" she bursts out. "Exactly." She huffs and shakes her head, making her burnished curls swirl around the edges of her beautiful face. "It seems like even more is at stake now—"

"Why do you say that?"

"Last night my parents gave me a check for a lot of money, money they've been saving since I was a little girl. They want me to use it as a down payment on a house," she reveals.

"Well, that's great! I mean, wow, that's really wonderful news, though—"

"Is it?" she argues. "If the business goes under, they are going to need that money. I don't want to tie it up in a house or a new car or whatever if six months down the road they have to close up shop. Not only will they be left high and dry, but what will I end up doing?"

I understand why she's upset, and I don't want to be dismissive, so I think carefully before I speak—not something I am particularly good at. "You're a very smart lady, Hannah. You'll always be able to find a job. You have an MBA, and there will always be a need for someone with that education and your experience..."

She just stares at me, trying to think of a rebuttal, but maybe I've finally given her an argument she can't rebut. I continue, "But look at me, on the other hand. I never even got my degree. Friday's Formalwear is all I've ever known. If my family's business goes belly up, I really will be screwed. What else am I going to do?"

"Well, I'd hire you." A sheepish grin spreads across her lips. "Well, I think I would. Pending any skeletons in your closet...or that of your family's." She winks.

"Fine," I concede, trying to remember how we got off on this tangent in the first place. *Oh, yes, the family feud.* "So, my sister Jessica is your brother Mo's age. But I don't think I have any of her yearbooks. You know, she and my sister Renee are stair-stepped in age with your two oldest brothers, but then there was a gap before Russ and I were born."

"How old is Russ? Maybe his freshman yearbook would have been their senior yearbook?" she calculates.

I shake my head. "Nope, there's a five-and-a-half-year gap there."

"Damn it. Well, where do your sisters live?" She taps her finger against the edge of her wine glass, which is now empty.

"Far. What about your brother?"

"He's in Chicago..."

"What if you just called him up and asked him?" I

suggest.

She gives me a look like I just told her to fly to the moon.

"What? You don't talk to him?"

She sighs. "We aren't close. He's always been pissed that I was Daddy's choice to take over the business. But he wasn't willing to get a degree or even learn about the industry. He dropped out of college after like one or two semesters. Daddy wanted someone who could keep up with the latest trends and changes, and Mo didn't want to be that person."

"That makes sense. Well, I could call my sister Jessica, I suppose. But first, maybe I'll see if I can find any of her stuff at my parents' house. I know she didn't take everything when she moved out all those years ago. She ran off with some boy—she later married him, but still. I want to say there are a few boxes of hers up in the attic. That first apartment they had was approximately the size of a postage stamp."

"I think it's worth a shot. So you're totally curious now too, right?" She leans toward me, biting that bottom lip again, just like she was when I kissed her.

Is she trying to kill me?

It takes everything in me not to walk over there and claim her lips again. *Gotta stay professional*, I tell myself. "I'm more interested in coming up with our next tactical exercise. What do you say I gather up my theater geek friends this weekend? We can get them all liquored up and ask them to help us take down the enemy. What do you say?"

"Okay, but only if you promise to look for that yearbook."

"Fine. Now, come up with something else you can

do in the store tomorrow to further the cause," I ante up.

"Alright. I think the tiny penises order is coming in tomorrow." The way she says "penises" in a whisper is absolutely adorable.

"Can I give you a hug? As a show of good faith?" I spread my arms out, hoping she'll fall prey to my charm.

She flashes me a tiny smirk as she moves forward, walking right into my embrace. As I take in a deep whiff of her vanilla and gardenia scent, I remind myself that we're comrades now, soldiers in the war against Über Brides.

You're not supposed to want to kiss your fellow soldiers, right?

EIGHT

I'm trying harder to be subversive. It just doesn't come naturally to me. But some people do make it rather easy.

"Hey, uh, sorry, you can't bring a dog in here," I say to the couple who has just waltzed right up the main aisle of the store with their perfectly groomed Pomeranian trotting behind them on a pink, jewel-studded leash.

The bride (I'm assuming) scoops up the little fluffball and holds it close to her chest. "This is my emotional support animal," she whines. The groom (once again, assuming) shoots me a glare as if he can't believe I've dared to tell his betrothed no.

"Sorry, we only allow support animals if they're wearing service vests and are accompanied by official documentation," I say through my clenched teeth. The clenched teeth are part of a new customer service smile I've recently perfected. I'm told it looks very natural. It was the stock boy who told me that, but who cares?

"Maybe I'll just take my business elsewhere!" she huffs and whips her heavily highlighted tresses behind her shoulder.

"Uh, okay." I shrug. *That's kind of the whole point of my being here, right?*

But before I can chalk up another victory, her companion rolls his eyes. "Here, give me Princess. I'll go wait in the car while you order the flowers."

She shoves the dog in the guy's face, and he pivots on his heel to storm out of the shop, triggering the electronic bell over the door when he swings it open dramatically. I have come to despise that sound. I'm so glad my parents' shop doesn't have one.

"So, you're interested in some flowers?" I ask, meeting the woman's gaze again. She looks almost helpless, like she doesn't know how to function without that little dog attached to her. Maybe it is an emotional support animal, after all.

"Yes. Our wedding is next weekend, but the florist where we've already booked the rest of our arrangements is unable to get the flowers we need for the altar at the church and the head table centerpieces." From the sound of desperation in her voice, you'd think she was on the waiting list to receive a kidney or something.

"Oh, what kind of flowers are we talking?" Über Brides had already negotiated contracts with at least three florists in the area. It really is supposed to be a one-stop bridal mega extravaganza, or whatever. Basically, it's crappy customer service provided by barely-better-trained-than-monkeys sales associates, forcing ridiculous price cuts from local vendors in exchange for so-called buying power, and then hiring a couple drivers to pick up stuff and deliver it to wedding venues. That's how they pull off the "Über Magic," as they call it.

"It's a Warrior Lily," she tells me with an arrogant sniff. "Can you get those for me?"

Warrior Lily—never heard of it, but considering this is Operation Wedding War, I'm loving the sound of it. Maybe I'll order some for me too, especially if they are expensive.

"Hold on, let me check." I gesture for her to follow me back to the counter where my trusty computer is waiting for my fingers to stroke its keyboard. I type in a few things, stare at the screen, type in some more, let my eyes dance across the search results...

"Can you hurry it up? I don't want my fiancé and dog to have to wait in the car any longer than necessary!" She lifts her little up-turned nose so I can practically see up her narrow nostrils.

"Oh, yes! Can you tell me how big you want the arrangements, and what other flowers you might like to have along with your...uh...Warrior Lilies?"

She rattles off a whole list of crap, which I diligently pretend to type in. Then she asks in the world's snottiest voice: "Sorry, was that too much for you to process?"

I squint at her, refusing to believe she just took that tone with me.

"I just know how uneducated the people in these stores are," she continues, stretching out a hand to admire her perfect manicure.

My jaw tightens to such an extreme level, I'm

surprised it doesn't shatter. I want to tell her so bad that I have a freaking MASTER'S degree, but somehow I hold myself back.

"No, I got all of that. I just need your name, address, phone number." I poise my fingers over the keys and give her an expectant glare. "Sorry, was that too much for you to process?"

She scoffs at me but doesn't fail to rattle off the information I requested. "And you're sure you can get the Warrior Lilies? I don't even care how much they cost."

"Oh, you're going to get them alright." I make a few more keystrokes then lift my eyes to her, a smile spreading across my face when I think about the hell I am about to unleash on this first class c-word.

I just ordered four funeral arrangements with satin RIP sashes draped across them. Jason would be so proud.

"Hannah, this is Meric, Lindy, Jack, Claire, Sonnet, Drew, Chris, Brynne, and Shark," I introduce as I point to each of my friends.

"Wait—" After Hannah's eyes flash to Claire, possibly in recognition, they snap right back to Sonnet. "You got married last year, didn't you?"

A wide grin stretches across Sonnet's face as she

nods.

"And you got your dress at Delmarva Beach Brides, right?" Hannah chirps.

"That's right. How did you know?" Sonnet's dark eyes bounce between Hannah's.

"Sonnet is such an unusual name! My parents own that shop, and I remember seeing your photo and name on my mom's corkboard. She always keeps a snapshot of each year's clients with their wedding dates on them. I bet you were a gorgeous bride!" Hannah gushes.

"Oh, you're so sweet. Your mom is the best! I loved working with her." Sonnet reaches out to squeeze Hannah's hand warmly. "I just had the best experience there, and so did all my bridesmaids. Right, ladies?" Brynne, Claire, and Lindy all nod and murmur in agreement.

"What a perfect segue way to why you've all been summoned here tonight," I interrupt before ushering the gaggle of folks into my kitchen. On the bar that opens onto the living room, I've placed two coolers with an assortment of adult beverages. And any moment now, the pizza delivery dude will be arriving with my six large pizzas, including a vegan one for Sonnet and Jack. "Drink up, everyone!"

There are some curious rumblings from my guests, but everyone does as instructed, arming themselves with their "weapon of choice." I shoot Hannah a smile. "The second phase of Operation Wedding War is almost underway."

"Fingers crossed they all go for it," she whispers back as she grabs a wine cooler and heads into the living room. She's immediately scooped up into a conversation between Lindy, Sonnet, and Claire.

Once everyone seems to be comfortably seated on my furniture and the extra chairs I've brought in, I position myself in the corner near the flat-screen TV that's mounted on my wall. "Okay, so how many of you noticed that Über Brides just opened up on Route 1 in the old VonMart?"

Nearly all the hands go up. Not Meric's or Shark's. I wouldn't expect my two best friends to have noticed, though. Meric is an accountant, and besides Lindy, I'm pretty sure he only notices things of numerical value. Shark is a rugby player, a real manly man and a self-professed bachelor like myself. I would never expect him to notice something like a bridal store.

"Okay, well, for those who don't know, Über Brides is a national chain, a bridal superstore that claims to be a one-stop shop for brides. They literally handle every aspect of a wedding from the attire to cakes to transportation companies. And, as you know, my brother and I operate Friday's Formalwear, which has been in my family for over forty years, starting with my grandparents. Hannah's family owns—"

"Wait!" Claire shouts then gasps, bringing her hands up to her lips in shock. Everyone's heads whip around to look at her. "You guys are the Fridays and the Robinsons, aren't you? I can't believe I'm just now putting two and two together."

Hannah buries her face in her palms, then sneaks a glance at me from between her fingers. Everyone else's eyes are darting between Claire and me, waiting for further elaboration.

"I knew Delmarva Beach Brides were the Robinsons...that's where I got my gown for both of my weddings." She laughs a little as she slings her arm around her husband Jack's shoulders. "And didn't you get your tux at Friday's, honey? Remember them telling us about the family rivalry they had with the Robinsons?"

"Oh, yeah, you know what?" Jack says, scratching at his salt-and-pepper beard. "I do vaguely remember something along those lines...but I don't remember what the family feud is about. Do you?" He glances back at his wife.

"Oh, it's not important now." I wave him off dismissively. The last thing we need is for Hannah to go off on a tangent trying to speculate about her grandmother and brother and who knows what else. "The important thing is that both of our family businesses are being threatened by Über Brides, and we want to take them down."

Drew rubs his hands together. "That sounds awesome! I'm in!"

Sonnet shoots him a glare. "Don't you think we should find out a little more first?" She turns to me. "How are you planning to 'take them down,' exactly?"

I lace my fingers together and crack my knuckles so loud that it makes Tank whimper from her crate in the spare bedroom.

"Oh! I was beginning to wonder what you'd done with Dolly!" Hannah says, glancing up. "Why is she locked up? Poor thing!"

"Tank is hardly a poor thing—"

"Tank? Dolly?" Lindy asks from across the room. "Which is it? I thought her name was Tank?"

"It's a terrible name, isn't it?" Hannah posits.

"Yeah, how can that cute furry little thing be called Tank?" Lindy agrees.

"Folks, we're getting off topic here!" I try to wrangle everyone's attention back to me and Operation Wedding War. That seems to do the trick. For my efforts, I finally receive quiet and attentive looks from my guests.

"So, Hannah and I have joined forces—despite our family history—and she is currently working for the enemy. She's been able to do a few low-level things like ordering the wrong invitations, a bunch of useless bachelorette party favors, and she's loosened the seams in the tuxes for a wedding this weekend—"

"And today's feat: I ordered funeral arrangements for a wedding instead of, you know, wedding ones!" Hannah interjects with a huge, gloating smile on her face.

"What?" my head whips toward her.

"Wow, that's kind of mean," Lindy decides, folding her arms across her chest.

"Oh, if you could have met this privileged biatch, you wouldn't think that at all!" Hannah defends herself.

"Anyway, we need to think much bigger and grander!" I sweep my hands into a dramatic gesture. "We need to get people to call corporate and complain, and we need to stage a lot more sabotages. That's where you guys come in!"

"I'm not following you, man," Drew states. I turn toward him and find his brows furrowed in confusion. I thought with him being a practical joker type of guy, he'd be all over this. I'm not surprised the ladies are a bit more skeptical. Drew's wife is sitting with her arms crossed over her chest and the beginnings of a scowl on her face.

"Alright, here's the deal. Hannah and I were

thinking about how we didn't want to ruin any actual weddings...well, not too badly anyway. So, instead, we were thinking we needed some actors to help us pull off a couple of the stunts we have planned—"

"I can vouch for your stunts after the whole thing with Meric's dog!" Lindy pipes up, causing laughter to erupt across the room like a sudden spring shower.

Finally, some recognition for my canine hostage negotiation skills!

"Right! And who better to help than people who wrote and produced a musical! And those who were starred in it?" I look right at Meric and Lindy.

"We're not all actors," Brynne points out. "But I'm definitely willing to try. Chris would probably be better at it than I would, though." She throws a kiss to her boyfriend.

"I'm no actor," Shark interjects, "and I don't think I ever could be. So why the hell am I here?"

"Does your family still own the horses and carriages they use for Return Day in Georgetown?" I question.

Meric looks stumped. "What the hell is Return Day? And, Shark, you own horses?" He shakes his head. "Geez, ya think you know a guy—then you find out he's been hiding horses from you!"

Shark leans forward, propping his tattooed arm on the side of the sofa. "Return Day is a big deal in Sussex County. After each local election, the votes are tallied and the winners are paraded around the Georgetown circle in a horse and carriage—"

"That's so bad ass!" Drew exclaims. "I mean, I already knew about Return Day, but I didn't know anyone who owned horses." Then he turns to Shark. "That's really cool, man."

Shark's face always seems to be fixed in a permanent scowl, but he looks extra-scowly today. He and Sonnet could have a scowl-off. Though I think hers might be more of a resting bitch face.

He finally answers, "Yeah, we have a few horses and two carriages. Why?"

"I have an idea for you, man. We'll discuss it later, but I wanted to know if you're on board."

"As long as no horses are harmed, then sure." He crosses his full-sleeve tattooed arms over his chest.

"Well, not permanently harmed...maybe just a bit of gastrointestinal discomfort," I explain but then realize I've said too much. "I have lots of other ideas too! Chris, you're a cop—I have some ideas for you. Jack, Claire, how do you feel about portraying wedding photographers?"

Jack stands up and looks around the room. "I don't know you too well, Jason, and Hannah, I've just now had the pleasure of meeting you, but I'm a strong believer in supporting local businesses. Claire and I consider ourselves local business owners what with our theater productions and all. Drew's a local business owner, and Lindy, Sonnet and I all teach at the Delmarva Academy, which is a local private school."

"What I think my husband is trying to say," Claire stands up next to her man, "is that we're on board—however you need us. We don't want Rehoboth Beach to lose family businesses that have been woven into the fabric of our community for decades. So, just let us know what you need from us—as long as it won't require bail money."

"Hey, that's what you've got me for!" Chris pipes up, and everyone laughs.

"So I think tonight went well?" Hannah questions as she helps me clean up the rest of the mess. I told her she didn't have to, but she insisted.

"Yeah, I told you everyone would be happy to help. Now we just have to figure out all the logistics."

She smiles as she tosses a stack of dirty paper plates into the trash can. "Shark's laughter about what you want him to do with the horse and carriage is still ringing in my ears!"

I chuckle, remembering the look on his face. Totally priceless. "Have you seen that episode of *Seinfeld*?"

She crinkles up her nose. "No? That's from *Seinfeld*? I've never watched it."

My eyes practically pop out of my head. "You've never seen *Seinfeld*? That's my favorite show of all time!" I grab her hand and pull her toward the living room.

"Where are we going?" She pulls back to resist me, her brown eyes narrowed.

"You have to watch it. I have every single season on DVD. Come on!"

"Oh, don't be silly," she protests, trying to wrangle herself free.

"No, no, you're not getting out of this one. You are hereby sentenced to three episodes of *Seinfeld*!" I joke around with her.

When she continues to protest, I pick her up and carry her to the loveseat, plopping her down on the left-hand side, her normal spot. She's erupted into girlish giggles by the time her ass hits the cushion, and now I'm laughing too.

"Three episodes? That seems a little harsh, don't you think?" She's still laughing at me.

I grab the remote and slide in next to her. Laying a hand on her thigh, I predict, "Once you've seen three, you'll want to just keep on going..."

"Is that so?" I don't miss the way the muscles in her thigh tense as the heat from my hand seeps into her skin.

"Wanna make a bet?" I don't know if it's the three or four beers I had or just because I've grown so comfortable with her, but that part of my brain that usually rejects my crazy ideas before they get too far developed doesn't even bat an eyelash.

She leans toward me, stabbing me with her dark, shining eyes. "Yeah, let's make a bet. Go ahead. Make your wager."

"Fine. So...if you laugh at any point during the first episode, you have to give me a kiss..."

Her eyes widen, then she tosses me a smug smirk as she folds her arms across her chest. "Fine. And if I don't?"

I really thought she'd balk at the whole kiss idea...but hmmm. She didn't. "Then...your choice?" I challenge her, watching another smirk creep across her face as she devises her counter-bet.

"Remember all those tiny penises I ordered?"

My eyebrows lift. "Yes?"

"Photo of you surrounded by tiny penises uploaded to your Instagram page—"

"How did you know I have an Instagram page?"

"Uh…" A sheepish grin takes the place of the smirk. "I may have stalked you just a teeny tiny bit." She puts her thumb and forefinger a short distance apart to indicate a small amount. "What do you say…deal?"

"You have a sick and twisted mind," I tease her. "I love it." I probably love it because her mind has grown immeasurably more sick and twisted under my tutelage. So, pat on the back for me.

"Alright, let's get this over with." She takes a nervous breath and arranges her hands on her lap as I dig the set of DVDs out of the cabinet under my TV. I have to Google what episode we need, then I queue it up on the blue-ray player.

We start to watch, and I notice she's sunk down farther and farther into the cushion. Her shoulder is pressed into my side, and I can't fight the urge to slide my arm around the back of the couch and then very slowly—stealthily—move it down until it's around her. It's that classic junior high movie theater date move, right? She doesn't seem to notice; she's too engrossed in watching Jerry and George conspire about how to get a marble rye back into George's future in-law's apartment. I am on pins and needles, waiting to hear anything remotely resembling a laugh, a chuckle, a giggle, a guffaw escape her lips.

"Oh my gosh, Jason! This is so silly!" she bursts out suddenly, punching me in the arm. "That's what you want to do with Shark's horse?"

"Shhhh," I say, leaning in close to her ear. "Just

watch."

We get to the part where Jerry has to steal the marble rye from the old lady outside the bakery, and then he takes off running down the street with a wild look on his face.

She cracks up.

It is the most beautiful sound I've ever heard.

"Aha!" I shout, jumping up from the loveseat. "I win!"

She reaches up, grabs my hand and yanks me back down beside her. "Shush! I want to see how it ends!"

And just like that, I've created a fellow *Seinfeld* fan.

When it's over, I turn off the blue-ray player and pivot to face her. Now that the screen is dark, there's only a dim light coming from the kitchen illuminating Hannah's gorgeous face, her wide, glistening eyes, her sculpted cheekbones, her impossibly kissable lips.

"So, I guess you won..." she says softly. It's not so much a statement of defeat as it is one of expectation.

"I won't kiss you if you don't want me to." I mean, I'm a gentleman. The last thing I want is for her to feel like I'm taking advantage of her.

Her voice squeaks out, even softer than earlier, "It's not that I don't want you to, Jason."

"It's not?"

"That's not why I left the other night. I didn't leave because I didn't want to kiss you—"

I want to respond. I want to voice any one of these gazillion thoughts swirling around my head, but I don't seem able to make any of them into words.

She reaches out and strokes a finger down my face, a lightning bolt streaking through me at her warm touch across my stubbly cheek. "I left because I didn't want to stop at kissing..."

NINE

I've pilfered a couple tuxes from the shop, and I don't think Russ even noticed. It's my day off, and I've promised Hannah we are going to nail this carriage ride thing today. The logistics have been a nightmare, and Shark is about to throat punch me, but I think it's going to be well worth it.

The wedding is taking place at a lovely church in downtown Rehoboth, only blocks from the ocean. Who wouldn't want a horse-drawn carriage to carry them from the ceremony to the reception at the Atlantic Sands? Hannah sold the bride on the romantic notion of the resounding clip-clop of hooves making their way down the Avenue with all the tourists straining to see the fairytale bride and groom on their happy day.

Plus I promised Shark a hundred bucks. *See, everyone is happy!* This plan has to work.

Shark unloads the horse and carriage from his parents' ginormous trailer, and it's beautiful: a glossy black with "Kelly Carriage Company" emblazoned across the side in a shiny gold curlicue font. "Wow! Do you guys typically do weddings?"

"Yeah, all the time," he assures me. "It's usually my brother Declan who handles it, but due to the...special nature...of your request, I figured I better do the honors."

I pull out a huge can from the shopping bag I'm carrying and set it on the fence post next to the carriage. "Think this will work?"

"I brought my most flatulent horse," Shark assures me, patting the large brown beast's head. The horse gives a little snort, then flicks his ears.

"Okay, let's give it a shot. Hope he's hungry!" I pull a can opener out of the bag and make quick work of the lid.

"Rudy is always hungry." He grabs the can and offers it to the horse, whose lips pull back, exposing his teeth as he sniffs it. It doesn't take long for his entire muzzle to disappear inside the can. "Oh, yeah, he loves it."

I smile at the way the garland of flowers Hannah sent over is scalloped across the back of the carriage along with a "Just Married" sign. It looks perfect. She's going to be at the church to take some photographs so we can capture the moment for posterity's sake—and social media posts, of course. Her boss, Patsy, was thrilled Hannah had taken the initiative to make these arrangements. I don't know how thrilled she's going to be when the scathing bad reviews come in!

"I sure hope this works." I glance down at my watch. "We've only got about ten minutes to get to the church. Is that enough time?"

"Yep, we're all ready to go when you are. So what is it we're hoping for exactly?"

"Lots of gas or droppings, the more and louder the better. Enough to make the bride and groom complain about Über Brides all over social media, maybe call up corporate, if we're lucky." I swing my leg up onto the floor of the carriage and pull myself into the velvety cushioned bench.

Shark joins me on the carriage bench and slaps the reins down on Rudy's back as he gives him a command that sounds like a loud smooching noise. *Alrighty then.* We lurch forward and make our way out of the alley between Delmarva Art Connection and a bed and breakfast next door.

We pull up to the church minutes later, and Hannah appears out of nowhere clutching a camera. Her bouncy curls are blowing in the breeze, and so is her full skirt. I catch a glimpse of her silky brown skin and take a deep breath, hoping I can keep my concentration on our mission. I can't help but think about the party last week when I had all my friends over to ask for their help with Operation Wedding War. All we did after everyone left was kiss—okay...I may have made it to second base—but I haven't been able to get her off my mind. We agreed to try to keep our focus on driving Über Brides out of Rehoboth, but what I really wish is—

"Hey, Jason, Shark!" she calls. "The ceremony will be finishing up any moment. The bride is wearing a gown from my parents' shop. It's gorgeous." She walks up, her hand angled over her face so the sun isn't glaring in her eyes.

"Um...did you sell her the gown?" I question, my

brows furrowed. "Didn't she think it was weird you were working at Über Brides now?"

"No, she bought the dress last year. Don't worry, she won't suspect anything. I don't even plan for her to notice me here, but I wanted to snap a few pics for my mom, and, of course, of the horse and carriage. You guys look fantastic, by the way! I definitely want a horse and carriage if I ever get married. But not one who just ate a can of Beefarino. By the way, that's not a real thing, is it?"

"We improvised," I assure her. I had already tossed the evidence in the dumpster in the alley where we were parked.

Before she can respond, the church doors burst open, and sounds of laughter and chattering fill the air. "Here they come!" She flashes me an excited smile as people begin to spill out of the building and make their way down onto the sidewalk. All the children are pointing at the horse, and everyone is smiling and gushing about how lovely the carriage is.

I have a momentary pang of guilt that I'm about to put a serious damper on some happy couple's wedding day. But I have a war to win. *And all's fair in love and war, right?* Besides, it's not like it will ruin their day. It's only a short twenty-minute jaunt over to the Atlantic Sands, if even that. So they have to smell a stinky horse butt for a few minutes. *Whatever.* Losing my family business would mean a lifetime of misery for me.

"Howdy," Shark says to the groom as he helps his newly minted wife up into the carriage. "I'm Shannon, and this is Jason."

"Shannon?" I mouth, looking at him with huge eyes. I've known him for years, and I never knew that was his real name. I'd sort of convinced myself that his parents had actually named him Shark.

He's ignoring me, though, looking back at the couple to make sure they are all situated before we press onward. He makes the kissing sound at Rudy again, and we jerk into motion. I glance back to see the bride and groom happily waving to all of their wedding guests.

We don't make it more than ten or fifteen feet before Rudy drops a massive foul-smelling dump. I put my hand over my face to hide my smile, but when the smell hits me...*oh my god.* It's like a skunk and rotten eggs had a giant mutant baby! I know it's going to take a little bit longer for the smell to hit our passengers and—

"Oh!" the bride's voice pierces the air.

"Wow!" the groom chimes in. I glance back just in time to see him clutch his nose, trying to block the disgusting odor.

We make it about twenty more feet, and Rudy lets another bomb fly. It seems like he has diarrhea. All I can say is "Mission Accomplished!" I give Shark a pat on the shoulder.

He turns his head to the backseat. "Everything okay back here?"

"What the hell is wrong with that horse?" the groom shouts, clearly agitated.

"So sorry, it seems he's having some digestive issues," Shark explains in what suddenly sounds like an Irish brogue.

"Nice touch, buddy," I want to say, but I'm laughing too hard to get any words out of my mouth. I'm laughing so hard, I have to keep my face straight ahead, or the bride and groom are going to see me absolutely busting my gut.

I only wish Hannah were here to enjoy this hilarious and thoroughly revolting moment with me!

Hannah

My sister Ruth is the typical middle child. As soon as I tell her I'm trying to find a yearbook from Mo's senior year, she shifts her gaze to the floor as if I've just told her Mo has a terminal disease or something. She hates any type of family drama. It's like it makes her physically ill unless she is able to help smooth it over.

"Why can't you just ask him?" she suggests. "I'm sure he could tell you anything you want to know."

"He's all the way in Chicago," I argue, "and I haven't spoken to him since Christmas. I just don't feel comfortable calling him up and—"

"Is it because you're afraid Tracy will answer the phone?"

Yeah, that was the other reason the rest of the family didn't get along with Mo. Not only had he stormed off to Chicago, indignant that Daddy didn't want him to take over the business when he retired, but he married this truly hateful person named Tracy. Actually, you know what? I'm not going to hesitate to label her as she truly is: *a biatch*. You know I only use that word for someone who really deserves it.

"Why do you need it, anyway?"

I know she's not going to appreciate my reason, but

I don't know why I was expecting her to just hand over her freshman yearbook so I could dig up some dirt on our oldest brother.

"I'm doing some research," I tell her.

"I understand you've been doing a lot of 'research' lately." Her eyes widen and she purses her lips, which makes me think she doesn't necessarily approve. "How is that all going?"

"It's going well. I've already made a few people so mad they've complained to corporate. My boss has a phone call with them next week, as a matter of fact. They might be sending in reinforcements soon."

"Oh, well, I guess that's a good thing?" She gives a tiny shrug. "Does the yearbook have something to do with Über Brides?" She smooths out her straightened hair, arranging it around her shoulders. She's always had the nicest hair; it's always been smooth and long. She got the only thin genes in the family too. Plus she's one of those people who is so sickeningly sweet and thoughtful, it's almost hard to be around her sometimes. I always have to remind myself of my own strengths when I'm around her.

"Hannah?" She snaps me out of my daze, making my eyes jerk back to hers.

"Oh, well..." I hate lying to her. I mean, just looking into those milk chocolate brown eyes is like taking truth serum. What if I told her? What if I just came right out and told her I was working with Jason? His brother knows, after all. What if Ruth knew too? What if I could have an ally?

"What is it?" She lays a gentle hand on my forearm as her lashes flutter with concern, her brows knitting together.

I blow a long breath out and look around to see if anyone else is paying attention. It's Sunday dinner at my parents' house. That means all the Robinsons in a fifty-mile radius are present and accounted for. "Okay, promise you won't tell?"

"Yes, of course." She gives me a smile, the best *you can trust me smile* she can muster.

"Don't freak out," I implore her. The smile fades, and the knitted brows return, along with a bit of a squinty glare. "Uh...I'm working with Jason Friday to sabotage Über Brides." I blurt it out so fast, I don't get a chance to change my mind.

"You're what?!" she squeals, and this time she slaps my arm in shock. "Girl, you cannot be serious!"

I sigh. "I'm serious. And—"

"And?" Her eyebrows arch.

"Well, did you ever notice how cute Jason was when we were in high school?"

Her mouth forms an O as she stares at me, her eyes bouncing between mine. "You CANNOT BE SERIOUS RIGHT NOW!"

"Shhhhh!" I put my finger to my lips. "They'll hear you. Come on! I need to tell someone. It's killing me!"

"So Mama and Daddy don't know you're seeing him?" she presses.

"'Seeing' is a strong word...but we did kiss a couple of times," I reveal.

"Oh my god," she breathes out, fanning herself with both hands. She is not the type to take the Lord's name in vain. If Mama heard that, we'd have both gotten a lecture.

I clear my throat, trying to gather my wits about me

so I can explain the rest. "When I first found out about Über Brides, Daddy made some kind of comment about what the Fridays might think of that development. And I got to thinking about it, so I looked Jason up on Facebook to see what he's doing now—and it turns out he's managing their store, along with his brother Russ."

"Oh, I remember Russell Friday!" my sister exclaims, grasping at her chest. "He was a hottie too! And our star quarterback." She does a dramatic swooning movement which includes fake collapsing on the bed.

I laugh. "He's married now with a little girl. But anyway—I just decided to call Jason up and see if he wanted to put our heads together to figure out how to steal business away from Über Brides and hopefully get them to close their doors forever."

"So you're not doing it entirely on your own like Mama and Daddy think?"

I shake my head. "No, Jason is the idea man. I just execute the orders." I laugh. "Well, I have thought of a couple things myself, but that guy...his mind is brilliantly deviant!"

She joins me in my giggles. We're so loud that I'm struck with the fear that Mama or Grandmama are going to bust in at any moment. "Shhhh, okay?" I whisper, my face heating up from all the extra blood flow. I feel like we're little girls again, conspiring to hide a secret from our parents.

"And you kissed?" she whispers back, her eyes wide. "If they find out they're gonna be livid!"

"I know, I know..." I huff out another breath, trying to get my racing heart to calm down. "But that's why I need the yearbook. I've been trying to weasel some information out of Mama and Grandmama about what happened to cause the huge rift between our families, and from what I understand, it has to do with Mo. At first Mama and Daddy tried to act like it involved our grandparents, but that was clearly just designed to throw me off the scent. I just don't understand what could have happened with our brother, and, if it was something that important, why I don't remember it. I mean if it happened when Mo was in high school, surely I'd be old enough to remember. Do you?"

My sister focuses her chocolate eyes on the wall over my head for a moment, letting her mind flip through her memories of Mo's high school days. "Wait...yes...something is coming back to me..."

I lean forward on the bed, trying not to fall off in anticipation. She's a few years older than me, so she is in a much better position to remember this stuff than I am.

"I remember Mama and Daddy yelling about something. And Grandmama and Granddaddy were here too. It was late at night, and we were all supposed to be asleep. And then the next day, Mo got grounded..."

"Really? I guess I didn't hear that—or I blocked it out somehow. Why did he get grounded?"

She taps her finger against her cheek as she tries to retrieve the long-buried memory. "I can't remember—it had to do with a girl though, I'm pretty sure..."

"I wonder if it was Jessica Friday!" I gasp. "It has to be... Darn it, we need that yearbook!"

"Okay, now I want to know too. I thought Mama and Daddy always said it was Grandmama and Granddaddy who had had the falling out with the Fridays."

"Yeah, that's what they tried to tell me the other

day. Why would they lie to us about it for so long? It doesn't make any sense to me." I purse my lips while I try to imagine all the possible scenarios. "So can you get the yearbook?"

"Yes. I can try to bring it over tomorrow after work. Is that okay?" Ruth asks, staring at me through hopeful eyes.

I nod. "Yeah. The intrigue is killing me. Or you can look it up when you get home and call me?"

She giggles and holds up her index finger. "On one condition."

"What's that?"

"You tell me how the kiss was with Jason?"

When my phone rang later that night, I was hoping it would be Ruth with the details she'd gleaned from Mo's senior yearbook. Unfortunately, it is Patsy. The fact that she is calling on a Sunday evening makes my heart pound against my ribs as my finger hovers over the answer button, trying to decide if I should press it.

Maybe she's calling to fire me? I wonder. That would ruin our entire operation. I take a deep breath knowing if I don't answer, I'll never be able to sleep tonight wondering what she wanted. And I'd still have to face her tomorrow one way or the other. "Hello?"

"Thank God you're home, Hannah," she gasps out, panting heavily.

"It's a cell phone. It goes where I go," I try to say as cheerily as possible. "What's wrong?"

"Can you go to the store for me?" Her voice is as shrill and unpleasant as always.

"What? Right now? It's Sunday night... We're closed."

"I know, but I left some important papers on my desk, and Jeremy from corporate is probably going to have a coronary if I don't get him the numbers he's asking for by 8 PM tonight. I'm out of town this weekend so I can't get them myself. Plus they're breathing down my neck about the three new one-star reviews on our Facebook page. Can you see if you can delete those or something? And you don't even want to hear the rant some customer went on over at Yelp about the seams in their tuxes ripping out last weekend at their wedding—"

Yes! I fist-pump, wishing Jason were here to celebrate with me. I almost miss the rest of what Patsy has to say, I'm so excited.

"I don't know, Patsy, it's family time here today, and it would be really hard for me to get away—"

"I know I'm asking a lot, but if I don't get these numbers to Jeremy ASAP, they're almost certainly going to send someone down from corporate, and we might all lose our jobs—"

Huh. And close down, maybe? I can't help but smile, despite the sheer panic in my boss's voice. *Maybe Operation Wedding War is doing better than I thought?*

"Please? If you do it, I'll try to talk corporate into hiring some more help. I promise."

There's nothing like the sound of desperation to tug at my heartstrings. I am not very good at saying no. "Alright. Tell me what I'm looking for." I start to pull on my shoes as I head down the stairs. I gesture to my parents that I have to go out and mouth that it's my Über Brides boss on the phone. Patsy starts rambling about what it is she needs me to find.

I get in the car and start it up, the directions from Patsy still fresh in my mind. I want to leverage this as best I can. She's letting me into her office. She told me where the master key is. I have to call Jason and find out how we can work all this to our advantage.

But before I'm able to dial his number, I realize a text has come in. My sister has sent me an image. When I open it, I find it's a photo of a page from my brother's senior yearbook...

TEN

"They keep the master key in a drawer under the front counter? That is probably the dumbest place you could choose. Why not just dangle it from the ceiling with a big sign that says, 'Hey, thieves, here's the master key. Have fun stormin' the castle!'"

"I don't think you should be here, Jason," she says, totally ignoring my hilarious *Princess Bride* reference. If I find out she hasn't seen that movie, there's going to be a real *come to Jesus meeting*—a phrase I learned from her. "What if Patsy shows up?"

"If Patsy were planning to come in, wouldn't she have just gotten the damn numbers for her boss herself?" I turn back toward her, accidentally flashing the light right in her face.

"Hey! Watch it with that thing!" She rubs at her

eyes as I realize I'm blinding her and reposition the beam accordingly.

She doesn't want to turn on the main lights in case the police drive by and see someone was in the shop after closing. They might get suspicious, she said. And it doesn't matter to her that our local cop friend Chris Everson is already well aware of Operation Wedding War and even plans to take part at some point—as soon as I figure out the best way to use him. He's my ace in the hole.

I snag the key, and she leads me down the hallway to her boss's office. I hand her the flashlight so she can train it on the door while I bust in. "We can turn the light on in here, right?"

"Yes, of course," she breathes out. Her chest is heaving up and down in her gray Penn tee. She's also wearing cut-off sweatpants. I have never seen her dressed more casually, but I love it. It's nice to see her relaxed for once. At least clothing-wise. She's anything but relaxed demeanor-wise at the moment. But I guess I can't blame her.

"Okay, calm down. This is going to be fine," I assure her.

She rolls her eyes at me. "I hate it when someone tells me to calm down. It's always a man, too. I'll be however keyed up I want to be, thank you very much." She expels an exasperated huff before rifling through the papers on her boss's desk for the reports she requested.

"You know, there's got to be other shit we can do in here..." My mind works to unravel this new puzzle as Hannah thumbs through papers in a manila folder.

"Here! I found it—the weekly sales report." She holds it up victoriously.

I snatch it out of her hand and immediately begin to scan through the lines of figures. It's about two seconds before I drop the paper on the desk with a grunt. "Holy mother of—"

"Language!" She glares at me, her index finger pointed at me like she's about to wag it in my face.

"You know, I really hate it when someone wags their finger at me," I retort. "It's always a woman, too. I'll swear however goddamn much I want to, thank you very fucking much!"

She apparently doesn't think my joke is funny at all because not even a smirk plays on her lips. Instead, she picks up the piece of paper, and as she begins to examine the numbers, her honey brown eyes grow wider and wider. "Shit," she says—her one word really conveying everything we are both thinking and feeling at the moment. Plus, I know how rare it is for a curse word to come out of her mouth. Only something truly curse word-worthy could trigger that reaction from her.

"I don't know how they can gross that much in one week!" I shake my head in utter shock, the numbers I read still very much tattooed on my brain. "We don't even gross that much in a month. Maybe not in a quarter!"

"Well, their inventory is a lot more diverse...and those numbers are gross..." Her voice drops as she continues to stare at the figures. "Oh, wait. Well, the net is pretty ridiculous too." She points at it.

"Wow, how can they not have more overhead than that? How many employees did you say there were?"

"Eight," she answers. "Which I know sounds like a decent amount, but six of them are part-time. Patsy and I are the only full-time employees... Actually, I'm not even full-time. I only get thirty-five hours."

"So they don't have to pay you benefits, right?"

She sadly nods her head. "But Patsy said if I do this, get her these numbers tonight, she might be able to convince corporate to hire someone else. Probably just another part-time employee but—"

"Fucking Über Brides." My jaw is ticking I'm so damn mad. What the hell is wrong with people that they want to support this evil empire screwing over their employees and their vendors? I already looked up to see how much their CEO Victor Schneider makes in a year, and it's around five billion.

Five billion dollars!

I'm seething, I'm so angry now that I've seen these numbers. "We have to step up our game. I want them out of Rehoboth by the end of the summer."

Hannah glances up at me, her eyes looking so sad. "What we've done already doesn't seem to be enough. I mean, the busted tux seams folks were pretty mad, but even your bride and groom with Sir Farts a Lot the other day didn't seem overly upset."

"You weren't there, Hannah; the groom was livid. I have no doubt they'll be leaving a review when they get back from their honeymoon. They might even call corporate to demand their money back," I assure her. "That was an awesome prank. We can do it again to another couple too...Shark is game."

She sighs. "Everything we want to do takes so much planning—the execution will need to be flawless. I just have a feeling this is all going to blow up in my face pretty soon. And, oh—I totally forgot to show you this." She whips out her phone and hands it to me, open to a photo.

I stare, trying to make sense of it. It's a black and

white prom photo of a young, athletic-looking African American boy and a—wait, that's my sister Jessica.

"Where did you get this?"

"My sister found her yearbook. It was from her freshman year but Mo's senior year. Look—your sister and my brother were named Prom King and Queen."

"Wow, that's craziness!" I stare at it again, wondering how I didn't know about that. I was Prom King, and I don't remember anyone in my family saying my sister had held the title of Prom Queen when she was a senior. That's kind of a big thing not to mention...

"I'm so confused..." She exhales a long breath as she slumps down into her boss's chair and buries her face in her hands.

"About the yearbook photo?" I lean down to put my arm on her shoulder. I want to be supportive, but I can't have her breaking down now. I need her to stay strong. We both have to be one hundred percent committed to this.

"About everything," she murmurs, looking up at me with big, glossy tears hanging in her eyes. "The yearbook photo, Operation Wedding War, you—"

I reach out to grasp her hands in mine then lift her to her feet before sweeping her into my embrace. She fits there so perfectly, her head cradled against my chest. I swear I can feel her heartbeat fluttering through her gray t-shirt. I try to keep my hands from wandering down to squeeze her butt, which looks absolutely scrumptious in those cut-off sweatpants...but no, I'm being all comforting and shit, and I'm not going to let myself succumb to temptation.

She starts to sob into my chest when I pull her back to look at me. "Hannah, the only thing you need to worry about right now is Operation Wedding War, okay? The yearbook photo we'll get to the bottom of later. The stuff between you and me—"

Her chin jerks up, and I see a flash of something that looks like frustration tighten her features. "Stuff?"

It's my turn to let out a long sigh. "Yeah, I don't know what's happening here either, but I know I like you. I know when I'm with you, I don't want you to go... And I don't want to go either. I know I want to kiss you again...and again..."

"You do?" She tilts her head and looks at me, the corners of her lips just slightly curling upward.

"I do. Whatever is happening between us, I feel it... I'm just trying to remember the task at hand and not get too carried away—"

"Plus the thing with our families..." Just as quickly as they turned up, her lips shift direction, the corners now tilted down. Her face follows, her gaze trailing to the floor.

"Right, but, honestly if we can pull this off, then they'll forget about that stupid disagreement that happened twenty years ago, don't you?" I lift her chin with my finger, forcing her eyes back on mine.

"But if I can figure out what happened between Mo and your sister, maybe..." Her voice trails off. She realizes I'm right, but she never likes to admit it.

"Let's focus on this first, okay? You've got to call your boss back, and I have a couple ideas on how we can really piss corporate off." My wheels have been secretly turning this whole time, and damn, I'm a freaking genius.

Her voice trembles, "I, I don't think I can call her. I'm—"

"Yes you can, and here's what you're going to say." I grab the sheet of paper and take a couple of zeroes off all the figures. "Looks like Über Brides had a really bad week..."

Her eyes light up as she realizes what I've done. "Oh, yeah...quite a bad week." She flashes me a mischievous smile.

"You can do this, Hannah. Come on. Here, call her from her own phone." I reach down and pick up the receiver.

"Okay, fine, but if she gives me permission to hire another part-timer...I think it should be you."

I don't know how Russ is going to feel about that, but I figure we can work out something. "Deal."

"Do you know anything about this?" Patsy asks, her hands on her hips as she glances at the stack of boxes in the storeroom. "Someone ordered a thousand of these things!"

"Oh...that's weird. Whose name is on the order form?" My eyes trail over the boxes, knowing instantly they're the bachelorette party favors I fudged the numbers on.

Patsy looks down at her clipboard and frowns. "Stacy," she reads. "Dammit, that's the fourth or fifth time I've caught her screwing up. Look, Hannah, I know we're short on help right now, but I'm going to have to let her go—"

"Oh, no, please don't do that!" I protest. "We're already swamped. Can't I just train her better or something?"

Patsy lets out a huff of air as her pale eyes bounce between mine. She's such a strange-looking creature, so small and mouse-like, so pale she's nearly translucent. Ever seen a picture of a naked mole rat? I'm pretty sure that's her spirit animal.

"You can keep her this week while we hire someone else, but then we'll let her go when the new person gets up to speed," she tells me.

"Wait, you said we could hire someone in *addition to*, not replace someone we already have!" Besides, Stacy is my scapegoat. I really need her to stick around.

"The numbers we gave corporate were terrible. They're very unhappy, and we just got two more horrible reviews on Facebook. Did you hear about the wedding party that had trouble with their tuxes? It's almost like someone deliberately ripped out the seams..."

"I think that only proves we need *more* help, not less! I think we're getting such horrible reviews because we don't have enough employees to provide good customer service—"

She chews on that for a moment, but then the electronic bells chime to indicate someone has entered the store. It's a wiry dark-haired man with a short, perfectly groomed beard, accompanied by a taller man with broad shoulders and golden blond hair that's long on top with lighter blond highlights in the front. Patsy tilts her head at me, effectively ending our conversation.

I try to swallow down the remainder of my completely warranted indignation as I walk over to greet the couple. "Hi, can I help you with something?"

"Yes, we'd like to go over some plans for our wedding with a consultant? We need tuxes, a cake, flowers, a photographer, invitations—you know, the works!" The man's animated expressions match his exaggerated gestures.

"Okay, no problem." I usher them to the counter at the back of the store where we do consultations with couples. "We have lots of decisions to make!"

"Do you have any problem with two grooms?" the taller man questions.

"Uh, no, of course not." I give him a smile. "Congratulations to you both!"

"Oh, so you just assume we're the ones getting married!" the smaller man pipes up, his hands automatically flying to his hips. He stops and glares at me, shooting daggers out of his eyes.

"Whoa, uh, I'm sorry, I—"

"That's it!" he shouts, turning toward his companion.

Okay, maybe it's just a friend. I shouldn't have assumed, but wow, talk about an overreaction. I'm pretty sure he said "our wedding."

"It's okay, Jean-Marc, we'll just take our business elsewhere," his blond friend suggests, patting him on the shoulder.

"I will not *only* take my business elsewhere, but I will shout from the rooftops about this disastrous experience we've had today!" "Jean-Marc" continues to yell, making the head of every customer and staff member in the store swivel toward him in a split second.

I freeze with panic when I see the horrified looks on their faces.

But he doesn't stop there. He continues to spew his anger across the wide expanse of our showroom. "Rehoboth Beach is a gay community! We should have businesses that cater to our needs, and I won't sit idly by while this sorry-ass excuse for a homophobic-as-fuck so-called bridal superstore continues its scourge on our beautiful community! Brides aren't the only important people in a wedding, you know, you sexist pigs!"

"Oh, sir, I'm so sorry, we—" I force out through my nearly frozen lips. I'm just so blindsided, I can barely think straight.

"Come on, Raymond!" he continues, turning his head to his friend. "Let's go to Friday's Formalwear where we'll be treated with dignity and class." His head rockets back to me so fast I could have sworn he gave himself whiplash. "You better believe I'm going to call up your corporate offices and give them a piece of my mind, and after that, I'll be launching a social media campaign to warn others of the unacceptable treatment we received here today."

"But I—" I eke out.

It's too late. Jean-Marc and Raymond storm out of the store, and all but one or two customers follow shortly thereafter. I turn around to glance toward the back of the store, and sure enough, Patsy is standing right there with her mouth gaped open. Then my phone buzzes with a text from Jason.

Hey, did Claire's friend Jean-Marc stop by? He and his buddy are going to come in and raise some hell. You can thank me later!

I march right over to Jason's house after work. Well, when I say "march," I really mean "drive," but it sounds so much more adamant and deliberate if you use the word "march." Plus, you know, the whole war metaphor thing. I pound on his door, but he doesn't answer, and when I peer into his garage, I notice his car isn't there. However, I can hear Dolly barking up a storm and throwing her tiny little body against the front door. *Poor thing!*

I sneak around to the side of his house to see if there's another way in or maybe a hidden key. I circle the house all the way around to the back, which has a cute little patio I can envision with a smoking grill and a wicker table set all decked out for a barbecue. When I try the back door, I find I'm in luck. I hear the pitter-patter of Dolly's little feet come racing from the front door to the back door, and she's so excited, she skids across the tiled floor in the kitchen and nearly crashes into the garbage can. *Oops!* That was the most adorable fail of the century.

I pull out my phone and give Jason a head's up: *I came over to talk to you, but you're not here, so I broke in and stole Dolly. See, you're not the only one who can dognap!*

I've heard the story of how he and Lindy rescued Meric's dog from his ex last summer a zillion times. It's a cute story, but it has nothing on the stories we're quickly racking up at Über Brides. Today's outburst with Jean-Marc and company is right up there with Sir-Farts-A-Lot the horse!

"Come here, pretty girl." I locate her leash on the

washing machine near the back door and bend down to clip it on her tiny wriggling body. "I'm only going to call you the dignified name of Dolly, alright? You are much too beautiful to be called Tank. Yuck!"

She seems to agree as she jumps up to try to lick my face. I take her right back out the back door, and she strains against her leash, anxious to get onto the grass where she immediately takes an enormous dump. *Nice. I'll let Jason clean that up later.*

It's only a few minutes later that Jason's shiny black truck pulls into his driveway. He beeps his horn at me, then steps out with a gorgeous grin spread across his face. "I didn't expect to see you today."

"Disappointed?" I question, my eyebrow arched.

"Hell no." He bands his arms around my waist and pulls me toward him for a kiss, an embrace I promptly wiggle out from.

"What's with the PDA? I thought we were trying to keep this—" I gesture between our two bodies, "—to ourselves?"

He chooses to ignore my question. "So how was it? Did Jean-Marc steal the show?"

"Steal? It was the only show in town. And it made almost everyone in the store leave. I can't wait to see what he posts on social media." I take a breath when I realize I'm racing through my words so fast Jason can probably barely keep up. "He is going to follow through on his threats, right?"

"Oh, yeah. He and Claire are carefully crafting a statement to post on social media and to send to the corporate office. Plus I'm pretty sure his friend was recording it." His grin widens even further. "This may do it, Hannah. It may be enough to get them to fire

143

Patsy, you, and if their sales numbers are dismal when it's the busiest season of the year, I can't imagine them staying open too long."

"How do we know they won't just dig their heels in and double down their efforts? Patsy keeps saying they're going to send someone down from corporate— and it doesn't sound like a good thing when she says it." Dolly has managed to wrap her leash around my legs approximately four times, so if I were to step, I'd promptly keel over. Jason laughs when he notices and takes the leash from me so he can unwind his dog.

"Oh, hold on." He digs his phone out of his pocket and takes a look at the number calling him. "It's Pete again. I just know he's going to ask me to go to his show tonight. You don't want to go, do you?"

"Wasn't the first time torture enough?" I shrug. "Seriously, your friend's band sucks. Hasn't anyone ever told him?"

"Nope. I think we all just suffer through." It is rather tedious to get invitations from him all the time, but I try to be a good friend and catch his shows when I can.

"Does he support any of *your* work? Has he ever rented a tux from you? Or referred any business to you?" I ask.

Jason's eyes narrow as he considers my question. "No, and you know what, his sister is getting married this summer, and I am pretty sure they got their tuxes from freakin' Über Brides! He's even in the damn wedding!"

"Are you serious? That's low." I shake my head. Whatever happened to *quid pro quo*?

"Hey, let's go inside. Are you hungry?" He takes my

hand and begins to lead me back around to the rear entrance.

I am hungry, but not for food. There's something about the way he looks right now with his five o'clock shadow starting to outline his sharp jawline and the way his dark, wavy hair is mussed up after he runs his long, thick fingers through it that has me thinking crazy thoughts. I already know what his lips feel like on mine...how would they feel on other areas? How would mine feel grazing over other parts of his skin?

His Adam's apple bobs when he swallows as if he's just read my devious thoughts. Am I really that transparent? I watch his biceps flex when he reaches down to scoop Dolly up into his arms. He waits for me to enter the house first, but I'm more interested in checking out the rear view. I know he was scoping my backside out last night in those cut-off sweats. I'm not completely oblivious to how round and curvy my booty looks in them! That's the main reason I didn't change before meeting him at Über Brides.

I smooth my skirt down around my hips, take a deep, cleansing breath, and head up the steps and inside the back door. I try to remember that I'm a good girl, he's a good guy, our families are mortal enemies and we're currently engaged in the battle of the century: the little guys against the bloodsucking corporate giants. *So why have I never wanted to be a bad girl more than I do right now?*

He drops Dolly to the floor, and she scurries off to her food and water bowls. I watch her, amused by how she stuffs her whole face eagerly into the food dish. Taking me completely by surprise, Jason grabs me around the waist and spins me around to face him. I'm stunned by the look in his eyes. He always looks witty, like he's about to crack a joke, but this look...it's different. It's hot, intense. *Downright steamy.*

"What are you doing?" The words tumble out of my mouth, but it's immediately apparent he has no intention of answering me.

In seconds he has me pinned against the pantry door, his lips ravenously feasting on the delicate skin below my ear and down my neck. Desire surges through me as I thread my fingers through his wavy dark hair. Just when I think it can't get any more passionate, his lips claim mine, pulling me into a sweet surrender of biting, sucking, and dueling tongues. My body is on fire, every nerve begging for more of him.

I'm tugging at the hem of his shirt while he's fumbling with the zipper on my dress. I press into him, giving his fingers a bit more room to work, and as soon as he lowers it to my waist, he shifts so I can rip his shirt off in one fell swoop, like I've just performed a magic trick.

Holy crap...it does seem like magic. I was not expecting him to be so...ripped! I mean, I was pretty sure he wasn't a complete stranger at the gym, but sweet mother of Baby Jesus...his defined pecs and abs are the perfect complements to the arm muscles I've been admiring for weeks now. The straps of my dress slide off my shoulders under his gaze like they're begging him to trail his fingers down my smooth skin. It doesn't take long for him to get the hint, and soon those fingers are off to explore other locales as well. I gasp as one slides beneath my lacy bra.

"Jason, I—"

His mouth lifts to my ear, where all I hear for the first several seconds are the heavy pants of his hot, lusty breath, melting away any other protests or words my brain might have been trying to form.

Nope, other parts of my body are taking over now, *thank you very much*. You had your chance to stop this, Brain, *and, frankly, you're too damn late!*

ELEVEN

It's a little unnerving to go to an interview knowing that the night before, you bumped uglies with the person who will be interviewing you.

Okay, Hannah would be wrinkling up her nose at my terminology there. I mean my "interviewer," of course.

My silly joke only adds to the smile on my face as I make my way from the parking lot to inside enemy camp: *i.e. Über Brides*. I'm all ready to seal the deal after a text conversation with my brother last night that went something like this:

Me: Hey, can you cover the store for a few of my shifts for the next month or so?

Russ: Why the hell would I do that?

Me: It's time to deploy Operation Wedding War Stage II: Super Offensive

Russ: Super Offensive? That's the best you could come up with? Your creativity is really slipping, bro.

Me: Bite me. I am going to get hired part-time so Hannah and I can go in for the kill.

Russ: Dad would be so proud.

Me: Come on, you know this has to be done.

Russ: Fine. Give 'em hell, bro.

I adjust my tie and head toward the counter, where I expect to greet the lovely Hannah Robinson before she ushers me back to the room where they do the interviews. I'm assuming there's such a place since she doesn't really have an office.

Memories of the night before are making it really hard to get into interview mode. I clear my throat and tighten my tie—any tighter and it's going to cut off my circulation. I'm sure this interview is just a formality, but I wonder if we'll have any privacy? I'm not sure I can be trusted to keep my hands off her after what happened last night.

It was incredible, by the way. I am pretty sure that's obvious from the dopey smile on my face. I was hoping she'd spend the night, but when I got up to take Tank out for her last walk before bed, Hannah followed me, insisting her parents would be suspicious if she didn't come home. She mumbled something about them thinking she was a good Christian girl.

Oh, there wasn't anything good and Christian about what happened last night, that's for sure. It was totally unexpected. It's like we got inside the house and passion just overcame us. We were both powerless to stop it. It was pure magic.

I arrive at the counter and look up expecting to see Hannah's beautiful face, but instead it's a waify girl with dishwater blonde hair and a nametag that reads "Stacy."

Oh, okay. No problem. I'm sure if I just ask for Hannah—"Hi, I'm Jason...Fr...uh...Fritzinger, I have an interview with—"

Hannah was going to doctor the paperwork so there was actually nothing legally filed, no W-4 or I-9. That means I won't get paid, but that's okay. I am here for access to Über Brides' files and computer systems, and to help Hannah, of course.

"Hello, Mr. Fritzinger." I hear the voice before I see where it's coming from. It's a screechy, raspy, grating type of voice. The body it belongs to comes into view, a short, heavyset pale woman with stringy fake red hair and a pointed nose. She wears glasses on a chain around her neck and carries a clipboard. "I'm Patsy. I'll be doing your interview today."

Out of the corner of my eye, I see Hannah arranging some bridal gowns on a rack. She flashes me an apologetic look. My heart sinks. I wonder if she is upset about last night?

No time to think about that now, I have to try to get this naked mole rat woman to hire me.

"Hello, nice to meet you!" I flash my most charming smile and follow her back to her office, the office where we broke in and doctored the sales reports not long ago. I have to pretend like I've never been here before.

She goes through the requisite questions, like what experience do I have and why do I want to work for Über Brides, and just as we're about to wrap things up, Hannah appears at the cracked door. "Hey, sorry for interrupting, but Patsy, someone from corporate is on the phone."

Patsy emits a long, put-upon sigh as she scrambles to her feet and stomps out of the office. My eyes snap to Hannah's. "What happened?"

"She said she has to handle this stuff. Corporate is breathing down her neck!"

"Great! My last name isn't Fritz—whatever I said it was—and if she finds out it's Friday, she's going to know I'm working for the other team!" I whisper through clenched teeth.

"Have you filled out the paperwork yet?" There's a look of desperation on her face, and I can see she's trying to come up with a plan.

"No. She hasn't hired me yet." I blow out a heavy breath with my bottom lip extended, feeling it hit the end of my nose. I have no idea what we're going to do, but if Patsy finds us talking like this, not only will my cover be blown, but so will Hannah's.

Her eyes brighten momentarily before she turns to rifle through some filing cabinets across from Patsy's desk. She hands me some forms on a clipboard with a pen attached. "Here, fill these out—"

Patsy suddenly reappears at the door, and somehow her face looks even less pleasant than it did three minutes ago, although I'm not entirely sure how that's possible.

"Fill these out, Jason," Hannah continues. "We're happy to have you on board. I'll come back and pick them up in a few minutes." She ushers me out into the hallway before poking her head back in to address Patsy. "I'll take care of all the paperwork for our new hire, no worries."

"Thanks, Hannah, you really are a godsend. Now corporate is claiming we sent someone funeral arrangements instead of wedding ones! Can you imagine?" She shakes her head before pinching the bridge of her nose. "How I haven't become an alcoholic yet is beyond me."

"Oh, that's strange! I wonder how on earth that could have happened," Hannah says in her fakest surprised voice. "Just go relax, Patsy. I've got this! Jason can start tomorrow, is that alright with you?"

"Yes, of course. Thank you so much. We're happy to have you on board!" She yells out the door in my general direction.

Trying to contain her bubbling laughter, Hannah quickly shows me to the storeroom across the hall where there's an old metal desk covered with an ancient lamp and telephone. This must have been left by the previous owners because the day planner covering the surface of the desk is from 2007. *Nice.*

"Just make it all up," she whispers to me with a wink. "Glad to have you on board, Mr. Fritz-whatever you said your name was." She traipses out of the office, but not before whipping around to blow me a kiss.

"It's really nice to have a pretty face to look at when I'm working," I say to Hannah. "I'm used to my brother's ugly mug."

She glances up from the reports she's reading and gives me a quizzical look, like she didn't quite make out what I said.

"I said, 'It's really nice to—'"

"Yeah, I heard you," she snaps back.

"Uh, sorry...I didn't mean to offend you. I was trying to give you a compliment. Sure beats looking at my brother Russ all day." I run my fingers across my chin where the hair is finally starting to grow back. I shaved for my interview a couple days ago, but now I'm letting it grow back in. Hannah claims Patsy doesn't really care what I look like. The only way I was getting away with it at Friday's Formalwear is because my dad hasn't been there to give me shit about it.

"Jason..." She looks up from the lines and lines of figures again.

"Yes?" I have a feeling I'm just talking to myself at this point. She's completely engrossed in those numbers.

"Something here isn't adding up." She points to a few figures and gives me a confused look.

"I need some context. What am I looking at?" I take the spreadsheet from her and peer down, trying to make sense of it.

"These are the deposits over here. These are the expenses over here. These lines are for employee salaries. What do you notice?"

"There are twelve lines?" My eyebrows arch as I count them again to make sure.

"Yes. And how many employees do we actually have?"

"Uh...nine?"

"Yes, but actually only eight because you're not really on the books." Her lips purse. "There are fake employees on this report. Look at these ID numbers...they are too similar to be different people."

"What in the world? You're right!" I study the salary amounts. "And this guy is paid even more than you are, almost as much as Patsy is making."

Her eyes widen. "Let me look up the code on the system." She turns to the computer at the consultation counter and taps in a series of numbers, her long nails flying over the keys.

A record shows up for someone named Eric Wilson. Under title it says "Assistant Store Manager."

"Holy shit!" I exclaim, then realize I need to lower my volume about a zillion decibels. "She made him up! There's no Assistant Store Manager!"

"If there were," Hannah huffs, "it would be me! This guy is completely fake."

"And Patsy is pocketing the money, I bet. How in the world is she getting away with this?"

Hannah takes in a deep breath then blows it back out in a long huff. Her eyes are narrowed, nails drumming against the counter. "Because it's a huge company, and no one knows what the hell is going on. They're not doing internal audits. No wonder she doesn't want someone from corporate to come down here."

"What are we going to do about it?" I glance around the store to see if anyone is looking. There's a couple looking at cake toppers a few aisles over, and a bride and what appears to be her mother fingering some ivory-colored gowns. Otherwise, it's been a pretty slow day. That's a good thing. Maybe our campaign is working? I've noticed two more negative reviews on Facebook just this week.

"I would go to corporate myself with the evidence, but I think they might just look the other way. But what if we document the hell out of it and take it to the media?" she suggests.

I like the way she thinks. "Yeah, and not even small-time like the local paper. Let's go to Baltimore, Philly, DC...NEW YORK!" I start to envision headlines and stone-cold serious anchors reporting on the huge scandal happening at Über Brides-Rehoboth Beach.

"Tonight after Patsy leaves, I'll start compiling some stuff, and we'll figure out a game plan. Maybe your friend Claire has some contacts? Didn't she write for *The New York Times*?" She looks like she's trying hard to conceal a victorious grin.

"Oh, tonight? I was going to ask you about something..."

"Like what?"

"Like, would you go on an actual date with me...tonight?"

I wish I could take a picture of the expression on her face now. It's one of surprise and joy, all rolled up into one. But the corners of her lips suddenly tilt down, and her brows knit together.

"It's my parents' anniversary tonight," she says as if she's just now realizing it. "I'm not going to get to stay late after all. I'll have to work on the evidence tomorrow."

"Oh, okay." I scratch the end of my stubbly chin. "Tomorrow night after you do that? I am being forced to go see Pete's band again."

She groans. "That sounds more like torture than a date. I thought you wanted to do something nice for me?"

"What do you think your parents would say if I showed up at their anniversary dinner with you on my arm?" I reach down and take her hand, lacing our fingers together under the counter so no one can see. I'm getting really tired of keeping this thing between us a secret—even if it is a weird thing with no label, and I haven't quite figured out what to call it yet.

"I don't think they'd be too happy." She lets go of my hand and moves out from behind the counter. I feel a rush of cold air filling in the gap where her body was close to mine moments before.

"Did you ever talk to your brother about the yearbook?" I am sure she hasn't. Otherwise, she would have told me, right? Though we've been pretty busy trying to dismantle the Über Brides Empire and keep from attacking each other in the storeroom.

She expels a deep sigh. "No, my sister was going to try to do some recon for me, but she's failed at her mission, apparently. I haven't heard from her."

"Well, that was definitely your brother and my sister on prom night. Our families seemed to be getting along just fine at that point, so something must have happened after that. And I have a feeling Jessica knows. Maybe I should just ask her?"

"Yeah, can you just ask her? Mo and I have never gotten along that well. That's why I wanted Ruth to talk to him on my behalf. She's the middle child, you know, the peacemaker type. She gets along with everyone."

I smile at her. I can't imagine that knowing the story would change the way I feel about her—assuming I even know how I feel about her. I know this much: I want to keep seeing her. I want to do that thing we did the other night after work again. And again. Really, I can't imagine it getting old. Not with her.

"I can't believe Patsy is embezzling money," she says as if she wants to force the conversation back to its original topic. "We're going to make the most of this. We have to. This could be our path to victory."

I look at her, admiring the determination in her eyes, the curve of her jaw. Her bronze skin is glowing, her long lashes batting adamantly as she speaks. She's wearing her hair a little different today with a pink headband taming some of her curls, but they're still framing her face so beautifully. How can she be so sweet, so smart, so perfect—and yet completely off limits?

I want to take her on a date. I want to stroll down the Avenue with her on my arm, showing her off to everyone who passes by. I want to take her to meet my parents and tell them I may have found someone...someone I never expected to find.

But I can't.

All because of this stupid family rivalry. I know I keep telling her it's not important; we'll figure it out later. But I need to know. I can only keep so many secrets. No one in my family knows about our attack on Über Brides except Russ. And I think it's high time I just spill it to my parents. They deserve to know what's going on. They deserve to know that the business they poured their blood, sweat and tears into is going to persevere— and that I didn't do it alone. Hannah Robinson was by my side the entire way.

Hannah

"Mama, Daddy, happy anniversary!" I shout as I enter through the back door carrying a huge bouquet of flowers and attached balloons.

"Oh my gosh, aren't you the sweetest thing ever!" Mama gushes as she reaches down to kiss me on the cheek. "Your brothers and sister will be here soon. And Rose too, of course!"

The house smells amazing. I can't believe she had time to cook—and not that she should have, anyway. It's her wedding anniversary! "Didn't you work today?"

Mama flashes Daddy a concerned look and then fixes her gaze back on me. The smile on her face looks forced. "We didn't have any appointments today, so we closed at noon."

My heart sinks. That is not what I wanted to hear. I was going to tell them the latest shenanigans I've pulled over at Über Brides and how corporate is about to come down and raise hell because of all the mix-ups and irate customers they've fielded phone calls and letters from as of late. I really hoped the tide was turning in our war.

Ruth walks through the door carrying a huge cake and her three sons following along like ducklings. I pat each one on the head as I say their names: "Daniel, Noah, Elijah." Nothing but the best Old Testament names for my nephews. As soon as my sister sets the cake down, her brood gathers around her asking if they can go play. She nods and off they run to my parents' playroom they've set up just for their grandchildren. It's a kids' paradise in there with blocks, cars, dolls, books, puzzles, games, and so on. I almost want to pop out a kid just so he or she can play in that room!

I want to get my parents occupied and drag Ruth away for a bit so I can ask her again if she found out anything else about the yearbook. It's been almost a week now, and I haven't heard a peep from her. Maybe she got too busy to investigate further. She flashes me a look as soon as Mama goes to take the roast out of the oven that shows she is just as eager to talk to me.

Giggling, I grab her hand and drag her off to my room. I'm sure my parents won't think anything of it. We executed that exact maneuver all the time when we were teens.

"So?" I gasp as soon as I pull the door shut.

"So? You tell me!" she fires back.

I wrinkle my nose. "You're the one who is supposed to be finding out information," I remind her. *She's always been kind of flighty. Come on, Ruth, don't let me down now, sis!*

She grabs my hands and squeezes. "First tell me what's going on with Jason and the War."

I told her we were calling it Operation Wedding War, but apparently she's decided to shorten it to just "War." It's kind of funny since the thing going on between our families is also a War. For someone who considers herself to be somewhat of a pacifist, I've sure gotten embroiled in some pretty serious conflicts.

"Well, we found out today that my boss is embezzling money from the company!" I share, eager to see her reaction.

"Oh my gosh!" she squeals. "Are you serious?"

I nod, struggling to contain my excitement. "We are going to collect as much documentation as we can find and go to the media. Not just the local media—the national media. Jason's friend has some connections we are going to try to leverage."

"Wow! That is amazing! I'm sure Mama and Daddy will be thrilled. Did you hear they closed the store early today?" Her smile fades accordingly.

I nod. "I know, that's not good, but I think we're on the threshold of a serious breakthrough. And we have quite a few more tricks up our sleeves in the next couple weeks. Just have to wait for the right...'victims.'" It's interesting how I hear Jason's optimism reflected in my voice.

"So what about you and Jason?" Her eyes widen as they fix on me, anticipating my response.

"Well..." I lean forward, my hands dropping down into the pockets in the full skirt of my dress. I rock back and forth on my feet a few times, trying to decide what juicy tidbits to share.

This is my very conservative, prudish sister. She got married to her high school sweetheart a few months after graduation and then started popping out beautiful bouncing baby boys. She's never missed church a day in her life, and she even teaches Sunday School.

I obviously can't tell her what happened between Jason and me the other night at his house. Not that anything like that has happened since then. I mean, sure, there's been plenty of kissing and a bit of random groping when we're pretty sure no one is looking, but we have to be super careful because there are video cameras all over the dang store. And even though our boss is blatantly stealing funds from the company, I have a feeling they wouldn't take too kindly to the two of us getting it on in their back room either.

"Well, you know, the same stuff," I finally settle on.

"So you really like him?"

"I do, but—"

"But?"

"Well, it's not like I can bring him home for Sunday dinner, is it?" I stare at her pointedly as once again the smile vanishes from her face.

"I thought that was why we were trying to figure out what happened all those years ago? And I wish you would because I don't like keeping this secret from Mama and Daddy," she confesses.

"Yeah, well, you don't have a choice right now," I remind her. "Besides, you were supposed to be helping me get to the bottom of it. I thought you were going to call Mo and ask him."

"Oh, right. Well, I'm sorry I was really busy this week. The boys had dentist appointments, and you know the younger two are still playing T-ball this spring, right? And then we have swimming lessons starting up. And Noah has—"

"It's okay, Ruth. I know you're busy. It's fine, anyway, don't worry about it."

Even if I did want to put this whole family feud behind us, Jason and I really need to focus our energies on Über Brides right now. I really need to keep my hands to myself until we get this story out to the media. Then maybe customers will stop showing up, and Mama and Daddy won't ever need to close up Delmarva Beach Brides early due to lack of appointments again.

"But I thought you really like him?" she presses. I

think she's only slightly less anxious for me to find a man and settle down than our mother is.

"I do," I breathe out. "But we have to focus on Über Brides. That's our top priority."

I like him too much. That is the problem in a nutshell. Even right now, I miss him, and I wish he were here. I just know Mama and Daddy would love him if they gave him a chance. He's smart and funny and charming. I'm not sure how they'd feel about me dating a white guy, and I'm *positive* they would be livid that he's a Friday, but I know he'd win them over...eventually.

But if we're not able to pull off saving our store, wanting Jason to be part of my life in a real way—not in a secret way—won't even matter. If we lose the store, then the real casualty of this war—of both of these wars—is going to be me.

TWELVE

"**O**kay, so you know your friend's band still sucks, right?" I question, flashing Jason an eye roll across the table.

"Damn it, you're so sexy when you say the word 'sucks'!" He can't help but laugh. He was trying to be all sultry and innuendo-y but failed miserably. "I plan to make this up to you after the show. I hope you know that."

"Is that so?" I narrow my eyes at him. "And exactly how do you intend to do that?"

"You'll see!" His wink sends a little shiver down my spine.

Why does he have to be so cute? It would be a lot easier to resist his charms if he were ugly. His beard is growing back in, and I have to admit I'm a sucker for a guy with facial hair, as long as it's neat and tidy. His is barely more than scruff right now, and I just want to run my cheek across it to see if it's gotten any softer since the last time I kissed him. Which was about three minutes ago. So probably not.

"How can they play this often and still suck so bad?" I try to keep the subject from devolving to the gutter, which is where my mind will go if I give it any leeway at all. "I mean, it seems like they have gigs several nights a week. The old adage 'practice makes perfect' doesn't seem to apply to them, does it?"

He chuckles. "No, no, it most certainly does not."

As soon as he says that, my brain sparks the idea for a hilarious sabotage for Operation Wedding War. "So, I know something cruel and evil we could do..."

"Oh yeah?" He leans forward, his dark eyes wide with anticipation. He loves that he's brought me over to the dark side. I swear every time I come up with a plan to help further our operation, he gets a little excited. And I think you know what I mean by "excited."

"Right, so you know how your friend Drew's band is one of our partner bands at Über Brides? One of the bands on the list we give clients to choose from?"

His eyes bulge out even more when what I'm thinking dawns on him.

"Yeah, so maybe instead of sending The Gallant Misfits, we send Pete's band instead?"

He takes my hand into his and lifts it to his lips, pressing a soft, warm kiss against my skin. "I love the way your mind works. It's truly brilliant."

"Oh, that reminds me, I did something else today you'd be proud of. Forgot to tell you since you weren't there today." He worked at Friday's Formalwear today so his brother could have the day off. I'm really only supposed to get him two days a week at Über Brides. I'm waiting for Patsy to ask me about his paperwork, but so far, so good. I'm wondering if she hasn't brought it up because she's afraid I'll figure out her own secret.

Yeah, too late for that, biatch! I've got her number now. And though I can't completely blame her for embezzling money from one of the most evil corporations in America, I'm going to use every shred of evidence I've collected against her to blow this story out of the water. I can't wait! All we need now is for Claire to provide us with a contact at *The New York Times*. In the meantime, I've already reached out to *The Washington Post*, *The Baltimore Sun* and the *Philadelphia Tribune*. I'm just waiting to hear back. Surely their editors will recognize the journalistic gold they're sitting on when they read my email.

"So, don't hold me in suspense!" He pats the top of my hand. "Here, let's refresh our drinks first, and then we can make a toast to whatever it is your brilliant mind has devised this time."

I roll my eyes at him as he signals for the waitress. Meanwhile, I'm watching his buddy Pete and his band set up, thinking about how angry some bride is going to be when they start to play at their wedding. I mean, it's cruel, but it won't ruin their whole day, right? Is it too much? *Well, they can always ask the band to stop playing...*

With fresh drinks in hand, Jason redirects his gaze to me. "So, spill it. What did you do today at work, Sugarbunz?"

Oh, damn it, he hasn't forgotten my parents' pet name for me. "Well, I was inspired by Jean-Marc's tirade a week or two ago. By the way, I am surprised we haven't heard more about that..."

"Oh, did I tell you they got it on video? His friend was wearing a little body cam."

"What? Are you serious?" Now I've already forgotten what I was going to tell him. "Why haven't they shared it yet?"

"Because Jean-Marc was leaving for a cruise right after that little performance, and he hasn't had a chance yet. But it's coming. It's coming soon. Don't worry!" He rubs his hands, together doing his Monty Burns impression again. "So, tell me what you did!"

"I ordered a cake-topper for a bride and groom today that was two grooms instead!"

"Oh, that's wonderfully evil!" He holds up his drink. "To my wonderfully evil girlfriend!"

I freeze as soon as the word comes out of his mouth.

I don't like the look on her face when the word "girlfriend" accidentally tumbles out of my mouth. I try to play it off by finishing my sip and then changing the subject to something else. Then I actually start praying Pete will strike up the band at any given moment. Who would've thought I'd be anxious for them to start playing?

But, nope, Hannah is still staring at me with her

mouth slightly agape. I can't quite read if it's shock or disgust controlling her expressions right now, but whatever it is doesn't look good.

Finally, some words come out: "Girlfriend? I really think—"

"I'm sorry," I mutter. "Really sorry...if that's not what you want. I, uh—"

"Actually..." A smile now plays on her lips that were pursed into an O just moments ago. "I kind of like the sound of it, but –"

Ah, that's a word I was afraid I might hear. "But what?"

"Well, I don't feel right having a secret boyfriend that my parents can't meet," she tells me. "I'm not really into the whole keeping secrets thing. This has already been out of my comfort zone, even though they know I'm trying to bring Über Brides down from the inside. Your parents don't even know *that* much, and I don't know how I feel about it."

I'm feeling emboldened. *Thanks, alcohol!* "So, what if I just told them? What if I just came completely clean about how we're working together...and dating."

Her eyes bulge out. "You'd do that? You'd just drop a bomb on them like that?"

I shrug. *Drunk me would.* "What's the worst that could happen? They're not going to disown me."

"How do you know?" she fires back. "And doesn't your dad have heart issues?"

I nod and blow out a sigh. I hear the telltale screech of Pete's microphone coming to life. Our time for talking and being heard is limited. "What if I call my sister and find out the scoop on her and your brother?" I offer.

Hannah's face brightens. "I'd rather you do that first..."

My sister Jessica and I don't really have a close relationship. I mostly see her and the kids on Christmas and maybe once during the summer. It's not like she lives that far away, just up in Pennsylvania with her husband, who is an architect. She's also like ten years older than me, so when I was old enough to bond with her and stuff, she was a teenage girl who thought little brothers were a disgusting plague visited upon poor, innocent young women.

"Hey, Jess, it's Jason." Thought I'd start off with something easy.

"Yeah, I can see that." She's always had a dry sense of humor. I can tell from the sound of her voice that she's not smiling.

"Do you have a few minutes?" I inject my salesman tone into my words. I mean, that's what I do for a living, right?

"Not really, but I never do, so just tell me what you want." Her tone is so cold, I have to remind myself I'm doing this for Hannah so I don't tell her off and hang up the dang phone.

"Alrighty, I know you're busy, so I'll make this as brief as possible. We were looking at a high school yearbook, your junior yearbook, as a matter of fact, and there was a photo of you and Morris Robinson as prom queen and king." *Why not just cut to the chase, right?*

There's dead silence on the other end.

"Jess? You still there?"

She makes a weird strangling, throat-clearing-type sound. "What is it you want to know?"

"Was that photo taken before our family feud began with the Robinsons?"

"Yes," she replies stiffly.

Alright, thanks for the info, sis. I decide to press for a little more. "Did you have something to *do* with the feud?"

"Uh, no, of course not!" she fires back defensively. "It was all *his* fault."

"Why? Were you guys dating? Did our parents have a problem with it?" Okay, so I am getting a little bit over-excited here.

"Calm down there, Sherlock." I hear some static and garbled yelling, like maybe she is shouting at one of her kids. "Look, it's not a good time, like I said."

"If I text you, will you answer? Like, when you have time?" Maybe that will be a more palatable option for her? And then I'd have whatever she says in writing to take to Hannah.

"Fine. I don't know why you're dredging all this up, though, Jase. It's ancient history. We've all moved on."

"Well, the Fridays and the Robinsons are still very much at war," I remind her. "You're just not here to be a part of it."

"Does this have something to do with Über Brides coming to town?"

"What? How did you know about that?" Panic immediately surges through my body, so intensely I nearly forget about the Friday/Robinson thing.

"Mom told me. Apparently she is trying to keep it from Dad, but if their sales don't pick up in the next couple months—"

"What? She hasn't told me!" I protest. Mom hasn't said a damn thing about this quarter's sales. That's she and Russ's thing—I handle more of the advertising and outreach, plus our social media. And ordering. They are the numbers people. But usually he or she tells me if we have a slump so I can start an ad campaign or a sale or something. Summer has never been a time we've had to worry, though. The dead of winter is typically our slow season. *Fucking Über Brides!*

"Well, mothers and daughters have to have something to talk about." Jessica lets out a long sigh. "I gotta go, Jase. Text you later."

I run my fingers through my hair then glance around the room for the nearest wall I can pound my head against. Deciding that giving myself a headache would be pretty much the worst thing I could do at this juncture, I send off a text to Jessica reiterating the same questions I posed earlier that she failed to answer.

A few hours later she sent this:

Mo and I dated for two years. When I broke up with him, he spread a ton of terrible rumors about me. I ended up getting kicked off the cheerleading squad and was basically a social pariah my entire senior year. That made Mom and Dad mad. His family accused me of doing mean stuff to him too. Thus the feud.

"If they dated for two years, how come I don't

remember it?" Hannah handed the phone back to me after reading the text Jessica sent multiple times. "I was seven or eight years old. I think I'd remember the girl my brother was dating."

"I honestly don't remember either, but then again I don't think my sisters brought their dates over to the house much. I can ask Russ since he's a little bit older. I am pretty sure the boyfriends were all scared of Dad—"

She giggles and looks up at me with such an adorable smile, it takes all of my will power not to sweep her up into my arms and devour her luscious lips. From the way she bats her eyelashes, I swear she just read my thoughts.

"Oh, by the way," I remember to tell her, "Jessica said my mom knows about Über Brides."

Hannah's honey brown eyes enlarge. "She does?"

"Yeah...and our sales haven't been good this quarter, my mom told her." Admitting that pretty much took the wind right out of my sails.

"Ours either. My parents actually closed up early the other afternoon because they didn't have any appointments," she reveals. "What if all this isn't working? We're both already on the inside. If we can't leverage that, what can we actually do?"

"We *are* leveraging it; it just takes time," I argue. "And I am sure once this story about Patsy's embezzlement hits the media, it's going to take a toll, not just on the Rehoboth Beach store but the entire company. What if this sort of thing is going on at all their stores?"

She takes my hand into hers and squeezes it as her eyes lower to the floor. She sucks in a breath and just stays there for a moment, wordless. She doesn't have to look at me for me to know she's worried.

"I want to believe everything is going to be alright," she finally confesses, looking up to meet my gaze. Her eyes are rimmed with teardrops, turning her eyes into two shiny liquid pools I want to drown in. A stab pierces my heart at the thought of her scared, anxious.

This time I don't try to fight my urge to take her into my arms. "We can do this, Hannah. Just trust me."

She blinks, and a tear goes rolling down her sienna cheek, slipping off her jaw and landing somewhere below. I don't want any more tears to fall. It's breaking my heart to see her so upset and to feel so powerless to stop it. I've never felt that before. I've had plenty of girls cry around me, especially if they didn't get their way. It always seemed like some sort of manipulation, but I know that's not what this is.

Hannah's entire future hangs in the balance. As does mine.

I pull her away from my chest to meet her gaze again. "I know it's hard to trust me when we aren't supposed to even know each other. Obviously something happened between our families long ago, and there's never been any reconciliation."

"I don't know why Mo would purposely spread rumors about your sister, especially false ones. And your sister didn't say what the rumors were?"

"I asked. She never answered."

"I'm going to have to talk to my brother," she resolves, looking off into the distance as if to underscore her determination. "It's the only way."

"Okay, Hannah, but listen to me, alright?" I use my index finger to tilt her chin back toward me and her gaze follows. She swallows, and I spot another tear glistening

172

where the other just fell from.

"What?" Her lips turn up ever so slightly when she sees the resolve in my eyes.

"We are going to figure this out. We are both here for the long haul, and we're not going down without a fight."

I realize the lines are so blurred that it sounds like I'm talking about our relationship as much as I'm talking about our family businesses. As hard as we've tried to keep our feelings separate from our professional partnership, they keep wanting to meld together.

She nods, taking in my promise, which is delivered with so much confidence that I believe it too. I have no choice but to believe it. *Fake it till you make it*, my mom used to say. The thought of that brings a smile to my face. "Who knows? Maybe we'll really join forces and merge our two family businesses someday? Can you imagine?"

Her eyes narrow as she scans my face, apparently trying to determine if I'm joking. "Like our parents would ever go for that!"

"It won't be their decision too much longer," I remind her. "They're getting close to retirement age. Once we take over, the sky's the limit as far as I'm concerned."

"You really think we could merge Delmarva Beach Brides and Friday's Formalwear?" She purses her lips like she's trying not to laugh at the idea.

"Hey, it's a crazy world out there." My smile is so wide now, it's crinkling my eyes. "Who would have ever thought a Friday and a Robinson could fall in love?"

Her body goes rigid in my arms as her eyes pop open to stare at me. She doesn't say a word. She doesn't have to. It doesn't change the way I feel, the way I've been feeling for quite some time now.

"What would we call it, anyway?" she ponders, apparently ignoring my declaration.

I know she's not ready to say it right now. But she will be. I pull her into my arms again, my lips seeking the warmth of hers. When her fingers tangle in my hair and her body yields to mine, I know it's only a matter of time.

THIRTEEN

Every time I go to call my brother, I hang up without pressing the button to connect. I know it was hard for Jason to call his sister, but at least he and his sister aren't enemies.

It was very hard for my brother Mo to accept that our parents chose me to take over Delmarva Beach Brides when they retire. The store was opened in the late 1980s by my grandfather, my father's father, the original Morris Robinson. In the early 2000s, my father took over. He's also the oldest son and Morris Robinson, Jr. When my brother, Morris Robinson III was born, I don't think my brother was the only one who assumed he'd take the reins someday. Everyone did. It was his birthright.

Mo had gone to college at Delaware State, but then dropped out and came home to help Mama and Daddy with the business. I was pretty young when that happened, so I didn't think anything of it. I didn't realize I was going to be the chosen one until I finished my undergrad and expressed interest in going for my MBA. I remember a long talk with my mother and father about my future goals. I had worked at the shop every summer since I could remember, and I couldn't really imagine doing anything else with my life, even though I planned to work in New York City for a few years to really get a good feel for the industry before beginning my graduate studies.

The day my father asked me if I would like to take over the reins someday, I was completely floored. He told me he thought I had a great head on my shoulders and would be one best qualified and educated to take over Delmarva Beach Brides. He said I'd made him so proud, and I was his first choice to carry on the legacy his own father had created decades before.

Daddy called a board meeting, which consisted of my brothers, brother-in-law, my grandmother, and my mother to let everyone know what he had decided. By the end of the week, Mo had put in his two-weeks' notice, which my father was angry about, so he told him to just get out. He was hoping Mo would stay on, and we could be one big happy family who put the success of the business above our own personal pride.

No wonder no one wanted to talk about the rift between us and the Fridays if it involved Mo. No one really wanted to talk about Mo at all. He had run off with his girlfriend Tracy to Chicago, where he began working at another formalwear store and since had become a partner. It was an older gentleman who owned the store, and from what I understood, he didn't have any children he could pass the baton to, which put Mo in position to someday own it outright.

Mo later got married and now has two kids, but I have only met them once. They came home for Christmas a couple years ago, but it was an awkward affair. What really happened between Mo and Jessica Friday? The curiosity is killing me. It's been a nice distraction from the pressure I'm under at my fake job. Oh, and, you know, the whole *we might lose our family business* thing. Hey, who knows? Maybe Mo got out when the getting was good? Chicago is a much bigger place than Rehoboth Beach. It can handle a Über Brides and several mom and pop shops too.

I blow out another deep breath then take in one more, fueling my resolve with plenty of oxygen. If Jason were here right now, he'd put his arm around me and tell me I can do it. I finally manage to press the call button, and my heart begins to pound in my chest while it connects and begins to ring.

"Hello?" his voice comes down the line sounding a little gruffer than I was hoping for.

"Mo? It's your baby sister."

I used the phrase "baby sister" because that's what he always used to call me. I thought maybe it would make him nicer to me…you know, if he still thought of me in an endearing way.

"Heyyyyy, Sugarbunz, what's up?"

He actually sounds happy to hear from me? Weird. He wouldn't call me Sugarbunz, my father's nickname for me, if he wasn't happy.

"How is everything going in the Windy City?" *Small talk is good, right?*

"Oh, you know, busy busy. Tracy and I can barely keep up with the girls; they're getting so big."

"I bet! You'll have to send me some recent photos."

I'm smiling, which translates into my voice as it carries down the line. There's an awkward pause, and I realize he's not going to fill it in. After all, I called him.

"So, you probably wonder why I've called..." *Where is all that courage I had a few minutes ago?*

"Well, you don't have to have a reason to call me," he says. "You're my baby sister. It's great to hear from you."

"That's great, Mo. I'm glad you feel that way." I'm surprised but encouraged by his response so far. I decide to go big or go home. Always a solid plan, right? "So, hey, I was wondering if you could tell me a little bit about what happened with you and Jessica Friday back when you were in high school?"

Silence.

Yep, that's just about what I figured.

"Mo?"

"Oh, sorry," he answers, his deep voice sounding like it is traveling through the space-time continuum to get back to the right decade. "It's a *real* long story, Sugarbunz."

"I've got time," I fire back. *No pressure,* I want to add, but don't.

"*Real* long. And not really something I've wanted to revisit. Hell, not even Tracy really knows what happened. All she knows is I lost my scholarship."

"What? What are you talking about?" That doesn't seem to have anything to do with what Jessica told Jason. "What does your scholarship have to do with Jessica Friday?"

He sighs. I can just imagine him rubbing the rapidly approaching migraine out of his temples.

"Can you just give me the executive summary?" I'm getting desperate here. Once again, I don't add that.

"Alright." There's silence again, and I hear him breathing in and out, possibly collecting the nerve and energy to summarize the story. Whatever it is, I can tell it's deeply upsetting to him, and I feel bad that I'm even asking, but I also feel like a great deal hinges on whatever he might tell me.

"Jessica and I worked on a huge project together for this national competition. Well, I was competing—it was for a scholarship to the state school of my choice. I was going to go to the University of Delaware."

"What kind of competition?"

"It was a business competition. I had to do a big research paper, propose a business idea, and put together a business plan," he explains.

Wow, so he *was* planning to study business! I am a little floored by this revelation because he was always so negative about me going to school to pursue an undergraduate degree in marketing and then, eventually, my MBA. No wonder he was miffed that Daddy wanted to turn over the reins of the family business to me!

"So what happened?" I press. I feel like I'm getting so close to the truth!

"Jessica and I had a huge breakup—and she was so angry about it, she went to the school principal and guidance counselor and told them she'd written my research paper for me."

"What? Are you serious?" That was *definitely* not mentioned in the texts Jessica sent to Jason.

"Yes, and when they found out, they contacted the scholarship committee, and just like that, my scholarship was stripped. That's why I ended up going to Del State instead," he shares. "And the school stripped my valedictorian title as well."

Wow. Just wow. That changed the entire course of his life!

"Why did you guys break up?"

"Stupid teenage bullshit," he tells me.

"So...wow...that's quite a story." I start to tell Mo what Jason's sister told him, but then I realize I can't share that because it would mean admitting to being involved with Jason. All I can do at this point is take his story back to Jason so we can compare notes.

But something is definitely not adding up.

"Okay, so your brother says my sister ruined his scholarship. And my sister says your brother ruined her reputation. They could both be true," I conjecture as I stack several boxes in the storeroom and pray they don't come tumbling down.

"I asked him what the break up was about, and he said 'stupid teenage bullshit,'" Hannah tells me. "But what I don't understand is why my parents first told me to talk to my grandmother about it, unless they were just trying to distract me. It doesn't have anything to do with her."

I shrug. "Who knows? It seems like every time we

get close to figuring it out, there's another layer we can't quite uncover."

"How much longer can we keep this façade up? How can we keep seeing each other *and* working here *and* trying to destroy Über Brides before someone finds out? I feel like we're racing the clock—and we're losing." Her eyes are wide and full of panic.

"You haven't heard anything from the media outlets you contacted yet?" I hand her the water bottle she set on the shelf behind me. If she can't be calm, at least she can be hydrated. The way we've been going at it in the evenings at my house, I have a vested interest in her energy and hydration levels.

She shakes her head. "I only contacted the major papers. Maybe I do need to go to the *Cape Gazette* first. Or even the TV station in Salisbury. I was thinking bigger, but maybe it's better to keep a local focus—at least to start with."

"Surely someone will listen," I agree. I glance up at the ceiling where the camera is in this room. I spent yesterday disabling all the cameras in the store. The only ones still working are two in the showroom and the one over the counter. I couldn't have us risking being found out by any security footage, though it's become pretty clear to me that Patsy doesn't check it, and neither does anyone else.

Knowing no one is watching, I take the opportunity to stroke a finger down Hannah's cheek before pressing a kiss to it. "You work on that this afternoon, and I'll take care of ordering, okay? I might get to have some fun with it." I give her a wink. "Of course, nothing will be more epic than the thousand tiny penises you ordered."

"Oh, right!" Her face instantly perks up. "That

reminds me of something I did this morning."

"Oh yeah?" My eyebrows arch as I wait to bear witness to her brilliance.

"So, someone came in to pick up their order for wedding favors. It was supposed to be two hundred of those little bubble wand sets, right?"

I nod and can't help the smile creeping across my face because she looks like she's going to crack up laughing before she spits out the punchline of her joke.

"I just happened to send them on their merry way with two hundred tiny penis soaps instead!" She nearly chokes, she's laughing so hard by the time she spits out all the words.

"Oh my god, that's excellent!" I praise her, wrapping my arms around her and drawing her close to my chest.

"Yeah, they both make bubbles, right?" She shrugs. "I guess Stacy got a little confused."

I can't help but join in her uproarious laughter. *Poor Stacy.* That girl has been our scapegoat for many a shenanigan, and she's completely clueless about it. Patsy always instructs Hannah to reprimand Stacy after each epic screw-up, but Hannah never does. Ignorance is bliss, I suppose.

I suggested we pin some stuff on someone else, possibly Brandon because he's a bit of a hipster douche, but Hannah really gets some sort of deep-seated entertainment out of using Stacy. For someone who looks so sugary sweet on the outside, Hannah sure can be totally devious and rotten sometimes. I think that's what made me fall in love with her. I was a little worried when we first started this that she'd be a little too Miss Goody Two Shoes for my tastes, but that persona is solely confined to her looks. She wears these sweet little floral dresses and conservative cardigans topped off with a pearl necklace around her neck. But strip away her 1950s-looking wardrobe, and she's wicked smart and cunning. It's sexy as hell!

Oh, and yes, I did just say the L word. Again.

No, she hasn't returned the sentiment yet, but I think she's getting close. I think if we could put this family squabble behind us, that would do it. She'd be all mine. She just wants us to be able to date openly and have me over to her parents' house for Sunday dinner after church. Hell, she probably wants me to get all spiffed up and go to church with her family too. And you know what? I've fallen so damn hard for her that I'd do all that in a heartbeat.

We just have to figure this stupid thing between my sister and her brother out.

"Hey, is that your phone ringing?" Hannah's smooth voice bursts the bubble of my thoughts. I glance up at her, and her lips curl up into a smirk. I think she knows I was daydreaming about her. About us. And I'm not even embarrassed about it.

I aim my ear toward the counter where I left my phone in the other room. "So it is. Be right back." I leap over a few boxes we have yet to open and bound down the hall. I swipe my phone to answer when I see it's my brother calling.

"You have to come to the hospital," he breathes out fast. "Dad just had a heart attack."

Hannah

I can't help but be distracted the rest of the afternoon wondering how Jason's father is. I'm still offering up silent prayers for Mr. Friday when I arrive home that evening. My parents aren't home from work yet, which I try to view as a good sign. That means business must have been good today at Delmarva Beach Brides. I decide to start dinner so it will be ready when they arrive.

My parents have not asked me lately about the money they gave me. I have not cashed the check yet. When I told them I wanted to know what had happened between the Robinsons and the Fridays, I wasn't joking. I know I threatened to tear up the check, but I'm not doing that just yet. Instead, I placed it on my dresser in my room, and every time I walk past it, I cast a glance at all those zeroes and wonder how they will end up getting spent. Will I actually be buying myself a house, or will I be saving it to embark on a new life and career someplace else? Maybe someplace far from Rehoboth Beach.

"Oh good, you're home," my father says as he comes in the back door.

"Where's Mama?" I keep watching for her, but he seems to be alone.

"She had to go babysit your nephews," Daddy explains as he sets his briefcase down on the kitchen counter. Yes, my father still carries a briefcase to work.

He's so old school.

"Oh, that's weird. Did Alan have to work late? Well, I started dinner." I shrug and turn around to give my father a smile, but when I catch sight of the grim expression on his face, that smile slides right off my lips. "What's wrong?"

"Alan had to take Ruth to the doctor." Daddy loosens his tie and props himself up with one hand on the counter. He looks positively worn out.

"Oh. Is she okay?" It's not like Ruth to get sick. It's not like Alan to have to take her to the doctor. It's not like Mama to watch the grandkids right after work on a weeknight—not unless something is really wrong.

"No, she's *not* okay." My father takes in so much air that his cheeks puff up before he blows it all out and closes his eyes briefly.

Okay, something is clearly going on here. First Jason's father has a heart attack, and now my sister has taken ill. "What's wrong with Ruth?"

"She's been upset about the secrets you've been hiding from your mother and me. Sit down, Hannah. We need to have a talk."

My heart starts to pound against my ribcage as I pull out one of the wooden chairs and perch myself at the kitchen table. My father doesn't bother to go change clothes like he normally does when he arrives home from work. Still in his suit and tie, he silently takes the seat across from me, the pained expression on his face never easing. If anything, it's become direr, the deep grooves between his bushy black brows warning me I'm not going to like this conversation one bit.

"Hannah, look," he begins, reaching across the table and taking one of my hands into his, "you know how much your mother and I love you, right?"

"Of course I do, Daddy." I swallow down a lump in my throat. "You're scaring me. What's going on?" I feel the blood drain from my face as I urge him on with my wide, panicked eyes.

"We love you, and we admire you so much. You've always been strong-willed, and you've always been so good at choosing to do the right thing. Some kids have to be guided and corrected and disciplined, but you've always had such a strong moral compass. You never got involved in drugs or alcohol; you never hung out with the wrong crowd. We've always trusted you to make good decisions."

My eyebrows knit together as he speaks, wondering where in the world he could be going with this conversation and what it has to do with my sister taking ill. Did she tell them about my relationship with Jason? Is that why she feels sick?

I should have known not to trust her!

"That's why we felt so strongly about putting the future of our company in your capable hands. Of course you need to learn some things first. Of course you need some time to grow because you're still young, but we know you're a star, Hannah. It's been apparent since day one."

"I'm just not following you, Daddy. What did I do wrong?" He's done nothing but compliment me so far...but he's obviously setting me up for something else.

"What you did wrong is lie to us." He takes his hand from mine and folds both of his together on the tabletop in front of him. "You didn't tell us you were working with Jason Friday on the project with...you know who."

He won't even say Über Brides. I'm surprised he

could get Jason's name out of his mouth.

"Daddy, please let me—"

"And from what Ruth says, there's even more going on than that." I have never heard such strong disappointment in my father's voice.

Wait.

Yes, I have.

I was a kid, but I remember hearing him talk to Mo. I can't remember if it was when he dropped out of college or when he left for Chicago. I think it was both.

"Daddy, Jason's actually a wonderful man. And he's a great businessman—"

"There's a reason we never went into details about our family's relationship with the Fridays," Daddy shares.

My eyes flutter back to his, leaving the memories of his sharp words to my brother all those years ago in the distance. "What's that?"

"When your brother and Jessica Friday began dating, we were wary. We knew the Fridays had been in business in Rehoboth Beach for about a decade longer than we'd been open, but obviously, it was interesting to us that our son would choose to date a girl whose family owned a business in the same industry. I mean, it sounds like a natural affinity, doesn't it?"

"It sure does," I agree.

"They dated for several years," he continues, "and our families began to grow somewhat close."

"We did? Why don't I remember it then?" Jason and I had both tried to remember each other's family being in our lives when we were growing up, but neither of us could. "I don't even remember Jessica coming over here."

"Your mother and I got together with the Fridays on several occasions, usually for dinner. But with us having so many kids—they have a large family too, if memory serves—it was too hard to converse with all of you around. So we always shipped you over to your grandparents' house on the nights we dined with the Fridays. We wanted to talk business and were actually close to—"

He stops abruptly and stares off into the living room. I'm not sure what he's looking at, but whatever it is has distracted him. Several seconds pass, and I finally prompt him, "What, Daddy? What were you close to doing?"

"We were actually thinking of merging our businesses," my father admits.

"What?!" My eyes have grown so wide I feel like they are going to pop right out of my skull. "You were thinking about becoming partners?"

He nods. "I know, it's hard to believe. But that was all ruined—"

"When Jessica and Mo broke up?" I guess.

"Yes. And that horribly vindictive—well, you know what word I want to use, but I could never actually use it—she ruined your brother's scholarship. He was so angry, he almost didn't go to college altogether, and then when he got there, he goofed off and ended up failing out. I knew right then and there I could never turn the family business over to him."

"You did?" Wow, I can't believe I never knew any of this stuff. "Why did they break up, though? And why wouldn't anyone talk about it?"

"We thought they were going to get married," he

explains. "They had been together for two years, and we thought when Mo was out of college and Jessica was done with high school and college, they would get married, and our families would start the process of uniting our businesses too. But she was caught cheating on him…"

"Wow, really?" Funny how she didn't mention that to Jason when they spoke. Mo didn't mention it either, come to think of it.

"Yes, and when Mo dumped her, she decided to make his life a living hell, accusing him of cheating on his scholarship competition entry. He was not only stripped of his scholarship, but the school also stripped him of the title of Valedictorian."

Now that my father knows I've been working with Jason, I blurt out, "But Jessica told Jason that Mo went and spread a bunch of rumors about her, and she ended up getting kicked off the cheerleading squad and lost a bunch of friends and everything."

My father huffs. "They weren't rumors. She was going behind Mo's back with one of his friends, another kid on the baseball team. Actually, she was messing around with a few of his teammates. It was disgusting behavior, totally unbecoming of a young woman."

"I see." I really can't think of any other words at this point. But I'm starting to understand how this thing got so blown out of proportion.

"That's why we told you never to speak to any of the Fridays at school," he explains. "They had two older daughters and two younger sons. We had three older sons and two younger daughters. We didn't want anything like this to happen ever again. Not to mention the fact that her parents were livid when I no longer wanted the merger. I didn't feel like I could trust them after what their daughter did—"

"But *she* did it, not her parents," I argue.

"Yes, but they excused her behavior. And they said Mo deserved what happened to him. But he didn't cheat!" my father insists. "They nearly ruined his entire life, and they didn't even care. All she did was get kicked off the damn cheerleading squad. Big deal!"

I'm sure it was a little more traumatic for her than that, but I'm really trying to see this whole thing from a neutral vantage.

"Jason has been nothing but supportive since we started our assault against Über Brides. When I asked for his help, I had no idea what to expect, but to be honest, most of the ideas we've used have been his. And now we've collected a lot of evidence against my boss that we're trying to take to the media. We're about to make a very big shake up, and we think it's only a matter of time before we affect not only the Rehoboth Beach store but the entire company." You can hear the pride in my voice. I'm still worried we won't be able to win the war, but we've already won so many battles. We've already accomplished so much. We just have to keep marching forward.

My father just shakes his head. He's not proud of me anymore.

"Your sister told your mother that there's more going on with you and Jason than just business stuff," he says. "Is that true?"

I clear my throat. I am not good at lying to anyone, but particularly not my parents. "Not really. It's just a...you know, a summer fling." I shrug.

"You can't trust a Friday," he reiterates. "Just be careful, Hannah, alright? Don't fall in love with the guy.

We don't need history repeating itself."

FOURTEEN

Does *anybody* actually like hospitals? You always hear people go on and on about how horrible hospitals are. I don't even think the doctors or nurses like being here. I glance around the gray walls of the waiting room, my eyes trailing over the generic floral furniture and watercolor artwork, the ugly geometric patterns in the carpet. Russ and I have been here in shifts. He's at the store now, and I'm here. His wife and daughter are sitting across from me, Jemma fast asleep in her mother's arms.

Jen lets out a sigh that is contagious. Then I catch her yawns. I just know my mother will come through those big double doors any moment with some good news. As though I'm suddenly clairvoyant, they swing open, and here she comes, rushing through with a panic-stricken look on her face.

"Jason," she gushes out, opening her arms to me as she rushes forward. I meet her halfway, and when we collide, I notice out of the corner of my eye that Jemma stirs in her sleep.

"There's my precious angel," my mother says, breaking away from our embrace to look at her angelic carrot-topped granddaughter. "You didn't have to come, Jen. I don't want her to catch anything here. Ugh. Hospitals are so horrible."

"What's going on, Mom? How's Dad doing?" I need to distract her from the baby if I have any hope of gaining information. But tearing a grandmother's gaze away from her infant granddaughter is not an easy feat.

She finally straightens up and turns her body to form a triangle with me and her daughter-in-law. "They took John to surgery. He has another blockage."

"Oh, no! Is he going to be okay?" Jen squeals, making Jemma squirm even more.

My mother lets out a huff. "I told him a million times he had to stop eating all that junk food. Fried everything! No one ever listens to me. What do I know, I—"

Her volume rose enough during her rant that Jemma's eyes pop open, and the poor babe takes one look at her surroundings and begins to wail. Can't say that I blame her. "Let me take her," my mother offers. And just like that, I know I'm not getting any more information from her.

"Let me go call Russ," Jen says, standing up. She looks relieved not to have a baby attached to her.

"How long will surgery take?" I ask my mother, but she's too busy settling herself in the chair and getting

Jemma perfectly arranged on her lap to answer. I'm glad the baby is here, though, because at least Mom is smiling. If that gets her through the next few hours while Dad is in surgery, then that's the best I can hope for.

"I'm going to go make a phone call too." I wave at my Mom, but I don't think she even notices me.

I have tried to save my phone battery, so I haven't checked it since I first arrived. It took nearly an hour for my mother to come out of the ER. From a quick glance, I can already see I have three texts. One is from Pete asking me about coming to his show tonight. At least this time I actually have a good excuse to decline his invitation. One is Patsy from work asking if I will be in tomorrow. Apparently my dad having a heart attack is not an automatic excuse.

My heart leaps when I see the name *HR* in my texts. *Give me an update when you can.* That's all it says. Simple and to the point. No emoji. No "xo." Just completely straightforward.

But I'm thrilled to hear from her nonetheless.

I realize my father's heart attack sets me back on my plan of telling my parents about Hannah. It's clear they already know about Über Brides—that's probably what gave him the heart attack. But now that he's going to be recovering, I am going to have to keep my relationship with her under wraps a little longer. It's not what I want, but how can I be selfish? My dad is in surgery, for crying out loud!

"Hey, it's me," I say as soon as Hannah answers.

"How's your dad?" She's as simple and to the point now as she was over text. I can hear the urgency in her voice, though.

"He's in surgery." Mine doesn't sound any less urgent.

"I'm praying for him," she tells me. "I probably better let you go."

"Wait, why?" She has spoken few words, but I can tell something else is going on. She's usually so bright and perky. She's not subdued solely because of my dad—there has to be something more.

"It's been a long day," she tells me. *Like that explains it.*

"How was the rest of work?"

"We got a scathing Yelp review today. Patsy was all fired up about it. Oh, and Stacy finally got fired."

"What, are you serious?" There goes our scapegoat. "What was the final straw?"

"The cake topper," Hannah shares. "Apparently the bride was none too happy, not even after Patsy offered her $100 store credit."

"Wow. Well, guess we will have to start pinning stuff on Brandon then," I muse.

"Yeah." She sighs. Someone who didn't know her might think she was sad about Stacy, but I'm sure that's not what's going on.

"Is there something else?" I push just a little. I'm willing to do whatever I can to keep her on the phone. Anything is better than returning to that depressing waiting room to sit and stare at the generic watercolor paintings of ships and lighthouses.

"No. I'm just turning in early tonight. But please give me an update when your dad is out of surgery, even if it's late, okay?"

I promise her I will, and then she hangs up. She's

definitely keeping something from me. I wish I could go over there and talk to her in person. If I could look her in the eyes, I'm sure she wouldn't be able to hide whatever it is from me. Too bad she lives with her parents.

I hope that won't be the case for too much longer...

Trying to occupy my mind while I wait to hear back about Jason's dad's surgery, I call Claire Reilly. We exchanged phone numbers back when Jason had the meeting of the minds at his house a few weeks ago. She is not only an author, but she used to have a syndicated column with *The New York Times* called The Reinvention. Jason said he asked her a while back to give him the name of a contact we could go to with the evidence of Patsy embezzling money from Über Brides, but as far as I know, she never got back with him.

"Hey, Claire, not sure if you remember me, but this is Hannah Robinson from Delmarva Beach Brides?" I begin, hoping she hasn't forgotten me already.

"Oh, yes, of course! I don't know if I told you when I saw you at Jason's a few weeks ago, but I worked with your mother when I bought my wedding gown too. She is just lovely! I hope you'll tell her I said hello," she gushes.

"Oh, of course." She had already told me that, but it's cool. She's a busy lady with a lot on her mind. That probably explains why she hasn't gotten back with me about *The New York Times* contact.

"How is Operation Wedding War going?" she questions. "I just love that you guys actually gave it a title. I love titling things. It's sort of my schtick." She laughs heartily.

"Well, that's why I'm calling, actually," I explain.

"Oh, great! I've just been waiting for our assignment from Jason, but I haven't heard anything from him since that night we met."

What? But—

"Oh, okay. I thought he emailed you..."

She laughs again. "No, haven't gotten anything from him. Is there something I can help you with?"

I bite down on my lip to prevent myself from saying something nasty about Jason. I have asked him at least four or five times if he contacted Claire, and he said yes! Why would he lie about that? He's just as invested in blowing up Patsy's story as I am.

"Actually, yes." I explain to her about Patsy and the evidence we've collected. "So we were hoping to have the name of an editor—maybe in the business department? Do you have any idea who we can talk to?"

"Oh, wow, that's some crazy stuff!" she agrees. "Might be damning not just for the Rehoboth Beach location but for the entire company!"

"I know!" Just thinking about having it splashed all over national headlines makes me giddy.

"I know the business editor who was there when I was writing for them has been replaced. Let me ask around and figure out the best person for you to speak with," she says.

"Oh, okay. I really appreciate it, Claire!"

"Of course. It's my pleasure. Jack and I are very much interested in helping you guys out, so please don't hesitate to let me know if there's anything else we can do. I'll get back to you shortly with a contact, alright?"

I feel a bit of relief wash over me, though I'm still irritated about finding out Jason didn't do what he promised to do. "Thanks again, Claire."

"Oh, and Hannah?" she says before we hang up.

"Yes?"

"Jean-Marc came back from his cruise, so he's going to be posting the video he and his friend took and trying to get as many views as possible on all the social media platforms," she tells me.

"Oh, wow, really?" My heart just skipped a beat thinking of it.

"Yes, ma'am. Hope it goes viral for you guys!"

I hang up and squeeze my eyes shut as tears begin to sting behind my lids. I wish I could call Jason and tell him, but I need to let him have his family time. He needs to decompress. Operation Wedding War is stressful enough without having a family member under the knife.

Not only that, but the conversation I had with my father earlier tonight keeps running through my head over and over. I thought about going back downstairs to talk to my mother when she finally returned from Ruth's house—and of course, to see how Ruth is—but I just couldn't make myself go down there. I'm angry at Ruth for not being able to keep my secret. To say it caused her to be *physically* ill makes me *physically* mad. She's always been dainty and flighty. I should have known better than to trust her.

But beyond that, I've been thinking a lot about what my father told me happened between my brother and Jason's sister. If what he says is true: Jessica was caught cheating and then when Mo broke up with her, she was hell bent on ruining his life, it really does sound like a horrible set of circumstances. My father had been hoping to partner with Mr. Friday so they could merge their businesses. Maybe if they'd been able to do that, we wouldn't be facing the crisis we're facing now with Über Brides. The two businesses together would have been stronger and better positioned to compete with a national superstore.

Jessica might have ruined a lot more than Mo's chance to go to U Del on scholarship. She might have unknowingly sabotaged both her family business and mine.

My phone has blown up with texts all night. I vaguely remember hearing it buzz—it'd been set to vibrate—but I was too enamored with my dream to attend to them. There was a brick house with a little green fence all around the backyard. And there were two little kids chasing a dog around, back and forth, in circles, tiny little feet traipsing through the lush green grass of the yard. And the dog was Dolly. I have no doubt.

It left me with a warm and fuzzy feeling until it abruptly burst, and I realized it was morning. I grab my phone and scan the texts, looking for the "J" first.

He made it through surgery fine. I'm taking today off.

That's all it says. *Succinct.* But I guess I was also rather succinct when I contacted him the day before. There are three more texts, one from Claire with a name and phone number to contact. Nope, two from Claire, the second being a link to a video on Facebook. The final text is from Patsy: *Get in here ASAP.*

I don't have time to watch the video. I throw off the sheets and blankets and stumble for the shower. Despite the urgency in my boss's text, I can't shake the tranquil feeling of the dream that enraptured me for most of the night. Whose kids were running around in the yard? At first I thought maybe they were my sister's little boys till I realized one was a girl. Mo's daughter?

No, the kids had lighter skin, a beautiful golden color, shimmering in the sun. It was much lighter than mine.

And the dog was clearly, unmistakably Dolly.

When my mind makes itself up that the dream must have been about having Jason's babies, I very nearly toss my cookies. *We are certainly not at that point,* I think with an adamant headshake, *and I very much doubt we ever will be.* Not after that conversation last night with my father.

I get to the store about thirty minutes later, well before opening. Patsy is pacing the showroom floor, her cell phone in one hand and the cordless phone from the sales counter pressed to her ear.

"Yes, ma'am. Of course. Well, I—" she started but was evidently cut off. A long pause ensued. "No, there's no reason for you to—" Another pause. "I have already fired her."

She flashes me a look, and she's so rat-like, I have a hard time determining if she's angry, sarcastic, or upset. Maybe all three?

"No, it was definitely out of context. I don't think there's anything wrong with—" Another pause. "No, of course not. Yes, we can do that. Okay, then."

She hangs up the cordless phone and stuffs it in the front pocket of the large, bulky tunic she's wearing. Her gaudy costume jewelry necklace bounces against her chest as she makes her way to me faster than I've ever seen her move. "Did you see Facebook this morning?"

I shake my head, pretending not to know what's going on. She pulls out her cell phone, presses something and hands it to me. A video begins to play, and it's obviously inside our store. I recognize Jean-Marc, then I come into view. It's edited to start at the spot where I mistook his friend for his fiancé, and then it spews on and on in all its Jean-Marc glory. He was really working the crowd, that's for sure. He sounds even more irate on the video than he did in person, and if I remember correctly, it was a tough enough pill to swallow in its first iteration.

"That's you, right?" she asks, yanking the phone from my hand.

"Well, yes, but—"

"Corporate is supremely pissed off!" She purses her lips and shakes her head, and I still can't tell if she's mad at me or corporate. "They're so pissed off, they want to come down here and bring down the hammer on someone."

"What happens if they come down here?" I question. She's threatened that they might *come down here a* few times now, and I've never really understood what would happen if they did. And, they're on the West Coast, I think, so I'm pretty sure the appropriate direction would be "over," not "down." But I digress.

"Trust me, that's the last thing we want." She puts a hand on her hip for emphasis. "If they come down here, we're all getting fired. Me, you, everyone!" She gestures her hand in a giant circle to indicate how disastrous the consequences would be.

"Bad enough they'd close down the store?" I push, hoping for the answer I want to hear.

"Who knows? They've closed stores before when they've underperformed, but it's pretty rare. This isn't so much underperforming—except how off that one week of sales was, still don't understand those numbers—but we've had so many complaints. I don't think you've been properly training our new hires."

Oh yeah, sure, blame this all on me. That really angers me. I am not typically an angry person, but I've felt more anger in the past few weeks since this whole thing started than I've ever felt in my entire life.

"I didn't get much training myself," I say as calmly as I can.

She rolls her eyes. "Corporate is sending me some training videos I'm supposed to have you watch. One of them is on diversity."

Oh for crying out loud! I don't have to tell you how infuriating and demeaning that is. I know Jean-Marc didn't mean to get me into trouble, but I wish it would have been anyone else who'd been caught up in his hysterics. I'm itching to say something highly inappropriate, so I have to bite my tongue to keep the words from hurtling out. I wish Jason were here. He would calm me down. He would remind me that it doesn't matter if I'm in trouble—the greater good is that the whole store is on corporate's radar.

"A hundred and sixty-seven comments on Facebook," she seethes. "Look at all these fags and dykes! Who knew there were so many gay people in Rehoboth Beach?"

All the blood rushes to my cheeks when I hear her hateful slurs. Not even Jason could hold back my vitriol now. *Nope. That's it. Can't hold it in any longer.*

"I did," I fire back at her. "And Über Brides should have known too. If they had bothered to do any type of environmental scan or demographic research before setting up shop here, they would have known there is a significant population of LGBT folks here. By the way, that's the term you should be using, not gay, and definitely not those other extremely offensive terms I cannot repeat. Actually, it's LGBTQIA plus, but—"

"Look," she cuts me off. "You better watch your mouth. There are cameras all over here. I just did you a huge favor and talked them out of sending someone from corporate down here. I just saved your job and told them you were my best employee. So I suggest you wipe that smug smile off your face and get your little floral-covered ass back to the computer in the storeroom so you can watch the videos they're sending you. Then there's a little quiz you need to take after each one so they know you've watched and understood. Is that clear?"

Wow. I have never been so patronized in my entire life. I solemnly nod and shuffle my way back to the computer to watch these stupid training videos. I've never felt more humiliated! All I can think is a) I'm glad there weren't any customers in the store and b) I'm glad Jason didn't see that. But then I realize that c) no, I really wish Jason were here right now.

I miss him so much, and it's not even been twenty-four hours since I saw him. How am I supposed to keep my distance from him when the pull is so strong? I hate not being able to tell him why I have to be standoffish right now, but he has enough to deal with. Between what Daddy told me and Claire saying he didn't contact her—after he promised he would—I just don't know what to do about him.

What if he's not the man I think he is? The man I need him to be? I just don't know if we can ever truly be on the same page.

As if she's reading my mind, Patsy shouts across the showroom, "And where the hell is Jason? He should be here by now!"

FIFTEEN

I had a late night and am extra groggy when my phone rings at eight o'clock. But as soon as I hear the sweet voice on the other end, I find myself perking up.

"Sorry if I woke you up. Is everything okay?" Hannah asks.

"Yes, of course, what's going on?" My heart is racing. The last time I got an unexpected phone call, it was my brother telling me my dad was in the hospital. I'm so exhausted; it's a good thing I'm taking the day off. Our part-time guy Scott is opening the store, and our administrative assistant Tiffany will be there as well.

"I—" She only gets that one word out before she

must think better of it. "How's your dad?"

I know damn well that's not what she was going to say. "He's doing well, thank you. I am going to go see him here soon. Russ and Mom are with him now. He's going to be in the hospital for a day or two. They placed a stent. It's a damn good thing Mom got him there as fast as she did, or it could have been a lot worse."

"Wow, I'm so glad he's going to be okay." After she says that, she's quiet, like I called her instead of the other way around. I haven't forgotten how off she seemed last night. It doesn't sound like things are quite right today either.

"What's going on there? Is Patsy mad that I'm not there?"

"Uh, yeah. She's pissy at everyone and everything, actually. Even I got yelled at," she discloses.

"You? But you're the golden child!" I laugh. She's an adorable butt-kisser. Patsy has no clue Hannah is actually conspiring behind her back to not only bring her down personally but the entire company as well.

"Not anymore." She explains, "Jean-Marc posted his video on Facebook, plus he tweeted it. It's getting a lot of views and comments."

"Oh, but that's great!" Best news I've heard in a while. I knew getting my crew involved was the way to go. You can't beat a group of theatre geeks for getting shit done. After watching them pull off *Yo Ho Rehoboth*, I knew this was going to be a walk in the park. And I still have more plans in store for them.

"Yeah, but I'm in the video, and now corporate is mad that I made a customer so irate, and I have to watch a bunch of training videos." I hear the pout in her voice.

"Well, you're taking one for the team, Sugarbunz."

I laugh, knowing how much she'll hate me using her father's nickname for her. "It shows your dedication to the cause...falling on your sword in front of the enemy."

"Why didn't you talk to Claire like you said you would?" she blurts out.

"What?" After my heart had just calmed down, it starts racing again when I hear the sharp accusation in her voice. "What are you talking about?"

"I called Claire Reilly last night, and she said she never got anything from you about a contact at *The New York Times*," she huffs out.

Oh, crap. "Well, I emailed her a week ago probably." I crack my fingers against my jawline while I try to figure out what happened. "You know what? I emailed her from my Friday's Formalwear account. I bet it went to spam."

She's silent for a moment.

"Well, what did she say?" I continue when it's clear she's not going to speak.

"She texted me a name and email address today." There is no joy in her voice, not what I expected when we're this close to bringing down the enemy.

"Will you please tell me what's going on?" I have the phone balanced between my shoulder and ear as I make my way to the bathroom. I'm trying to hold my bladder until we're done with our conversation, but I don't want to hang up when she sounds so sad.

"I don't want to discuss it right now. I'm at work, and you're supposed to be taking care of your dad and stuff." There's a slight tinge of resignation in her voice, like she's given up on me. On us.

I don't want that. I can't handle that. I need her.

"Hannah, please. I can take care of my dad and whatever is bothering you too. My shoulders are strong and can handle a pretty heavy burden. Can you please just tell me what's going on? I sensed something was wrong yesterday when we spoke."

Silence again. *Please talk to me, Hannah...*

"It's not your job to take care of me," she grinds out. "I'll talk to you later, Jason."

And just like that, she's gone.

After visiting with my parents, I end up at work anyway. It would have been better if I could've caught some more *zzzzz's* since I didn't get much sleep last night, but I can't stop thinking about Hannah. So I try to distract myself by capitalizing on the social media uproar Jean-Marc has started on Facebook. There are hundreds of local folks commenting on his video as well as LGBT advocates from across the globe. For the local ones calling for a boycott of Über Brides, I leave comments telling them Friday's Formalwear would be more than happy to make all their wedding dreams true—at least with regard to tuxes and accessories.

I'm just about to switch with Russ, who has just arrived from the hospital, when a new customer swings through the door. He's alone, which is pretty unusual. Most of the time the men who shop here come with their buddies, their moms, their fiancées, their girlfriends. This guy is all alone.

"Hi there," I approach him, "is there something I can help you with?"

He runs his fingers down the sleeve of one of the Christian Diors on the mannequin near the front of the store. With his slim frame and broad shoulders, it would look amazing on him. I don't hesitate to tell him so, but before I can get any words out of my mouth, he interrupts me.

"You look really familiar..." His eyes sweep down my body and back up again. "Do you also work at Über Brides? I swear I just saw you there a couple days ago."

I cough out, "Uh, no, huh. That's weird. I must have a doppelganger!" I soften my stiff words with a chuckle.

"Weird. Yeah, I suppose you do." He glances around the showroom. "I'm just looking around. I'll let you know if I need anything."

"Great!" I give him a beaming smile. "This is my brother, Russ," I introduce him, pointing to my brother as he steps out from behind the counter. "Friday's Formalwear is a family-owned business. You're in good hands here. I have to step out for my lunch break, but Russ will be more than happy to help should you have any questions or need to try anything on."

"Fantastic, thank you," he says and goes back to the Dior. I watch him pull out a little notebook and scribble down a few things, then slide it back into his jeans pocket. He then runs his fingers through his sandy blond hair before making his way across the room to a different display.

I still find it a little odd he's here on his own and taking notes, but maybe he's planning to bring his fiancée back later, who knows?

Soon I'm in my car and headed back to the hospital, thoughts of the strange unaccompanied blond man quickly displaced with thoughts of Hannah Robinson and what might have upset my beautiful comrade.

Hannah

My fingers are trembling as I pick up the phone. The reporter from *The New York Times* promised to call at 3:00 PM, and it's now 3:01. I thought my heart was going to explode when it finally rang. "Hello?"

"Is this Hannah Robinson?" her voice comes down the line, soft and smooth.

"Yes, ma'am. Thank you for calling me."

I tell her my story, well, minus the part about me being a corporate spy. I tell her I've been employed here since May and that I noticed some discrepancies with payroll reports. The first thing she asks me is if I've reported it to anyone at corporate.

"No, not yet. I was kind of hoping to leak it out like this," I answer.

"You might want to give corporate a chance to deal with it first," the reporter suggests. "Because the first thing we're going to do is ask them for a comment, and if *they* don't know and you *do*—well, it might not end well for you. You're a new employee, and I don't have to tell you there's no loyalty to employees who have been with a company for years, let alone someone new like you."

"Oh," is all I can squeak out. That makes sense. "So...call you back later then?"

I can hear the smile in her voice. "If corporate retaliates against you or doesn't reprimand your supervisor, then sure, definitely get back with us. But you have no proof that she's behind it or how long it's been going on as the records only go back to May."

"Well, that's when we opened," I explain.

"I know. But your boss came from a different store, right? So it would be more compelling if you had evidence it had been going on there too. It sounds like it's a small-time affair with one person involved and only over the course of a month or so. Maybe you could find out if it's been going on at other stores. If it's a company-wide problem, then—"

"But I thought you guys were the reporters. The ones who do the research..." I don't mean to sound snarky, but it's coming out that way, I guess because I'm disappointed by her lack of interest.

I briefly think about throwing myself under the bus and telling her about Jean-Marc's video, but I'm not falling on my sword that hard. Not today. My ego is still bruised from earlier.

"We do plenty of research," she assures me. "But we have to point our time and resources toward what we think will yield the best stories."

"Right. I understand." I thank her again and hang up, my mouth filling with a sour taste.

Glancing at the new comments on Jean-Marc's video, a few of which are extremely unflattering to me, I want to curl up in a ball and cry. I'm not going to do that, of course. I just—

I wish Jason were here.

There, I said it.

Even though I'm not sure if I believe he really did

contact Claire like he promised he would. Even though my father filled me in on what *might have been* with our two families, a future that was destroyed by young, fickle love. I still want him.

I suck in a sharp breath and decide to see if I can find an ally at the store Patsy came from. Maybe someone will confide in me that she's been embezzling from the company for longer than the six weeks or so she's been in Rehoboth Beach. After that, one way or another, I'm calling corporate.

I've done everything I can to appease Patsy by closing time. She leaves and I stay behind to hang up all the bridal gowns that have been tried on and put all the merchandise that's been moved around back in place. If there's one thing I can't stand, it's walking into an untidy showroom in the morning. I'm waiting on a call back from someone at the corporate office, and also from someone at Patsy's previous branch in New Jersey.

Just as I've finally decided to brave dinner with my parents, I see Jason pop through the back door, heading down the hallway straight toward me. It takes everything I have not to leap into his arms. I gauge the worried look on his face, and my mind immediately goes to his father. I hope he hasn't taken a turn for the worse.

"What's wrong?" I stammer out as he nears me. His arms are outstretched, and I am afraid I see a tear glistening in his eyes. "Jason?"

He doesn't answer. Instead, he sweeps me into his arms, lifts me off the ground and swings me around. It's a testament to his bulky muscles because I'm not a small girl, not with a booty like this on me. His grip is so tight around me, all the air squeezes out of my lungs, then he sets me back on the ground. The room is still spinning as my senses settle into place. "What's going on?"

"Nothing," he answers. "I just missed you."

"What's going on with your dad? Is he okay?"

"Yes, I told you that earlier." A small smile breaches his lips.

"But you look so worried—"

"About you," he cuts me off. "I'm worried about you because you won't tell me what's going on."

I sigh. I don't want him to worry about me.

Or maybe I do.

Ugh, I don't know.

"Come on, let's go talk," he tells me. "I'll take you out for dinner."

"In public? But what about our parents?" Then I remember his dad is in the hospital, and my parents already know.

"Do you still care about that bullshit?" He locks his eyes with mine, boring into my gaze as he searches for my response.

I smile. I do, or I wouldn't be upset right now. But like I said, my parents already know.

"Where to for dinner?"

"I'm feeling Asian tonight. Saketumi?" he suggests.

I nod. "Can you drive?"

"Of course I can."

We're sitting in the restaurant swirling plum wine in our glasses as we await our sushi. The lighting in here is perfect. It's cozy and romantic, and right now I would rather have any conversation at all with this man than the one I need to have.

"So are you going to tell me what's going on?" He doesn't waste any time cutting to the chase.

I roll my eyes at his forwardness, though that's one of my favorite of his many redeeming qualities. I can't deny that I'm better off being just as straightforward as he is.

"The other night—last night, I guess, though it already seems like eons ago now—my sister took ill, and my mother had to go watch her kids while she went to the doctor."

Concern spreads itself across his features. "Oh, I'm sorry to hear that. Is she okay?"

"Yeah, she's fine." I toss in another eye roll for posterity's sake. "She was feeling ill because she'd kept my secret about you from our parents, and she worked herself into such a tizzy, she had a panic attack, I guess."

"Wow. That's not good. I didn't realize you'd told her about us."

"Well, you'd told your brother, so I thought it was only fair if I told my sister," I explain. "Anyway, my father had a come to Jesus meeting with me last night."

His eyes widen. "I bet that was fun. What did he say?"

"Well," I take a sip of my plum wine, letting the

sweetness tingle on my tongue before continuing, "there seems to be a bit more to the story than the teenage angst rendition we were fed earlier by our respective siblings."

This time, his eyebrows quirk in response. "How so?"

"Apparently your sister and my brother were not only dating, but everyone expected them to get married," I reveal. "And there were plans to merge the family businesses."

He's speechless for a moment, practically frozen, with his mouth gaping open. "And your dad told you this?" he finally eases the words out.

"Yup. He told me that my brother caught your sister cheating on him with a buddy of his on the baseball team, and then after he dumped her, she went ballistic and cost him his scholarship to college. It ended up changing the trajectory of his whole life."

"Well, we already knew that part of the story, but my sister said he was lying about her cheating on him. Plus, she said he spread vicious rumors all over school about how she'd done 'half the baseball team,' I believe were the words she used." He sounds a little keyed up defending his older sister. "Not only that, but he really *did* cheat on the scholarship project. She knew because she did some of the work for him."

"He says she lied about it," I reiterate.

"Well, someone's lying, alright," he says, his voice raw with anger.

Great, now we're fighting about it too. Yeah, I can kind of see why this has been going on so long.

I swallow down the rest of my plum wine. I may not be here much longer if this discussion continues to go south. "My father says our parents officially dissolved their business relationship, and apparently there were a lot of hard feelings. And it sounds like it devolved from there."

"How did I never know Dad was planning to take on a partner?" He scratches his head like he's already forgotten the nastier parts of our discussion involving our siblings. "I don't think Russ remembers it that way either."

"It could be that no one else knew besides our parents. Like maybe Mo and Jessica didn't even know," I conjecture.

"I have a feeling that either Mo or Jessica is lying," he states. "My sister was not a slut. There's no way she would have gotten it on with that many guys."

I huff back, "Well, my brother was super smart, and there's no way he cheated on that scholarship!"

Okay, so we're back to this, then?

He reaches across the table and grasps my hands, squeezing them into his much larger ones. They feel so warm. So strong. It's hard for me to remember why I was defending my brother so adamantly. I've barely spoken to my brother in years. He did get really ticked off at my parents and move several states away. That couldn't be *all* Jessica Friday's fault.

"We have bigger problems to work out," Jason reminds me. "I don't know what's going to happen with my dad, but I don't think he's ever going to be able to return to work."

My eyes shift down to the shiny tabletop. "I'm sorry to hear that."

"He saw the sales reports, Hannah. That's what set off his heart attack. That, and Mom finally told him about Über Brides."

"Oh no." I bury my face in my palm. "Why would she do that?"

"He wanted to know why the numbers were so low. He kept yelling at her until she finally told him."

"So now what?" I glance up at him, hoping his brilliant plans haven't dried up. He's the idea person. I'm the detail person. Together we make one hell of a team. Surely we have some more fight left in us?

"What happened with *The New York Times* contact?"

I fill him in on my conversation with the reporter, plus my attempts to speak with someone at the New Jersey branch where Patsy previously worked and with someone at the corporate offices in California. "I guess we just have to wait and see how that pans out...plus the video Jean-Marc posted, of course."

He nods. "Do you think they'll send someone from corporate here? You know the company better than I do."

"It's possible. I have no clue what will happen if they do. Patsy says everyone will get fired, and they'll just start fresh with new people." I shrug. I don't know whether or not to trust anything Patsy says at this point.

"We need a plan. I think you should invite corporate down yourself if you can talk to someone there." From the look in his twinkling eyes, he is on the verge of sharing another brilliant idea.

"Why would I do that? I risk getting fired, and then there goes our 'in.'"

He squeezes my hand in his once more. "Because you need to tell them we're involved in the biggest wedding on the East Coast—we outfitted the bride and groom, provided all the services—and we want them to witness what an amazing job we did!"

"But—" I stare at him, my eyes bouncing between his, trying to figure out what in the world he's suggesting. "I'm sorry, I'm just not following you."

"I don't have all the details worked out yet, but I promise you it's going to be the nail in the coffin. The equivalent of the atomic bomb." His lips spread into the widest, most devious grin I have ever seen.

I shake my head. "I don't know about you sometimes. You scare me." I can't help but laugh as I see how my confession only makes his smile grow. It's the most gorgeous smile I've ever seen, and I can't deny it makes my insides do all sorts of acrobatic maneuvers I've been trying to ignore for weeks.

"You love it!" he fires back, on the verge of laughing.

I can't stop myself from blurting out, "I love you."

We're both frozen in time for a moment, staring at each other with those huge cartoon hearts popping out of our eyes. And that's the exact moment the waiter arrives with a huge serving platter full of sushi, which he places before us with a grand flourish. Then, completely failing to see he's interrupted a beautiful, romantic moment, his gaze sweeps from Jason to me before he asks, "Everything look good?"

I nearly burst into laughter as Jason grunts that things are fine. As soon as the dude scurries away, Jason moves his plate aside and reaches for my hand again. I move mine too, looking down as he intertwines our fingers. I love the way they look together, the contrast of our skin tones, his wide, manly fingers and my narrow, well-manicured ones. He squeezes and looks deep into my eyes.

"I love you too." He smiles at me, his eyes lighting up when he sees the corners of my lips turn up to match his. "We need all hands on deck for this final scheme. First thing we're doing is going to our parents and getting them to get on board."

The smile is wiped right off my face, my eyes pulled into slits as I evaluate the sanity of the man sitting across from me. I may love him, but that doesn't mean he's not crazy. "Are you sure that's a good idea?"

"Trust me on this. It's a brilliant idea."

SIXTEEN

"**B**ut why do we have to talk to my parents first?" Her eyes are bouncing between mine, and a look of horror is gripping her features. If she ever needed the perfect expression for an extreme close-up in a slasher flick, this would be it. You'd think I was holding a knife to her throat.

"Because my dad's still in the hospital recovering from surgery," I remind her. "Let's give him a few days to rest up before we wreck his heart again."

"Your parents just seem so much more reasonable than mine." She folds her arms in front of her chest. "Mine are...well...they are set in their ways, to say the least. My mother is probably going to douse you in holy water and start quoting scriptures or something."

"What, they think I'm possessed?" I can't help but

laugh. "Come on, I know your parents are good people. If not, my parents would have never considered going into business with them. It's time we bury the hatchet, Hannah. We're going to need their help for this final battle."

"Are you going to fill me in, or what?"

"I did—we're planning the wedding of the century. All hands on deck. Yada yada yada." I scratch the scruff growing on my chin. "I thought we covered this before?"

"Details?" Her expectant gaze pierces through me.

"Details are more your thing." I grab her hand. "Come on. It won't be so bad. I promise." I help her into the passenger side of my truck and then take my place behind the wheel. Moments later we're squealing out of Saketumi's parking lot and barreling down Route 1. Good thing it's a weeknight, or we'd be crawling.

As it is, traffic is still thick. She starts to give me directions to her parents' house, and I begin to wonder if she's leading me on a wild goose chase. "I had no idea you guys live so far out," I tell her.

"It's not that far away." She shrugs. "Turn here."

There's a neighborhood with two-story houses, all with similar siding, porches and driveways. She points to a home on the left, and I swing into the driveway so fast, it forces her body into mine. I catch a whiff of her perfume, and it only strengthens my resolve. We're going to march in there and tell Mr. and Mrs. Robinson we've united, and there's nothing they can do about it.

I take her hand in mine and squeeze it tightly as we make our way down the sidewalk and up the porch steps. "They'll think it's weird I'm coming in the front door," she tells me.

"I hardly think they'll notice that when they figure

out you're with a Friday." I swallow down a chuckle as she rolls her eyes at me.

She turns the doorknob, and the door slowly creaks open to reveal a grand foyer with a sturdy oak staircase leading to the second story. There's a brass chandelier twinkling from a rosette in the ceiling and a huge, old-fashioned hall tree holding hats, coats and umbrellas. Beyond that is the living room, and that's where she guides me, our hands still clasped together.

"Mama, Daddy?" her voice breaks the silence. After the sound of her question fades, all I hear is the *tick tock* of the grandfather clock in the corner of the room while two heads peer up at me over their respective newspaper and book. The whole thing seems like it's happening in slow motion, her father's bald head reflecting the light above him, and her mother's eyebrows arching so high they nearly disappear into her hair.

"Where have you been, Hannah? Who's this?" her mother questions. She seems calm. *For now.*

Hannah doesn't say anything at first till I clear my throat and jerk her hand a little. I'm kind of surprised she's so terrified of her parents. She is the strongest, most take-charge woman I know—but even I will admit the glare coming from Morris Robinson's eyes is fairly formidable.

"This is Jason Friday," she introduces me. "As you know, we're working on the plan to run Über Brides out of town. We want to discuss our plans with you." She glances back to look at me as if to ask if she characterized our presence satisfactorily.

"Hello Mr. Robinson, Mrs. Robinson." I dip my chin toward both of her parents as I acknowledge them. "Nice to meet you."

Her father stands up slowly, obviously nursing a bad back. He doesn't even deign to look at me. "I thought we told you not to associate with the Fridays." His words come out in a low snarl.

"Daddy, there's no way I could have done what I've managed to do without Jason's help. Did you see what's going on? We've had some friends help us, and one of them posted a video that's gotten over a hundred thousand views on Facebook today. We've gotten the attention of the corporate offices. They want to send someone down—"

"Which means we're ready for our grand finale," I cut in. "We're going to stage a huge 'celebrity wedding.'" I use air quotes for that last bit. "Not real celebrities of course, but we're going to make them think they are. I have some really stellar ideas, but your daughter is the detail person. She's the only one I know who can bring my ideas to fruition."

"That sounds like a whole bunch of hooey!" Mr. Robinson growls. His wife jumps up and is at his side in a flash. "Morris, why don't we give the kids a chance to explain?"

Hannah's mother's face is painted with concern. She looks torn between her daughter and husband, standing in the middle of them. "Hannah, can you tell us more about your plans?"

"We're just starting to figure it out," she explains. "But we need to know we have your support. We are going to need a lot of help to pull this off."

"So it's a fake wedding?" Mrs. Robinson is still trying to wrap her head around it.

"Yes." I give her my most charming salesman smile. If I can't sell Mr. Robinson on this, I can work on his wife and hopefully bring him around. "We have some friends who are actors, and they will play the bride and groom." *Never mind that I haven't officially asked them yet.* "And we're going to make it out that they're super rich, and it's a super high-profile affair. It's a chance for Über Brides to redeem themselves in the community after the negative press we've gotten lately."

"I did have a bride tell me that she got terrible service at Über Brides," Liz Robinson shares. "It sounds like you and Hannah have been doing something right."

"We're doing our best, Mama," Hannah interjects. "And we've also discovered our boss is embezzling from the company, and we're about to break that story in the media too." She flashes me a look that says, *okay, maybe not yet, but a little embellishment won't hurt, right?*

"So I don't understand how you're going to pull off a fake wedding." She purses her lips and looks from her daughter to me, completely ignoring the scowl burning itself into her husband's face.

"Well, it won't be easy, but we have a venue—my buddy Drew owns a gallery where we could hold it. We have some other friends who can play the photographers, band," I wink at Hannah and she giggles knowing exactly who I mean, "and we can have all the wedding gifts go missing, which requires calling the police. I have a cousin who's a cop, and I'm also friends with a state trooper."

"Well, goodness, that sounds like a pretty crazy ordeal," Mrs. Robinson says, looking like she is about to faint.

"We'll need an officiant," I continue, "and wedding guests—"

"Daddy, you're ordained," Hannah blurts out. "You could be our officiant!"

All of our eyes flash to Mr. Robinson, who looks like he'd be going postal right now if he were a postal worker. You know in cartoons how steam is always coming out of the really angry characters' ears? Yeah, I can nearly see that steam evaporating into the air as his rage becomes more and more pronounced.

"I will do no such thing," he finally breaks his silence. "This whole idea is ludicrous, and I'll have no part of it. Especially not if it has anything to do with the Fridays."

"Daddy, the rift between our families happened years ago now. Jason and I have investigated, and we got two entirely different stories. It's easy to see why everyone's been angry for so long, but I'm sure if you heard both sides of the story, you'd know both sides are equally at fault." She glances at me, reminding me of the little spat we got into earlier tonight over those two stories. I squeeze her hand to reassure her we're on the same page: *ready to put the past behind us and move forward.*

"Your sister cost my son his scholarship," Mr. Robinson seethes as he paces toward us. "He lost his scholarship and lost his will to even pursue higher education. If not for your sister, he'd be running Delmarva Beach Brides right now!"

"Daddy!" Hannah gasps. "That's not a fair thing to say. What about me?"

"What about you?" he roars at her. "You're ambitious, and that's wonderful, Hannah. But you always make everything about you. Well, I have news for you: it's not always about you. This company was meant for your brother. It was his birthright." She looks as though each word he spoke was a slap to her face.

Then he turns to me. "This is more than just a rift

between the Robinsons and the Fridays—it cost me my relationship with my oldest son, the rightful heir to Delmarva Beach Brides. I haven't even seen him in years! And it's all your selfish, immature sister's fault!" He's so angry now, he's shaking, his finger trembling as he points it toward me.

"I can't believe you just said that, Daddy!" Hannah's face has paled, and red cracks have appeared in the whites of her eyes. "That is the most awful, hurtful thing you have ever said to me! You made me feel like I was special and important. Like you were proud of me and wanted me to head the family business. Like I was the best choice. I never realized I would never be your first choice." A sob shatters her voice, causing her last few words to come out in a wail.

I expect her to rush into her mother's outstretched arms or to stomp up the stairs, but instead she rushes into my arms. I hold her as she breaks down, her shoulders heaving under the weight of her father's terrible words.

Now I'm trembling with anger too. I don't care what he says about my sister, but to hurt his own daughter? That is completely unacceptable. Especially when I know how hard she's worked, how many years she studied to position herself as the best, most capable CEO she could be.

"My sister went to the principal and guidance counselors because your son coerced her into helping him cheat. She wrote the damn research paper for him. That's the only way he got the scholarship. It's not her fault he lost it or that his title of valedictorian was stripped away. Maybe he cheated his way to that too?" I'm the one seething now, and all of this is erupting from me like a volcano, spewing lava and ash as far as I can possibly hurl it.

"Furthermore, he may have lost his scholarship, but the nasty false rumors he spread about my sister cost her her reputation. He told everyone in the school she was screwing the entire baseball team, cheating on him. That's not even true. After he used her to earn his scholarship, he dumped her. Why do you think my sister moved away from her family? She couldn't handle the ridicule he brought upon her!

"And not only that—" *Nope, I wasn't done yet, not by a long shot. I could keep going all night.* "—How dare you talk to Hannah like that? She has worked her ass off for your family. She might be getting a paltry paycheck from Über Brides right now, but she is basically running that place. And every bit of headway we've made toward getting that evil company run out of town comes down to her brilliant management skills. Not only that, but she has not *one* but *two* degrees, one of which is a freaking MBA! Don't you belittle her or act like she's second class just because she's not your firstborn son. You don't even deserve her as a daughter if that's the way you're going to treat her!"

"Get out!" Mr. Robinson shouts as he steps even closer to us. "Both of you, get out of my house, and don't come back!"

Hannah

It was a restless night, but when I wake up next to

Jason, I feel renewed. He pulls me toward his warm body, his arm wrapped around my waist protectively. I was hysterical last night by the time we arrived at his place. I only had time to grab a few things from my room. I know my father was angry and will probably reconsider kicking me out, but I grabbed the check he and my mother gave me a couple weeks ago. I can't imagine they'd ever rescind their offer—it's a graduation present, after all, and they kept insisting it was my money they'd saved for my college education. So I guess if worse comes to worst, I will just get my own place.

The thought causes dull pains in my stomach as I stretch and try to make out the time on the alarm clock. I keep thinking about the look on my mother's face when I said goodbye. She looked completely heartbroken. Devastated. I wonder what she said to my father after we left.

"You awake?" his deep voice rumbles in my ear as I feel him shift behind me, tightening his grip around my waist.

"I am now." I chuckle. It's been a long time since I've woken up next to a man. I'd forgotten how nice it feels. Or maybe I've just never felt this way about anyone before. The way he defended me to my father last night was—I can't even put it into words. I never thought in a million zillion years a member of the Friday clan would stand up like that for me in front of my own parents.

His lips graze my neck as he peppers my sensitive skin with a dozen tiny kisses. "How are you feeling this morning?"

My eyes still feel puffy from all the tears I shed last night. But you know what? I'm ready. I'm ready to get into work, find out what fresh hell awaits us, and get to work on planning this massive fake wedding.

"I'm okay." I shake my head. "No, I'm not *okay*, but I'm going to be *fantastic* once we figure this out. With or without my parents' help, we are going to kick Über Brides' ass."

"I like the sound of that." Taking me by complete surprise, he flips me over and pins me beneath him in mere seconds. "Oh, sorry..." He smirks as his gaze sweeps from my face down my bare chest.

"Sorry? What for?"

"For what I'm about to do to you," he answers, pressing another kiss to the edge of my lips and then another close to my ear.

"Oh, please. You never have to apologize for that!" I giggle as I wrap my arms around him.

Somehow, some way, everything's gonna be alright.

I opened up the store at eight o'clock, and the rest of the employees filtered in. Everyone but Patsy. I didn't think much of it because she's not known for her punctuality. And even when she is here, it's not like she leaves her office except to toss out a few commands and then return. I think if she comes out and bosses people around a little bit, it makes her feel productive. Then she can go back to scheming ways to embezzle money from the company.

There are two voicemails on my phone: one from

the representative I tried to reach at corporate headquarters and the other from the manager at the Über Brides location in New Jersey where Patsy used to work. I return the latter call first.

"Good morning, Matt Barnes," he greets me when he answers his phone.

"Hey, Matt, it's Hannah Robinson from the Rehoboth Beach store. Did you get my message?"

"As a matter of fact, yes I did. So, there's no way you could have known this, but there was a huge shakeup at this store a few months ago," he tells me.

"Oh, yeah?" This sounds juicy. I'm all ears.

"Patsy was the assistant manager and was working under this other woman named Theresa Bright. Well, corporate caught on to Theresa's scheme of faking employee records and drawing paychecks for fake employees. Patsy got herself transferred to the Rehoboth Beach store just a few weeks before corporate came in, investigated, and lo and behold, Theresa Bright is now awaiting her trial date for embezzlement."

"Wow!" I gasp. "So I guess Patsy learned it from her."

"Yes," he confirms. "I came down from the New York store, but the staff filled me in on everything that happened. Are you the assistant manager down there?"

"No. We don't have one."

"Oh, well don't be surprised if they come down and promote you, then. Sounds like you are really on top of things!" Matt tells me.

I hang up from our conversation and sit there for a moment pondering a few things. What if I stayed here? What if I accepted a promotion and actually ran this store the way it *should* be run?

Do I really want to work for my father after everything he said to me last night?

I glance around the store, surveying the long rack of bridal gowns and the shorter racks of colorful, glittering bridesmaid gowns. I look at the mannequins sporting tuxes and the aisles of all the other wedding accoutrements we sell here. If I stayed at Über Brides, there would be much more upward mobility than at Delmarva Beach Brides. There are regional directors and corporate executives. I have my MBA—this is what I prepared for.

I'm interrupted by the electronic bells and a bride carrying a cardboard box. I can't see her face, but when she gets closer to me and lowers the box, I notice her scathing scowl. She throws the box down on the floor. "Here's your junk. Half of them broke."

I expect to look down and see a box full of tiny penis soaps, thinking this may be the bride we gave the wrong favors to. But no, it's a box of different favors. They're supposed to be bride and groom lollipops. I pick one up, and sure enough, it's cracked right down the middle.

Oh, that's probably not a good thing. Oops.

"I'm sorry to hear you're dissatisfied with your purchase," I tell her with my customer service smile stretching my lips just so. "But we don't issue refunds for these."

It's not my choice. That's just company policy. We try not to ever issue refunds for anything. If the customer gets irate enough, sometimes we'll allow store credit.

"Great. Well, I can't use them at my wedding," she says, flipping her long brown hair over her shoulder. She glances around the store. "You know, I got my dress here. I've only tried it on twice, and it's already lost a bunch of beads and sequins. My friend used this place for her wedding tuxes, and half the seams in the guys' pants ripped. This place sells cheap junk. I'll never shop here or recommend this place again."

She doesn't say it in a threatening way. It sounds like resignation to me. Like fool me once: shame on you. Fool me twice: shame on me. She's never going to make that mistake again.

And that is precisely why I could never actually work here. I couldn't stand behind draconian return policies like that. I couldn't stand behind inferior products or lousy customer service. That's not what I went to school for. That's not what I believe in.

"You know, I've always heard Delmarva Beach Brides and Friday's Formalwear are the best places in town for wedding stuff." I give her a wink.

A little smile tilts the corners of her lips up. "You know what? I've always heard that too. I should have listened to my friends instead of trying to save a buck or two." She shrugs then turns toward the door. She begins to open it, setting off the electronic bells again. "Thanks for being honest with me," she adds and then disappears into the bright June sun.

SEVENTEEN

After lunch, Jason breezes down the hallway and onto the showroom floor. There's a spring in his step I didn't expect to see. "What did corporate say?" He reaches out to grab me around the waist and twirl me in place.

"Oh, crap, I forgot to call them!" I put down the stack of frilly garters I'd been trying to arrange on a display rack. "I got busy with a few things—" I sweep my gaze from the top of his ruffled dark waves to the brown shoes on his feet. "Did you go to the hospital? How's your dad?"

"He's doing great!" I'm so thankful to see a beaming smile grace his full, kissable lips. "They're releasing him today."

"That's wonderful to hear!" I clasp my hands together and stare at him for a moment.

"So what happened here while I was gone? Where's Patsy?" He looks around the showroom for her, though he knows as well as I do there's no way he'd find her on the floor actually working.

"She never came in," I answer, then I give him a rundown of everything else that happened this morning while he was out.

"Sounds like you need to call corporate." His face has taken on what I've come to term his *serious look*. "What if she got fired?"

"Seems like someone would have told us?" I shrug. "I didn't get any emails or phone calls, just the voicemail from the woman I spoke with yesterday.

Jason's brow quirks as the electronic bell dings. "Hey, I'll be in the back." He gives me a wink and then disappears as fast as lightning across the showroom and into the employees only area. I guess he doesn't want to help this customer?

It's a man by himself, which we don't see very often. I approach him wearing my well-worn customer service smile. "May I help you?"

"Hi, how're you doing today?" He gazes at me through gray eyes, looking slightly stiff and nervous.

"I'm well, thank you." My brows knit together as I take in the small notebook in his hand. "Is there something I can help you find?"

"Uh..." He glances around before turning his gaze back to me. "Are you the lady in the video that's been going around? I saw it on Facebook yesterday."

Oh crap. I was hoping I'd never be recognized. That's about the last way I ever wanted to gain fame or notoriety. I nod reluctantly and watch his smile brighten.

That's why he's here? To harass me about the video?

"I don't have any further statements to make about that, though," I tell him, crossing my arms over my chest.

"Oh, okay. That's fine. I was just wondering," he tells me. "Is your manager around?"

What is this guy's problem? He's creeping me out! Why did Jason leave me alone with this dude? I decide to play this smart. "Just a minute, I'll go check and see if she's in the back."

I walk as swiftly as my sensible pumps will carry me to the back, where I find Jason perched at the computer in the stock room. "Hey, why did you ditch me out there with that guy? He's a bit sketchy, don't you think?"

"He came into my parents' shop yesterday and asked if I worked here too," he explains. "I don't know what his deal is, but I didn't want to blow my cover."

That makes sense, at least. "Well, he wants to talk to Patsy, and she's not here. I think the whole thing is weird. He's carrying a little notebook."

"Why don't you take down his name and number and tell him Patsy will call him when she's in?" he suggests.

"Good thinkin'," I praise him and turn on my heel to go confront the weirdo. After repeating what Jason suggested, he takes out his notebook, scribbles a few things with a pen and then rips the paper out violently like he's pulling off a Band-Aid attached to a big clump of hair.

He turns to walk away, and I glance down at the paper with budding curiosity.

Talis Tilghman, The Delmarva Chronicle

I return to Jason and show him the note.

"Wow, he's a pretty big-time reporter over there," Jason says.

"I've never heard of him. How big can he be?"

"You just moved back," he reminds me, "so that's probably why you've never heard of him. I didn't know what he looked like. He's a lot younger than I expected, but he does a lot of exposé-type pieces. This is good, Hannah. Really good. You've gotta call corporate now, see what they say. Maybe Patsy got fired?"

I huff out a long, deep breath, rendering my lungs completely empty before filling them with determination. I pick up the phone in the stock room and dial the number for corporate that's listed on the corkboard hanging over the desk.

"Hi, it's Hannah Robinson returning Janet Bryson's call," I state. Jason gives me a thumbs up. A moment later: "Hi, Ms. Bryson."

"Hannah, I'm so glad you called us. We are currently investigating Ms. Laroche and your store's payroll reports and employee documentation. Thank you for bringing the discrepancies to our attention. So, I understand there's no assistant manager at your store currently?"

"No, ma'am. I've been acting in that capacity for—"

"I looked over your resume that Ms. Laroche uploaded to our intranet, and you have some very impressive credentials. From what I understand, Ms. Robinson, your family owns Delmarva Beach Brides, our direct competitor. I was just wondering why you aren't working for your family business any longer?"

I freeze as panic rushes through me like an avalanche barreling down a mountainside. It's cold and sharp, prickling all the nerves running down my spine. Jason must sense there's been something troubling because he rests his hand on my shoulder and squeezes firmly.

"I can understand your concern, Ms. Bryson—"

"Oh, please, call me Janet," she says.

"Okay, then, Janet, thank you. You see, my family and I had a falling out after I attained my MBA. That's why I've chosen to build my career with Über Brides. I think there's a lot more room for advancement and more opportunities to use my education," I state calmly and confidently. It helps that I just performed this mental exercise mere hours ago. Jason gives me a thumbs up as a wide grin spreads across his face.

"You've certainly got some moxie, Hannah," she says, sounding thrilled with my explanation. "I like it."

"That's great to hear, Janet." I repeat her name to solidify our relationship and build rapport. "So, Patsy didn't come to work today—"

"No," the head of corporate HR tells me. "She's been placed on administrative leave for the time being. Didn't she tell you?"

"No, ma'am." I shake my head, but I can't stop the smile lifting my cheeks. *Oooh, Patsy's in T-R-O-U-B-L-E!* That's what my brothers and sister and I used to chant when we were growing up and someone got in hot water.

"She was supposed to email you or leave you a voicemail," Janet says. "And she was to make it clear that the assistant manager is in charge in her absence, but I guess since there's no assistant, that would mean you should fill that role."

"I suppose so," I agree, winking at Jason. I can tell he's hanging on my every word.

"I don't know how long this investigation is going to take, but I do know there have been some other issues besides Ms. Laroche's payroll discrepancies. Do you know anything about those issues?"

My face drops. "What kind of issues? Can you be more specific?"

"We've had some customer complaints, and there has been a rash of poor online reviews since the branch opened last month. And then, just yesterday, there was a video of a poor customer experience that was shared on the social media."

I have to stifle a giggle at the way she says "the social media" like she has absolutely no clue what it even means. "Did you see it?" I question.

She scoffs. "No, I don't use the social media, but I heard about it."

"I see. Well, I'm sorry to hear there have been issues, ma'am, but I would like to work hard to correct those issues and make Über Brides-Rehoboth Beach the best it can be." *Yuck.* Just saying those words leaves a nasty sour taste in my mouth.

"That's what we like to hear," she assures me. "In any event, we have a small crisis aversion committee that visits stores with issues, and we want to schedule a visit to Rehoboth Beach at our earliest convenience."

This is what I have been waiting to hear—what we've been waiting to hear. I lean forward, my elbow resting on the surface of the desk while I wind one of my curls around a finger on my other hand. Jason leans too, seeming to sense the climax of the conversation is imminent. I then realize I can hit the speaker button. It's a little late, but better late than never. Jason gives me a thumbs up for the third time today.

"It takes everyone a while to pull their schedules together," she tells me. "But we can come in two weeks. Friday, June twenty-second. Does that work for you?"

"Yes. We'll be ready for your visit, thank you," I tell her.

"In the meantime, put together a list of clients who are getting married that weekend. We would like to interview some customers about their experiences with Über Brides-Rehoboth Beach. We'll also be doing a complete inventory and an audit of all your files. So make sure you're prepared for that as well."

"Yes, ma'am," I tell her. We're definitely going to need the fake wedding to distract them from the whole auditing thing. They'll figure out all the sabotages I've done and that Jason isn't a real employee. There's no doubt our covers will be blown.

She says goodbye, and I hang up the phone with trembling fingers. I turn to Jason, and he's wearing his *serious business* look again.

"So now what, partner?" I ask him.

"First we talk to my parents. Then we call another meeting."

I've warned my mom that we're coming over to discuss some business ideas with her. "What do you mean by 'we'?" she'd questioned.

"I'm bringing my girlfriend," I told her bluntly.

"Girlfriend?" I've never heard more happiness in a single word than what just dripped off my mother's tongue.

She may not be so happy when she finds out who said girlfriend is, but hey, at least she got more of a warning than Hannah's parents did. I know it's my dad's first day home from the hospital, but we only have two weeks. There is no time to spare and no room for error. *Which almost rhymes, but not quite.*

"Are you sure this is going to be okay?" Hannah questions as she climbs into my truck. "What if we send your dad right back to the hospital?"

"Don't worry, just let me do the talking. Speaking of which, did you hear from your parents today?"

She sadly shakes her head. "Nope."

Damn it. I can't believe they are treating her this way. And all because of me and my family. I'm so angry, I could scream, but I shoot her a reassuring smile instead, then reach over to squeeze her knee that's poking out of the full, vibrantly-colored skirt she's wearing. When I told her we were going to meet my parents, she changed out of the perfectly appropriate dress she wore to work and into this skirt and blouse that's really lovely, but she could have worn the other dress. Ladies' fashion is yet another thing I'll never understand about women. Men's fashion just makes so much more sense.

We pull into my parents' driveway moments later since they don't live that far from me. "You're going to do great," I tell her, then realize immediately that I shouldn't have said anything. Saying that just made her whole body stiffen and her eyes fill with dread.

"Just be yourself," I reiterate. "They'll love you."

She nods and follows me up to the front porch. My mom would kill me if I brought my girlfriend through the garage on her first visit to the parental unit's abode. Yep, another feminine mystery I don't claim to understand.

I find my parents relaxing in the living room. My dad's in his armchair with his feet propped up on the ottoman, and my mom is apparently playing a game on her phone. But as soon as they see us standing there, my dad switches off the television, and my mom puts her phone on the table beside her.

"Mom, Dad, this is Hannah," I tell them, purposely leaving out her last name.

My mother jumps up and rushes over with her hand outstretched. "It's so nice to meet you. I'm Wendy, and this is Jason's father, John. I'm sorry he didn't get up to greet you—he was just discharged from the hospital."

"Oh, no worries. It's great to meet you both. I'm glad you're feeling better, Mr. Friday," Hannah says as she shakes my mother's hand.

"Please, have a seat." My mother gestures toward the sofa. I lead Hannah over and allow her to sit before

I follow suit. "So what do you two want to share with us?"

I launch into a long, but very carefully prepared and organized speech about the work we've already done at Über Brides, basically making Hannah sound like an absolute queen (well, she is) and myself sound like her righthand man (well, I have been). Then I tell them how we've probably gotten our boss fired and how corporate is sending a "crisis aversion committee" down in two weeks.

Then I give them the pitch I gave the Robinsons for our fake celebrity wedding.

My mother's eyes keep growing bigger and bigger while the groove between my dad's eyes keeps growing deeper and deeper. It's not particularly encouraging, but I soldier on. *This is a war, after all, right?*

"That sounds—" my mother turns to survey my father's expression before finishing, "—completely crazy." She laughs. "Did you just make that up?"

"Uh," I scratch at my hairy chin, "make it up? You mean, come up with the brilliant plan? Why yes. Yes I did."

"I know it sounds a little—unorthodox—" Hannah cuts in. "But Jason and I have already done some pretty outlandish things. You should tell her about the horse and carriage!" Her honey brown eyes are gleaming as the memories fill her head.

"Horse and carriage?" my dad's ears perk up. "What on earth are you talking about?"

"Remember the Seinfeld episode with the flatulent horse and the Beefarino?" My parents are pretty big fans of the show—that's why I've seen every episode.

"You didn't!" My dad begins to laugh. He laughs so

hard, he chokes and starts to cough.

Oh no. I promised Hannah we wouldn't upset him enough to cause trouble, but I didn't take into account the possibility of making him laugh too much.

"John!" My mother rushes to his side and hands him his glass of water. "Try to take a sip." My dad does as instructed, and the redness in his face begins to dissipate, thankfully. Meanwhile, Hannah is shooting me looks of absolute panic.

"So what do we need to do to help?" my dad finally asks. "I'm still recovering, so I'm not sure how much help I can be, but with as much as you and your brother have helped out with the store while I've been feeling poorly, I owe you a debt of gratitude."

"Oh, Dad." I dismiss him with a wave. "It's our store too. We just want to make you proud and carry on the Friday legacy."

"There's something else you should know first," Hannah pipes up, leaning toward my father. She has a meek smile on her face, and when her eyes dart to mine, they're full of apology. "I don't want you to commit to helping with our plan until you know who I am."

Both my parents' eyes bulge as they stare at her. My heart rate begins to pick up as I try to anticipate what she's going to say and how the parental units are going to react. I bite my lip to keep myself from interrupting her. She's got the floor now as far as I'm concerned.

"I'm Hannah Robinson," she states, and she almost does a little curtsy. "My parents own Delmarva Beach Brides."

My parents are speechless.

I glance from her to my mother, to my father, and then back to Hannah again. I can probably count on one hand the number of times my parents have been rendered speechless, and two of those times involved my brother—when he announced he was getting married and when he announced he and Jen were expecting. Both were huge surprises.

"Hannah Robinson," my mother repeats. "I was not expecting *that*."

She doesn't sound...angry. Shocked is more like it.

Hannah leans forward again, folding her hands in her lap as if she is about to pray. She probably is about to pray—pray that my parents aren't going to *freak the eff out* like her parents did.

"I know there's a lot of bad blood between our families," she states. "My parents are currently not speaking to me because of their feelings about your family and what happened all those years ago between my brother and your daughter. Jason and I have really tried hard to get to the bottom of it, and it sounds like the only people who know the absolute truth of what happened are Mo and Jessica."

"Let's call them," my mother suggests, moving from her perch on the arm of my father's chair. "Let's just call them and lay all our cards on the table."

"Wow, really?" Hannah turns to look at me, and I take her hand into mine.

"My mom is a problem-solver," I tell her. "This is what she does."

"I actually suggested that years ago when this mess first started," she explains. "But no one wanted to listen to me. Your father was too damn stubborn—and mad about his business deal falling through—"

"And mad at *your daughter* for ruining it!" he interjects, his face beginning to redden again.

"Calm down, honey. Jessica was adamant that she helped the Robinson boy with his paper, that he had committed academic dishonesty by turning in her work." She walks toward her phone and picks it up off the table. "I wanted us all to sit down and hash this out with one of those, what do you call them—"

"Crisis negotiators!" my dad roars. "Can you imagine? Calling in a crisis negotiator to fix some stupid teenage love triangle?"

"Love triangle?" Hannah's ears perk up. "So Jessica *was* seeing someone else behind Mo's back?"

"Even if she was, she wasn't sleeping with half the baseball team like Mo told everyone." *Oh, shit, I'm starting to get defensive again.* My sister could have been screwing half the school; it's not like I actually knew at the time. I was too little to understand that stuff back then. And besides, who cares if she was? The only reason it was a problem was that Mo seemed to think they were exclusive. And apparently our families seemed to think wedding bells—and a business merger—were on the horizon.

"I'm calling Jessica," Mom announces as she turns on her phone and holds it out to us like it's some sort of threat. She presses a button and puts it up to her ear. "Hi, honey, it's Mom."

We all wait with bated breath to hear what comes out of her mouth next.

"So, your brother is here—yes, Jason. Yes, Dad's home from the hospital. He's doing just fine, but we're trying to clear up a few things. Jason's here with his girlfriend..." She pauses and looks up at me with a smile, like even if it's Hannah Robinson, she's still pretty stoked I have a girlfriend. *Thanks, Mom.*

"His girlfriend is Hannah Robinson," my mom

clues Jessica in. In the silence I can hear my sister's loud, screeching voice having some sort of overreaction. "Right, so we just want to put this to bed for the last time." More silence. Then: "Your dad is recovering from heart surgery. Our business is failing, and Über Brides is going to run our shop and the Robinson's shop out of business if we don't do something. Jason and Hannah are trying to save the day. But we need to bury the hatchet once and for all."

I squeeze Hannah's hand again as she gives me a hopeful look.

My mom pulls the phone from her ear and presses the speaker button. "Jess, I'm putting you on speaker. So just tell us what really happened, okay?"

"Fine, Mom. I don't know why we have to dredge all this up again from twenty years ago, but I'm going to just be honest with you."

We're all waiting on pins and needles as Jessica's voice fills the room.

"To be totally honest, Mo and I were just tired of seeing each other. And we didn't know how to tell you and Dad. You were so gung ho on the marriage thing and the merger thing..."

"Are you kidding me?" my father's voice bellows across the room. "You made up the entire thing?"

There's the slightest giggle on the phone as my sister tries to collect herself. "We had to come up with something so horrible and so outrageous that no one would try to fix it or try to change our minds. Me accusing him of cheating and him spreading rumors about me seemed to be the way to go. We didn't expect it to get so out of hand. We didn't know he'd lose his scholarship or valedictorian title. We didn't know I'd lose my cheerleading spot. But we just wanted to move on with our lives—without being together. And we didn't know how to tell you."

I don't think my parents are even slightly amused, but I can't help it. I begin to laugh. And it's one of those laughs that starts like a tickle in your throat and then moves down your esophagus until your whole torso is in on the action. It's the kind of laugh that you grip your stomach and hang your head down while all the blood rushes to your face and the sounds of hysterical chuckles come spilling out, using every molecule of air they can steal from your lungs. It's the kind of laugh that leaves you completely breathless and depleted. It's the kind of laugh that is completely, utterly, irrepressibly contagious.

And that's why moments later, we're *all* laughing uncontrollably.

EIGHTEEN

I did end up calling my brother later to verify Jessica's story. He corroborated her testimony and added that they'd pinky-sworn never, ever to tell the truth. But when I told him I was dating Jason, he just laughed and said, "Good luck, baby sis."

Patsy never returned to work. Apparently the evidence we amassed for corporate was enough to get her arrested because I saw in the paper that she was released on bail but faced embezzlement charges. I hope she doesn't know where I live.

Even if she does, it's not like I'm at that address anymore. I've been staying with Jason. I stopped by my parents' house tonight to get a suitcase full of my things. I purposely chose my father's bowling night to drop in.

"I've missed you so much, honey," Mama says, kissing my cheek. "I've wanted to call you ever since...the discussion the other night, but your father..." She shakes her head sadly as she finishes loading up the dishwasher and shuts the door.

"Daddy's not here, right?" I confirm. She shakes her head again, and I have never seen her so sad. I hate it. I hate that this has torn us apart, but I'm going to try to make it right. I have to at least try.

"Okay, listen, I need to tell you something. Can we go sit down?" If I don't ask her to stop working, she will probably scrub this kitchen from top to bottom with all her nervous energy. I just need her to relax for a moment and hear me out.

She nods. "Do you want some coffee?"

"It's a little late in the day for coffee, isn't it?" *Who is this woman?* Usually she won't touch the stuff after noon.

"I've been drinking a lot—of coffee, I mean," she confesses. "To stay alert during the day. I haven't been sleeping well."

"Come on, Mama, let's go sit in the living room." I grab her hand, which feels so small and delicate in mine, and guide her over to the loveseat where I wait for her to sit before I take the cushion right next to her.

"What's going on? Are you and Jason going to, you know," her lips purse as she struggles to get the words out, "get married?"

Funny that she's spent her entire life in the bridal industry, but the idea of me getting married to a Friday is too difficult for her to say. Hopefully what I want to tell her will change that.

"Look, Mama, the whole thing, the entire war between the Robinsons and the Fridays was made up," I tell her, dropping the bomb in one succinct sentence.

"What do you mean, 'made up'?" Her face has gone from despondent to confused.

I take a deep breath. "So, what I am about to tell you is the actual truth, and it's been verified by both your oldest son and Jason's sister, Jessica. Okay?"

"Okay?" It's definitely more of a question than a concession.

"They made it up," I tell her. "All of it. Now, Mo didn't realize he was going to lose his valedictorian spot, and he didn't realize he wouldn't get to go to U Del. And he told me that none of the stuff with Jessica had anything to do with him dropping out of Del State. He simply said he figured out pretty quick that college wasn't for him—so, in other words, he thinks the scholarship would have been wasted on him."

"And Jessica?"

"Jessica wasn't cheating on Mo. The story he initially told was that he caught her with one of his teammates, but somehow—you know the old proverbial game of telephone—it morphed into her with half of the baseball team. The details were pretty gruesome from what I understand. But neither of them realized she was going to lose her cheerleading spot or all of her friends over it," I explain.

"But why? Why go through so much trouble and do such hurtful things to each other?" my mother asks. "I don't understand why they'd do all that."

I shrug. "Teenagers aren't always the sharpest tools in the shed, you know?" I can tell she's still not quite getting it. "Mama, they weren't in love. They didn't want to be together—but they felt an immense pressure to stay together because of how you and Daddy and the Fridays wanted to merge your businesses. They were afraid to tell you they'd broken up. They were afraid everyone would try to get them to stay together—for the family business."

My mama soaks it all in. I watch her expressions change from those of confusion to those of understanding, softening the crinkles between her brows and pursed lips.

"So we have no reason to be at war with the Fridays?" she confirms as if it's still a lot to wrap her head around.

"No, Mama, they're really good people. And they know *we're* really good people. I met with Jason's parents a couple days ago, and they are lovely. His dad is recovering from heart surgery, but he's really anxious to do whatever he can to help us with our final mission."

"Final mission?" Her brows furrow again. "I don't like the sound of that..."

"It does sound ominous," I agree with a laugh. "But it's the fake wedding we talked about, remember?"

She shakes her head as the confusion works its way back onto her face. "So the thing with Mo and Jessica was made up, but the fake wedding is real?"

I laugh at the irony of it. "Life works in funny ways sometimes, you know?"

"I don't know how your father is going to feel about this..."

"I don't know either." I was too chicken to come over when I knew he would be here. But I am still angry at him for the things he said. And I honestly don't know how I am going to forgive him for saying those horrible things.

"You know he didn't really mean those things," my mother says as if she's reading my mind.

I squeeze her hand. "I don't want to talk about that right now. I have to focus on saving the business. I can tell you one thing: I may not have been Daddy's first choice to run Delmarva Beach Brides, but I *am* the right person to run Operation Wedding War."

"Operation Wedding War?"

I nod, another chuckle escaping as I fill her in, "That's what Jason and I have been calling it. We're the Allies. Über Brides is the Axis of Evil."

"That they are," Mama agrees.

"We're having a planning meeting tomorrow night at Delmarva Art Connection in Downtown Rehoboth. Wait until you see all the work Jason and I have already put into this. Now we just need a bunch of people to help us pull it off. We'd love to have you and Daddy on our team. We'd love to have you join the Allies."

My mother's lips tug down into a frown. "I can talk to your father, but you know how pig-headed he can be sometimes."

I nod. "Trust me, I know. We're looking for someone to play the minister, and I know Daddy would be perfect."

"He sure would be." She gives me a small, tight smile that lets me know I'm probably pushing my luck to hope he will be there.

I stand up. "Okay, Mama. I got a suitcase full of stuff for now."

She stands up to face me, and I realize in this moment how small she is. She's been shorter than me for a long time, but tonight she just seems older, frailer. I never thought of either of my parents as being old, and they're not really, not yet. But for some reason, it seems like she's lost some of her robustness, and that makes me sad. My parents are going to be passing the baton to the younger generation here in the next decade or two, and I've always hoped to be the one on the receiving end. I've always hoped to be the one to make them proud. Not that they aren't proud of my siblings, but I really did fancy myself the chosen one.

I guess that is why I was so heartbroken when I figured out I wasn't the chosen one, after all.

"Are you staying with Jason then?" Mama squeaks out.

I knew it was coming eventually, but I hoped she'd not be forward enough to ask.

"Yes, Mama."

I know without a doubt how she and Daddy feel about living with someone when you're not married. Fornication and hellfire and brimstone and all that.

But she doesn't give me a lecture. Instead she simply asks, "Do you love him?"

I silently thank God for not putting a sermon on her heart and lift my chin just a fraction of an inch as I tell her the honest truth: "I do. I love him very much."

I certainly never thought I'd be standing in my parents' living room confessing to them that I was in love with a Friday, but here I am.

"Why?" she follows up. "What do you love about him?"

I smile as I try to choke back the tears—happy ones, this time. This is something I've been thinking about a lot. I've thought about it so much because I wanted to be sure I really do love him. I put my brain through its paces, overanalyzing the living crap out of all of it because that is what I do. I'm a details person.

Jason just decided he loved me, and that was that. He's an idea person.

But we know that's not the way I work.

So I tell her. I tell her all the reasons my heart and mind agreed upon:

"He's smart and funny. He loves his family as much as I love mine. He loves his work, and he's committed to making his business succeed. He's loyal. He's honest. And most of all: he'd do anything for me, even give up his family."

She stands there looking at me. Her hands are at her side, and her face is neutral except for the tiny curl at the corners of her lips. She's not quite smiling, but she's definitely not frowning either.

"And Mama..." I lock my honey brown eyes on the woman who gave them to me, "I feel the same exact way."

"Take a look at this," I say as soon as Hannah walks in the door. I know she's just come from her parents' house because she's lugging a suitcase behind her and her eyes are red and rimmed with tears. I spin my laptop around to show her, and then I carry her suitcase into the bedroom for her.

When I return to the kitchen, I see she's propped herself up with one leg on the barstool, one on the floor, as if she was in mid-climb but stopped.

"How the heck did you pull this off?" she gasps, staring at me with huge, round eyes.

"Remember that reporter from *The Delmarva Chronicle*?"

"Talis Tilghman, was that his name?" She laughs. "It sounds like a freaking made-up name!"

I chuckle. "It does, but it's not. He's really interested in helping us with our mission, and he made this website for us. And guess what else?"

"What?"

"He's going to post a story about our 'celebrity wedding' on the newspaper's website so we can send it to Janet and her stupid crisis aversion committee before they arrive." I'm beaming so wide until I realize I forgot to ask her how her visit with her mother went. *Ack. I will get right on that.* As soon as she's done admiring our website.

"Is that Meric and Lindy?" She studies the screen, moving the cursor through the album of photos. "Where did you get all these?"

"Lindy's friend takes photos. They went out to the winery and took a bunch yesterday. Didn't they turn out amazing?"

"They look like engagement photos. Are Meric and Lindy actually engaged?"

If I'm not mistaken, I detect just a tiny hint of jealousy in her voice. But I could totally be imagining it.

"Nope, they're just dating, but they're really excited about playing the bride and groom at our fake wedding. Oh, and by the way, they are loaded—the characters they are portraying, I mean—so we have to go all out with this thing."

"How are we going to pull this off, Jason? I'm getting a bit nervous. We only have ten days to get everything arranged." Her face is all scrunched up with worry.

"I know. I have a bunch of people coming to our meeting tomorrow night," I assure her. "You'll see. Everyone wants to help. Everyone hates Über Brides. Hell, Jean-Marc has assembled an army of Gay Über Brides Haterz—his term, not mine—and they are all prepared to pitch in."

She sighs. I can tell she's overwhelmed by everything, but I know she'll feel one hundred percent better when she sees the details come together. That's just the type of person she is. She doesn't want to see the forest. She wants to see each individual tree.

"How did things go with your mom? Do you think they'll come tomorrow night?" I ask, pulling her into my arms.

"I don't know," she says as she buries her face in my chest. "I don't know if things will ever be right between my daddy and me again."

I pull her back to look at me. "I know how much you love him. If you didn't love him so much, you wouldn't have been so hurt by what he said."

Her eyes well up with tears just remembering the sting of his words.

"He was angry, Hannah. He was saying things he didn't mean because I was there." I squeeze her closer to me and nuzzle against her neck, taking in her delicious vanilla floral scent as her curls tickle my nose. "He'll come around. Maybe not by the time we have a fake wedding, but he will eventually..."

"I don't know, Jason. Even Mama seemed skeptical, and she's usually the most positive person I know."

"Just wait until we've officially run Über Brides out of town... He won't have any choice but to be proud of you then." I lean down and plant a kiss on her cheek, which is so soft and warm under my lips, it makes me want to give that kiss some companions a little lower...

"Proud of *us*," she corrects me. "He'll have to be proud of us. Because we're doing it together."

"That's right." I smile against her neck before placing a gentle nibble to that spot I know makes her go weak in the knees. "Now...I know some other activities we could pursue together..."

She lets out a high-pitched giggle. "Oh, I'm sure you do!"

NINETEEN

Hannah

My palms are sweating as I watch all the people settling into the metal chairs in the performance space at Delmarva Art Connection. It is shocking and completely humbling how many people are assembling from our community to help take down a retail giant, one that is squeezing the lifeblood out of so many local businesses. It's not just Delmarva Beach Brides and Friday's Formalwear that have united forces. We've raised a veritable army of other wedding vendors: photographers, bakeries, caterers, florists, jewelers. If it has to do with making a bride and groom's day special, those people are gathered here awaiting orders from Jason and me. I guess that really does make us the Generals in this crazy war metaphor, doesn't it?

Claire Reilly gives me a wave as she enters with her husband Jack. We've already asked them to serve as our photographers for this event. Only we have some tricks up our sleeves to make their roles incredibly entertaining.

Lindy and Meric come in right behind them. Tomorrow Lindy is meeting me at my parents' store to try on gowns. Though I doubt my father will come through in the role we asked him to play, my mother has donated the bridal gown from our store as well as the alterations. I just hope we can find something Lindy feels comfortable in but goes with the over-the-top theme we have in mind.

It's almost seven, and Jason appears from behind the stage curtain with Drew, who owns this joint along with his wife, Sonnet. I've heard she's a rocket scientist, so I'm sure if we need some brilliant ideas, she'll have something to contribute. "You ready?" Jason asks me, sliding his arm around my waist and pulling me close to place a kiss on my cheek.

It's so weird to be the subject of a public display of affection. I always see couples being affectionate in public and think "get a room," but now that I'm half of a couple, it seems sweet to me. Maybe I was just jealous before?

"I'm as ready as I'll ever be," I tell him with a soft smile.

"It's go time," Drew announces, handing Jason a microphone. Oh, wow, we're even using a microphone. *This is super official.*

"Hello all, I'm Jason Friday, and this is Hannah Robinson. First, we want to thank you all for being here tonight and for answering the call of duty to bring down Über Brides. I'm going to make this as brief and productive as possible, but I also want to make sure we're all on the same page, so please indulge me in this brief PowerPoint presentation."

Everyone groans and laughs as Drew points a remote toward a projector and turns it on. The picture materializes, and it's the face of Über Bride's CEO with devil's horns photoshopped on his head. Everyone laughs again.

"This is Victor Schneider, CEO. He makes five billion dollars a year, has been married and divorced not once, not twice, not even three times—we're talking *four* marriages and three divorces. He has a total of five hundred employees around the country, most of whom make less than fifteen dollars an hour. Many of them make less than ten dollars an hour."

Everyone boos and hisses. And the guy does look like a total twatwaffle. I had never seen a photo of him, but he has a pointy nose, pale soulless eyes, and a tan that makes it look like he spends every day at the beach. How can anyone making that kind of cash sleep at night knowing their employees are barely above the poverty line?

"His last wedding, which was in June of 2016, reportedly cost more than five million dollars. He clearly thinks weddings and brides are disposable because every one of his divorces was precipitated by his own infidelity."

More boos and hisses. Clearly this guy is King of the Asshats. And that's not even something I usually say. I think hanging out with Jason is rubbing off on me.

"As if we need even more ammunition against this guy, his products are cheap, too. Since Hannah and I have been investigating—"

I love how he leaves out the fact we are actually

working for them. I am pretty sure everyone knows that—or that we have inside help—but obviously Jason's not going to come right out and admit it at this meeting. I haven't discounted the fact that there could be a spy here, though I highly doubt it. The entire company seems to be almost painfully clueless.

"—we've seen dozens of complaints from local residents about bridal gowns that fall apart, tuxes that disintegrate, broken wedding favors, misprinted invitations—all backed up by unfair return policies and abysmal customer service."

"Let's nail this guy!" comes a shout from the back.

Jason smiles and takes a sip of his water while the crowd murmurs their agreement. "This guy's goal is to come into every major market and set up his store, pressure the local wedding vendors to enter into agreements with them that offer their goods and services at steep discounts, and drive anyone who doesn't want to play ball with him out of the market. How many of you local vendors were approached by Über Brides to sign contracts to be on their preferred vendor list?"

Several hands fly up.

"We had to sign," says a tall lady with a ruddy complexion and her auburn hair tied back in a low ponytail. "Brides want to go to one place and make all their arrangements, not go all over the East Coast looking for the best deals. They're used to buying things at big box stores. Why shouldn't weddings be the same way? It makes sense if you think about it."

"It might make sense if he wasn't cutting into your profits," Jason fires back. "If he offered you a fair deal, and you were actually able to make a sustainable living, it might be okay, but that's not their M.O. How many of you have seen profits slide downwards since Über Brides arrived six weeks ago?"

Many more hands shoot up into the air.

"It's been six weeks," Jason continues, "but what's it going to be like in six months? I won't say six years because none of us will be in business in six years at this rate. For businesses like my family's, which does formalwear, and Hannah's, which does bridal gowns...Über Brides has their own distributors for those products. They don't need vendors. So that means they are cutting us out of the market altogether, underselling in every sector. Sure, their stuff is cheap knock-off junk, but hey, you only wear it once, right?"

"So what's the plan?" someone shouts from the back.

"I'm getting to that," Jason says, turning back to the presentation illuminating the screen. "Hannah and I have already been able to make some progress in undermining their online brand reputation. Check out some of these reviews Über Brides has received on Yelp and Facebook." He slowly advances through several slides that mention poor customer service and inferior products.

"Because of this, and because the store manager is up on charges of embezzlement, they're sending in what they call their Crisis Aversion Team, or CAT for short. It's four members, the leader of whom is one Janet Bryson." The next photo shows Janet, a dark-skinned lady with sleek, straightened black hair. I had never seen her picture either. I have no idea where Jason found all these photos; all I know is he's been glued to his computer for the past three days.

"You know how they release the biggest action movies in the summer? You know, summer blockbusters? We want to do that—only with a wedding. Hannah and I have been calling this Operation Wedding War for a while, and this final part of our plan is the equivalent of storming the beaches of Normandy. Are you following me?"

There's an affirmative roar from the crowd as Jason advances to the next slide. It's a screenshot from the website he and Talis built for Lindy and Meric. "First of all, meet our lucky couple, Lindy and Meric. Come on up here, you two!"

They stand up from the front row, join hands and bound up the stairs onto the stage, still holding hands. Meric is tall and handsome with dark hair and his square stubble-covered jaw, and Lindy is a beautiful plus-sized lady with ivory skin, flowing brunette locks and gorgeous green eyes.

"These two are both seasoned actors and veterans of the stage right here at Delmarva Art Connection. You may have seen them last summer starring in *Yo Ho Rehoboth*, as a matter of fact. Meric Chandler is going to be playing an up-and-coming Broadway actor named Alexander Ray. As you can see we've created a website for him here." He clicks on a link in the presentation. and it brings up his bio and photos from shows he's supposedly done on Broadway, but are apparently just other shows he's acted in. I'm sure the one of him in pirate garb is from the aforementioned *Yo Ho Rehoboth*.

"And Miss Lindy Larson is playing Susannah Winston, a distant relative of the DuPonts, whom everyone in Delaware knows are basically American royalty. She's also the heiress to the fortune amassed by her father, who invented virtual reality. Here's a Wikipedia page about her," he clicks on another link, "and here is the article Talis Tilghman wrote up for *The Delmarva Chronicle* about their wedding." The headline reads: *Heiress and Broadway Star to Wed in Rehoboth Beach on June 23rd.*

I am so proud of us for coming up with all of this. It's absolutely brilliant how Jason came up with the idea to make them both semi-famous, and I helped fill in the details to make it all seem realistic and legitimate. Scanning the faces in the crowd, I see they also look duly impressed about what we have accomplished in such a short period of time.

"The wedding will take place on the beach, weather permitting, next Saturday, with the reception taking place right here at Delmarva Art Connection afterwards. Now, this is where all of you come in: we need flowers, a cake, a DJ, a caterer, decorations, and all the other stuff you'd have at a real wedding. I want to form some subcommittees and break into groups to discuss our plan of action. But just remember as you're coming up with ideas, the point of this whole operation is to DO OUR WORST. I know that's a complete contradiction to what we've always strived to do as business people. Weddings are certainly fertile ground for mishaps and mistakes to occur, but this is the one time we want to do absolutely everything we can to turn out a complete unmitigated disaster of a wedding. We want it to reflect so poorly on Über Brides that every newspaper, television and radio station on the Eastern Seaboard reports on it."

"That sounds like quite a challenge!" another business owner says as he rises to his feet. He looks around at his fellow business folks. "I don't know about you guys, but I'm all in. I'll head up the catering committee. We've been serving this community for twenty-five years, and I'll be damned if I'm going to let Über Brides take a cut of my profits or take away my customers!"

"I'm in too!" an older lady announces, joining the gentleman to her right. "I'll lead the floral committee. My husband Stan and I have owned Atlantic Floral Company for almost twenty years."

One by one, people step up and offer to take on leadership roles in our endeavor. My heart is nearly bursting at the seams.

"What about an officiant?" someone shouts from the back. "Don't we need someone to do that?"

"Yes," Jason says, picking the microphone back up from the stool where he'd placed it while the crowd was conferring. "My brother Russ is going to—"

The double doors leading to the lobby burst open as a thundering "No!" bellows down the aisle toward the stage. Swift, sturdy steps follow, and when the figure passes under the lights, I see the face of my father standing at the foot of the stage.

"Daddy!" I shriek.

"I'm going to play the officiant," my father announces, turning around to look at the crowd. "I'm not only an ordained minister already, but I am the owner of Delmarva Beach Brides. Hannah is my daughter, and I couldn't be prouder of the way she's stepped up to lead this community-wide effort. I've known since she was a little girl that she is a take-charge kind of person. She has an incredibly smart and sophisticated business sense, and there is no one on this earth I would rather hand over the reins of our family business to." He pauses and turns around to look at me. "I am so sorry for what I said to you the other night. I was angry, and I didn't mean any of that. I hope you can find it in your heart to forgive your old man."

My heart that was bursting moments ago has now completely exploded, and tears are flying out of my eyes as I jump off the stage and into my daddy's arms. "Oh, Daddy, of course I do!"

Lindy fingers some of the dresses before turning to me with a worried look in her eyes. "These are so beautiful, Hannah," she says, then her voice drops to nearly a whisper, "but I'm a pretty big girl, so I don't know if any of them will fit me."

I smile and wave off her concerns. "We'll alter it to fit you. It's no big deal. Besides, I have some bigger sizes in stock. I'm a big girl too, you know." I give her a wink. "You're absolutely beautiful, Lindy. You're gonna make a gorgeous bride."

She still seems a little hesitant. I've dealt with plenty of plus-sized brides, and it's always heartbreaking when what should be one of the most exciting and fun days of their lives—bridal gown shopping—is turned into something negative and stressful because of their size. Many times, it's the mothers of the bride or the salespeople who make things a zillion times worse. I always try to step in and put the brides-to-be at ease so they can enjoy themselves. Sometimes that means giving a pep talk. Sometimes that means pulling their mothers aside for a come to Jesus meeting about respecting and supporting their daughters. No matter what, I want Lindy to enjoy this experience, even if it's only fake-bridal gown shopping.

"I like these three," she says pulling the hangers off the rack and handing them to me. "I know you said they need to be over the top, and I get it. That's not really my style, but I'm doing my best to find something that will work."

"We can definitely compromise," I tell her as I lead her toward the enormous fitting room at the back of the shop. I get her situated then close the curtain but stay nearby in case she needs help. "So, how long have you and Meric been dating?"

She giggles, the sound a little muffled by the thick fabric of the curtain giving her privacy. "We met last summer when we did the show with Claire and Jack. I can't believe it's been a whole year!"

"That's great," I remark. "Do you think you'll be hearing real wedding bells any time soon?"

She pulls open the curtain and peeks her head out. "I sure hope so." She steps out to the center of the room with the train of the gown trailing behind her.

"What do you think of this?"

I gasp. She's a vision in beads and lace. It is way too formal for a beach wedding, but we aren't looking for understated elegance here. We're looking for something a spoiled heiress who has just snagged a Broadway star would choose.

She twirls around. "I think I kind of love it!"

"Yeah, and if you don't want the train getting in the way, we can always bustle it. That ballgown style is really flattering on you, Lindy!"

"I feel like a fairytale princess!" she coos, spinning around again to get a look in the three-way mirror at the very back of the showroom.

"You look like one too!" I walk around her, taking note of the fit and where it's going to need alternations. I'll need to pin it in place before she takes it off.

"I got my bridesmaid's gown here for Sonnet's wedding," she says as she turns to face me. "Your mother was such an angel. So patient with me. I just love her to pieces. I'm so glad I'm going to be able to help you guys keep your stores."

I take her hands into mine and squeeze. "Thank you so, so much. I would be a nervous mess right now if I didn't trust you and Meric to pull this off, and if I didn't know Jason was going to have everything under control. This is a pretty crazy thing we're trying to do!"

"It is. But you have assembled a great team. A strong, capable army!" She winks.

I give her a hug. "And just think, if you really love the dress, and you and Meric do end up getting married someday...then you already have it."

"Are you serious? I can keep it?" Her eyes expand to twice their normal size.

"It's a demo dress that we're going to alter to fit you, so yes. My parents have donated it to the cause. It's yours to keep."

"I can't believe I fell in love with the first dress I tried on!" she gushes. "Then again, I pretty much fell in love with the first man I really dated too."

I smile at her remark, but I can't help but think of my own dating history. Jason is definitely not the first man I've dated. I had a few boyfriends in undergrad, grad school and those years I spent in New York. But I think I can honestly say this is the first time I've truly been in love.

TWENTY

"Today's the big day!" I roll over and whisper in Hannah's ear after I turn off the annoying alarm. She stirs slightly, then her whole body arches as she stretches, pushing her delectable backside into me. *Well, we aren't going to get very far from the bed today if she continues to do that.*

She groans, "I'm not ready."

I gently flip her over onto her back so I can look into her eyes. "Not ready? Baby, we've been training for this day for weeks now. We've learned how to become the ultimate wedding crashers...and this mission is going to run like a well-oiled machine."

"I hope you're right. I just worry it won't be enough...that it won't make a difference." She begins to sit up, but I pull her into my arms instead. She reluctantly lays her head against my shoulder as I wrap my arm around her waist and trace the curve of her spine where it meets the small of her back.

"I have a few tricks up my sleeve," I tell her. I can't keep the grin off my face.

"I'm not a big fan of surprises," she reminds me. I've heard that a time or two. She will be a big fan of these surprises. *I guarantee it.*

"Tell me what you're still worried about, and I'll set your mind at ease." When she sighs, I prod her a little more. "Please? I want to make sure you're comfortable."

I can feel her walls start to crumble when she sighs again. "Okay, so...it's just that there's so much riding on this day, I can't even think past it right now. I need to be figuring out my future, where I'm going to live, what I'm going to do...but everything hinges on this. Are they going to fire me? Are they going to just bring in someone else and keep screwing things up for the small businesses of Rehoboth Beach? Or are they really going to get the clue that our community doesn't want them here?"

I take her hand into mine. "Hannah, it doesn't matter what happens today."

She jerks up, her eyes scanning my face as if I've suddenly grown another head. "What do you mean? Of course it matters."

I chuckle as I move myself into a seated position so I can look her in the eyes. "Today matters, of course. It matters in our war against Über Brides, and I am truly hoping that after today, we'll never have to worry about that evil company again. But as far as *you* are concerned and your future...none of that hinges on today."

"It doesn't?" Her eyebrows arch as she focuses her

honey brown eyes, still puffy from sleep, on me.

"Well," I begin, taking her hand into mine as I rest against the headboard, "first of all, you are the smartest person I know. You're going to do just fine no matter what. But as far as where you're going to live and what you're going to do..."

I'm watching her eyes grow wider and wider as I speak, and her grip on my hand tightens.

"I hope I factor into your decisions somehow?" A tiny smile appears at the corners of her lips when she sees the hope in my eyes. "I mean, I want to be where you are. I know that much."

She laughs. "I want to be where you are too."

"So, as far as where you'll live, well...I have this house and all..."

"I know you do," she answers, then lets out a sigh. "I love being here. I love being with you, but it's a temporary solution as far as I'm concerned. You met my parents. You know how crazy traditional they are. They don't want me to give the milk away for free, you know."

I scrunch up my nose. "Milk? Uh...I'm not getting any milk that I'm aware of."

A soft giggle erupts as she playfully slaps me on the arm. "You know what I mean...the whole 'why would he buy the cow if you're giving away the milk for free?'"

"What a horrible saying! You are *not* a cow, Hannah!" I tease her. I knew exactly what she was speaking of, but this is much more fun.

She throws a pillow at me, and when I retaliate by tossing one toward her, a pillow war ensues. But she never sees my secret weapon coming: I know all of her most ticklish spots, and she knows none of mine.

Though, after we start our day in the very best possible way, I'd say we both won this battle.

Hannah had been all business when we'd met Janet and her CAT committee the day before. They walked through the store, taking lots of notes and asking approximately four billion questions, which I'm sure my amazing girlfriend handled with a massively radioactive amount of aplomb. (*Please tell me you see what I did there.*)

It feels unsettling to have the enemy this close to us, but so far our covers are secure. Because I'm not officially in the payroll system, Hannah is completely on her own to deal with the committee. I'm just coming as her date for the Wedding of the Millennium. At least that's the way Talis Tilghman characterized it in his write-up in *The Delmarva Chronicle*. Apparently when Hannah invited the CAT committee to come see the "good work" their company is doing, they jumped at the chance, noting how impressed they were that we nabbed such high-profile clients.

"This is going to be a real feather in the cap for Über Brides!" Janet says as we gather on the beach waiting for the bride and groom to make their grand appearance. She sounds like she is faking a British accent. She already told us she's from Detroit, so I'm not sure where that's coming from, but it's weird as hell.

Guests are beginning to arrive, following the flower-lined pathways to the guest seating area that has been arranged on the beach. You wouldn't believe what went into securing this spot just steps away from one of the biggest hotels on the boardwalk. It's June—prime time for weddings—but somehow with all the connections that Claire, Drew, and Drew's state trooper friend Chris Everson have, they were able to get all the permits and everything we needed. From what I understand, even the mayor is going to be here, and he's fully on board with our mission.

We told our decorations committee to plan on two hundred guests, but it looks like way more white wooden chairs have been set up in the sand. There is a wide aisle in between the rows of chairs, flanked by white columns that are topped with huge planters holding fresh flowers and connected by vibrant ribbons in coral, teal and magenta. Just feet away from where the waves are crashing on the shore is a huge, elaborate arch—I'm not even sure what it's built out of because it's completely covered with florals and ribbons in the aforementioned colors, and they're all flying in the soft breeze coming off the water. It is absolutely breathtaking. Our decorations committee, which was led by Drew and Sonnet's neighbor Ken—who apparently has quite an eye for colors and design— deserves a huge pat on the back for their efforts.

Hannah grabs my hand and squeezes it, drawing my attention to her. She gestures with her head to the left, where her father and our groom are making their way across the sand to the arch of flowers. "Doesn't Alexander look handsome?" she asks in a loud enough volume so Janet and her minions can hear her.

"He looks great!" I agree. "You helped him pick out the perfect tux!"

I was the one who picked out his tux—being somewhat of an expert on such matters. *wink*

Mr. Robinson is wearing a dark suit with a long, fringed stole made out of kente cloth bearing two gold crosses on either side. His bald head is gleaming, and he's carrying a Bible in his hands. He winks at his daughter as he passes—I hope Janet and company didn't notice.

One disadvantage of being on the beach is that the waves are loud. *Duh!* But we actually have a sound and light crew thanks to Drew. His technicians from Delmarva Art Connection set up speakers, and they are so crystal clear, I am pretty sure I can hear Meric breathing in and out nervously as he awaits his bride. We, naturally, told the technicians to mess up the sound. So I'm expecting periods of blaring loudness intermingled with times it's a fuzzy, feedbacked mess. All part of the joy of "doing our worst," as has been our battle cry throughout this entire affair.

Finally, the music starts up, and the groomsmen and bridesmaids begin to saunter out onto the sand. I should actually be out there—Meric wanted me to be—but I needed to be behind the scenes so I can make sure things go off without a hitch. I told him to let my brother Russ stand in my place. My parents are playing the role of the groom's parents, so it seems to work. He also has our friends Shark and Ryan, who would likely be his groomsmen if he were actually getting married. On the brides' side are Lindy's best friend Megan, Sonnet, and Chris the state trooper's girlfriend Brynne, who is an ER doctor. We actually might need her expertise at some point in time this evening. I've warned her she's on call.

"Well, aren't those dresses...interesting!" Janet exclaims with sharply arched eyebrows. She turns to say something to one of her minions and then whips her head back to Hannah. "Did you help the bride and her maids choose those?"

"Why, yes, of course!" Hannah pipes up.

The ladies are being very good sports about wearing them—with their giant, ill-fitting off-the-shoulder poufy sleeves; tight, sequined bodices and full ballgowns blowing in the wind. Sonnet's is billowing out so much, it looks like the wind might just scoop her up and carry her off at any moment.

"That fabric is so—shiny!" Ling, the small black-haired lady on the CAT committee exclaims. She can't seem to tear her eyes away from the dresses, her mouth open in an O of shock and quite possibly revulsion.

"And the bride was happy with that selection?" Janet confirms after glancing at her colleague's horrified expression.

Hannah bites her lower lip ever so briefly before nodding. "Yes, ma'am." Then she corrects herself, "Well, mostly. They actually ordered a different style, but those were on back order, so we got these instead."

Janet purses her lips when our photographers, Jack and Claire, run back and forth across the sand capturing the hideous gowns with their massive cameras. They've attracted the entire audience's attention; they are being so disruptive. Without seeming to notice anyone watching them, they suddenly run toward each other and pose for a selfie with one of their cameras. Then Jack sweeps Claire into his arms and plants a huge kiss on her lips—which turns into tongue and a little bit of grinding action.

We are sitting near the back, so I have a pretty good vantage of the entire crowd, and everyone looks absolutely flabbergasted when their make-out session begins, a mood which quickly turns to disgusted as they continue. Finally, Mr. Robinson speaks up, his voice booming across the speakers, "It's time for the bride...shouldn't you two be taking photos?"

I glance over, and Janet is wildly fanning herself with the wedding programs we had printed up. We might need Brynne's help earlier than I expected!

Jack and Claire break their liplock just as the music changes over to "Here Comes the Bride." The sound is ear-shattering, and everyone quickly forgets the photographer's antics as the music blasts out of the speakers.

Seconds later, Lindy appears on the arm of what appears to be a very old man. From what I understand, her actual parents are here playing the roles they were already born to play. Her dad doesn't move very fast, plus it's on sand, so it's literally the longest bridal procession in the history of bridal processions. By the time they actually make it to the groom, Mr. Robinson, and the entire waiting bridal party, "Here Comes the Bride" has looped at least a dozen times at twelve gazillion decibels.

I never want to hear that song again!

On a positive note: Janet and Co. look like they are about to come unglued.

Finally, Mr. Robinson's voice breaks through: "Dearly beloved, we are gathered here today to celebrate the union of two of God's children—"

Suddenly the sound cuts out, and the rest of his sentence is swallowed by the sound of crashing waves. He beats at the microphone pinned to his chest, trying to bring it back to life, and there's a loud popping sound before the volume jumps right back to eleven. That's a *Spinal Tap* reference, for those of you in the back.

We've coached Mr. Robinson to bring out the

hellfire and brimstone, to use his best gospel preacher voice, and he does not disappoint in the slightest. As a matter of fact, he apparently invited several members of his church—where apparently he is not the regular pastor, but he does preach on occasion, according to Hannah—and they are livening up the service a great deal by interjecting "Hallelujah" and "God Almighty!" and various other exclamations at regular intervals.

It is quite possibly the very longest wedding sermon in the history of wedding sermons but finally—FINALLY he gets to the vows.

We told Meric and Lindy to write their own vows and to make them as crazy and outlandish as they could possibly make them, remembering, of course, that they are playing a Broadway star and a spoiled heiress—and they do not disappoint in the slightest.

"Susannah, my beautiful, succulent plum," Meric begins, "the apple of my eye. The cherry to my banana..."

That earns a few appalled gasps from the crowd, including one from Janet.

"I promise to love and cherish you in bad times...and in grape times, in sickness and in peaches and cream. When life gives us lemons, we're going to make lemonade. Orange you glad you agreed to be my wife?"

She doesn't even bat an eye, she just launches into her own equally obnoxious list of bad puns, only hers involves vegetables. *Of course.*

Moments later, Mr. Robinson asks for the rings, which are gathered from Megan and Ryan, except that Ryan drops his, causing a collective gasp to rise up from the audience. Then all the groomsmen fall to their knees, sifting through the sand to try to find the ring. Finally, Shark jumps up, which happens to be at the same time Ryan and Russ scramble to their feet, and they all run smack dab right into each other. What ensues is nothing less than a Three Stooges act of bumbling idiocy and slapstick humor.

The entire audience is in shock. No one has ever seen such a display at a wedding in their entire lives, and that includes me. I think Janet has passed out beside Hannah, and I briefly wonder if Brynne will have to step out of her role as bridesmaid to resuscitate a few of our guests.

Hannah shoots me a look as if to ask, *are you behind this travesty*? I put my hand up to block Janet's view of my mouth and whisper, "We said 'do your worst!'"

She gives me a nod of understanding, and the sound cuts in and out again as Mr. Robinson performs the ring part of the ceremony in which Lindy and Meric exchange the sand-covered rings. As soon as he pronounces them husband and wife, they share a beautiful, theatrical kiss, then turn to face their guests.

But everything comes to a grinding halt.

The celebratory shouts that arose from the audience when they kissed fade out. But no music starts. Instead, all eyes whip to the end of the aisle where Jack and Claire are busy making out—again.

Holy shit, those two are going at it. Tongues are flying, hands are groping, equipment is knocking around—gee, I hope none of it is getting damaged—

Mr. Robinson's hands fly to his hips, and he repeats: "I now pronounce you HUSBAND and WIFE! YOU MAY NOW KISS THE BRIDE!"

Jack and Claire snap to attention and bolt into place to take photos of the *real* kiss, then capture the bride and groom and wedding parties on their recessional down the aisle to—I kid you not—"Love Shack" by the B-52's.

"What on earth?" Janet exclaims so loud that I'm pretty sure half the crowd heard her.

"Isn't it great?" Hannah says, amused. "The bride and I have the same favorite song!"

"I've never been to a weirder, more obnoxious ceremony in my entire life!" her comrade Joseph posits. He looks like he's been personally assaulted.

They've seen nothing yet. Just wait till they get to the reception.

"Oh, we have arranged a special surprise for you since you're our guests of honor!" Hannah says as she stands up.

Just then I notice two carriages pulled to the edge of the pavement where it meets the boardwalk. I flash her a look—this one is a surprise to me.

"Oh, aren't those for the bride and groom and wedding party?" Janet questions, glancing from Hannah to me.

"The first carriage is for the bride and groom," she explains. "But the second one is for the four of you. You're going to love your horse. His name is Rudy!"

She shoots me a wink. *Yep, they ain't seen nothin' yet!*

"You're looking positively radiant tonight, by the way," I tell Hannah as we make our way to the table in the corner she's set aside for us and the Über Brides people.

"Thank you. You're looking mighty handsome yourself." She tugs the bodice of her dress, pulling it up to conceal a bit of her decadent cleavage. It slides right back down into place. Her lovely décolletage apparently wants to be on view tonight. I know I plan on stealing my fair share of glances.

"I have a ton of makeup on," she confesses as she swipes gloss across her lips lightning fast. "I never wear this much. I'm trying to think of it as war paint."

I hide my chuckle behind my hand. "Wow, the chocolate fountain is a nice touch," I remark, nudging my head toward the cake table. It's also hands-down the gaudiest cake I have ever seen in my entire life, and I've seen photos of my parents' cake from back in the 1980s that had these weird staircases running between the tiers. No idea what those bakers were smokin'!

"Isn't it? This whole meal promises to be spectacular," she whispers. "I gave the caterers pretty much free rein, and I don't know whether to be scared or excited."

"Did they say anything about the carriage ride?" I question. The four members of the CAT committee seem to be busy enjoying cocktail hour, but I'm sure their enjoyment will be fleeting.

She tries to restrain herself from laughing too hard, but I can see it's a losing battle. It's a good thing she wasn't drinking, or she would have spewed liquid across the entire reception hall. "Oh, yeah, they were not very impressed with Rudy," she manages to squeak out.

Speaking of the reception hall, the decoration committee once again outdid themselves. It looks lush and expensive but in a totally tacky way. There is more bling in here than whatever the blingiest thing you can imagine has. I actually spent a few moments trying to think of a good, funny analogy, but honestly, I don't think anyplace is blingier than the room we're currently standing in.

Hannah seems to notice me glancing around. "This place is nuts, right?"

"No doubt. They did an amazing job, and you know what?"

"What?"

"The best is yet to come," I promise her. *Or maybe it's a warning. I don't know.*

"That sounds vaguely threatening." She smiles as she crosses her arms over her chest. "Why don't you tell me exactly what you have planned?"

"There's no fun in that, that's why. Oh, look, the DJ is really getting into it!"

We got one of Drew's bandmates to play the DJ, and he's up there busting a move as he churns out basically the worst 90s pop and rap he can find. I mean if you think "Ice Ice Baby" is a good song, then you've come to the right place, but otherwise...you're S.O.L.

"What about the band? Aren't they coming?" Hannah looks at me with wide eyes.

"Pete's band? Oh, yeah, they wouldn't miss it for the world."

"Why aren't they set up?"

"Because I told them the wrong time." I give her a wink. And I just happened to rig a little surprise to happen when they run their freakishly long extension cord across the room to the only available outlet.

"You're a total genius, you know that?" She leans

down to kiss me on the cheek.

"You're not half bad yourself!"

Cocktail hour while the "photographers" snap photos of the fake wedding party and fake family members flies by. Of course, they weren't really taking photos. They are making sure everything is in place for Phase 2 of our plan. I don't think Janet and her minions have shut up about the "absolutely foul and disgusting horse" who pulled their carriage to the reception venue since we all convened at our table. He apparently made quite the impression on them. From what it sounds like, it was even worse than the first time we employed his service a few weeks ago. And Shark was more than happy to provide two carriages so our bride and groom could also ride in style to the reception venue. Naturally, the other carriage was pulled by a horse with a much healthier digestive tract.

We're all seated now and waiting for dinner to arrive. They've already served a salad which was the weirdest concoction I've ever seen. It had beets and pineapple and some weird lime Jello with carrot shavings in it, all stacked in some sort of configuration that was vaguely reminiscent of Stonehenge. I saw Janet and her crew eyeing it suspiciously, and I don't think they even managed to swallow down more than a bite or two.

We've barely recovered from that course when a waiter in tails swings by carrying a silver tray. "I have a special surprise for your table from the chef!" I take in the young man's pale, almost glowing skin, bright orange hair and toothy smile as he carefully sets the tray down in the center of the table.

"Oh my gosh!" I leap up from the table, my heart pounding a million miles a minute. Jason follows suit, scooting his chair back and standing up to see if I'm alright. "What on earth is that?" I gasp out.

On the tray are three blatantly phallic-looking creatures sandwiched between shells at one end. I am pretty glad I haven't eaten anything, because if I had, I'd have spewed it all over the table at this point—though perhaps that would have added to the "ambiance" we are trying to create.

"Those are geoducks!" Joseph, one of the CAT committee members exclaims, looking way more excited than anyone should be about such revolting objects.

"Come again?" Jason retorts.

"It's pronounced 'gooey-duck,' but it's spelled G-E-O-D-U-C-K. You're not supposed to serve them like that, though! They're supposed to be sliced up. Nice and thin is best. Would you happen to have a sharp knife?" he asks the waiter.

But the waiter pretends not to hear him and turns on his heel with a flourish after exclaiming, "Enjoy!"

"Oh my gosh, I have never seen anything so vile and disgusting in my life!" Janet shouts, clutching at her chest as though she, too, might become ill.

"They're just clams, Janet, calm down," Ling

chastises her.

"I'm not touching those with a ten-foot pole—"

The fourth of the comrades, Adam, starts to share his thoughts but is interrupted when there's a shrill scream from the center of the room. My eyes jerk to the right just in time to see one of the guests stand up. She's covered from her shoulders to her stomach in chocolate, which is sliding down her dress slowly but surely, turning her a rich dark brown color. Sure enough, the chocolate fountain behind her has toppled over.

"Oh, no, did our cord do that?" comes a shout from the stage area.

Sure enough, Pete and his band have just made their grand entrance. If the guests think them knocking over the chocolate fountain with the cords to their amps is bad, just wait until they hear them play.

"Is this one of the bands on our vendor list?" Janet asks as she lays her napkin on the table. I don't think she's managed to eat any of the food that has been served tonight. Perhaps she is saving room for cake?

"It is," I answer. "It wasn't their first-choice band, but they booked so late, this is all we had left."

"You would think a couple of their means could afford whoever they want!" Joseph pipes up. "Even, you know, someone well-known. Isn't the groom a star on Broadway for chrissake?"

"Everyone loves saving money!" I banter back. Jason squeezes my hand under the table.

We are getting ready for the happy couple to do their first dance, but there's a commotion on the other side of the room. I squeeze Jason's hand even harder and angle my head toward the sound, flashing him a look that says *what the bleep is going on?*

He returns a reassuring smile as someone I seem to remember being introduced as Jason's cousin runs to the center of the stage and grabs the microphone out of Pete's hand. There's a horrible screeching feedback sound as the din of wedding guests' voices and dining noises are suddenly snuffed out.

"I'm so sorry to interrupt everyone's evening, and I don't want to alarm anyone, but the wedding gifts have been stolen. Oh—along with the cake. Sorry guys," he says, looking down with a sad panda face at the bride and groom.

"What?!" Meric jumps up. "What do you mean, stolen?"

"Who steals a cake?" Russ shouts.

Janet turns to me with her eyes as big as the moon. "Didn't you hire security? This is a high-profile wedding! You always hire security. It's in our consulting guidelines!"

"That is our security," I say, pointing to Jason's cousin, whose name escapes me at the moment.

"The police are on their way!" he shouts into the microphone. He throws out his arms, signaling for the crowd to stay calm and quiet. Then he turns to Lindy and Meric. "We'll find your gifts and cake, we promise!"

At that very moment, the sounds of police sirens pierce my ears, and a collective murmur of panic rises up from the guests. Everyone is playing their parts so well, arguing about who would steal a cake and wedding gifts. There's so much going on that hardly anyone even notices when a crew of four cops burst through the double doors at the back of the room. I instantly recognize one of them as Chris Everson, but he must have gotten a few of his buddies to play along too.

While the other three stand at attention, Chris marches down the main aisle between the numerous tables with their gaudy, blinged-out centerpieces sparkling under the dim lights. He doesn't bother to use the stairs but jumps onto the stage in one giant leap, grabbing the microphone from Jason's cousin's hand—oh his name is Hank, just remembered—

"Good evening folks, I'm Corporal Chris Everson, Delaware State Police. Are you all aware that there's a huge demonstration going on right outside the building?"

My eyes widen before they snap to Jason's. He is struggling to contain his laughter. This must be the secret plan he arranged.

"And there's a smashed wedding cake all over the sidewalk!" he adds. "Looks like half-chocolate, half-vanilla. Might have had a raspberry-filled layer?"

A huge roar bellows out from the audience, and Janet once again looks like she is about to pass out. As if there's not already enough chaos and commotion, the smoke alarms in the building start to go off. In the eardrum-shattering cacophony, thick gray smoke infiltrates the room, and all the lights take on an oily, hazy glare.

"We're going to have to ask everyone to move outside in an orderly fashion," Chris speaks into the microphone. "I repeat, we need to evacuate this building immediately, folks!"

There's mass pandemonium as the guests scramble

to their feet. Plates shatter, tables are flipped, decorations are shredded as three hundred people move in the least calm and orderly fashion known to mankind toward the exits. In the midst of the screaming, feet stomping, and ear-piercing wails of the smoke alarms, police sirens and fire trucks arriving on scene, Jason grabs my hand and gives me a tiny, subtle wink I'm sure no one else saw but me.

I try to wait for most of the guests to pass by before I gesture for Janet and her posse to follow us out of the building. One glimpse at Janet's face tells me she is apparently out of words for the night. Her expression is completely stoic, like it's carved from stone. She doesn't even look at her comrades as they file out of the building before me.

They also don't see me reach down and squeeze Jason's hand before swinging it merrily as we march out of the supposedly on-fire building.

Sirens continue to howl as red and blue lights spin their flashing colors into the burgeoning dusk. The summer crowds of tourists are thick along the sidewalks, many stopping to watch the unfolding drama of screaming wedding guests as they flee the smoking building and nearly run right into an angry mob of protestors decked out in the most colorful attire imaginable, holding signs and chanting, "Über Brides Must GO! Über Brides Must GO!"

Their equally vibrant signs read, "Über Brides Hates Gays," "Über Brides, we want a divorce!" "Get the hell out of Rehoboth Beach!" and so many other things. When I look over to the edge of the crowd, one particular face stands out. It's Jean-Marc. He's bought his queer army with him, and they are taking a stand against this bigoted corporation.

But on the other side of the street is another protest. This crowd looks a little different, younger, a little nerdier. They're holding up signs that say things like "Über Brides Treats their Employees Like Shit," "Pay a living wage, Über Brides!" and the universal red slash NO sign with "ÜBER BRIDES" inside. Claire catches up to me, the camera still slung over her shoulder. "That's my son Elliott over there," she says, pointing. "He and his friends organized this for us!"

As the fire trucks pull up to the curb, and the firefighters shove their way through the crowd with all of their equipment and heavy gear, I realize a news truck has pulled in right behind them. A reporter and a cameraman hop out and begin to set up on the sidewalk.

"No!" Janet finally screams, the blood-curdling sound of her voice somehow carrying over the sirens, the chanting protestors, and the confused wedding guests. "No, you cannot film here! This is a private ceremony!"

"This is a public sidewalk, lady," the reporter says, looking over his shoulder before turning back to the camera.

My phone begins to ring in my strapless bra. No, a dress like this doesn't have pockets. I hate whipping my phone out from my cleavage in the middle of a classy affair like this, but I don't really have much choice. "Hello?"

"Hello, is this Hannah Robinson?" a calm, feminine voice questions.

"Yes, ma'am, how can I help you?"

"Are you the acting manager at Über Brides?"

"Yes. Why? Is there a problem?" I glance over at Jason, and he shrugs as if to say he has nothing at all to do with this phone call. I'm not entirely sure I believe him.

"Ma'am, we're calling to let you know the strip mall where Über Brides is located is currently on fire. We're waiting for the fire department to respond, but apparently they are on another call right now. We've requested back up, but—"

I pull the phone down and look Jason in the eye. Surely he didn't—

TWENTY-ONE

Hannah

I don't believe I've ever experienced such a range of emotions as I have on this day. Everything from uproarious amusement to utter joy to extreme panic all in a matter of a few hours. As the skeleton crew of Operation Wedding War faithful finally make their way back inside the building, I can't believe the mess that's been left behind.

"It's a good thing we have a clean-up committee," I tell Jason, who is right by my side.

We've just returned from the scene of the fire at Über Brides. It didn't start in our store but in the pizza joint next door. Apparently one of their ovens caught on fire, and then things went downhill from there. Jason swears he had nothing to do with it, but it seems a little too coincidental, if you know what I mean.

"It's an act of God!" my mother insists, and my grandmother nods in agreement. These two ladies and my father have been in the building this whole time, sitting here talking with Meric and Lindy, and also—surprisingly enough—the Fridays.

"What, the fire?" I question as we move through the mess toward the bridal table where the seven of them are gathered.

"The fire, the crazy stunt you just pulled off, the fact that you and Jason found each other," Mama answers, her eyes sparkling with tears. "It's just all too wonderful to be a coincidence. 'And we know that all things work together for good to them that love God, to them who are called according to his purpose.'"

"Romans 8:28," my father finishes her Bible quote.

I look back and see that Claire, Jack, Jean-Marc, Chris, Brynne, Drew, Sonnet, and Jason's cousin Hank are all gathered behind us in a semi-circle.

"Amen!" they all shout in unison.

"So what happened to Janet and Company?" Claire asks. "Did they leave?"

"After the fire at the store and the protests and the breaking news that two Über Brides employees have been caught embezzling money from the company, not to mention the video that Jean-Marc shot and the footage of the protests tonight going viral, uh, yeah, I think it's safe to say they're not coming back to Rehoboth Beach," Jason proclaims.

"Hallelujah!" Daddy shouts.

"To God be the glory!" Mama adds, and my radiant grandmother with a stylish hat perched upon her head shouts, "Amen!"

"We need to plan a celebration!" Claire decides. "The whole town came together, and we should all be proud of ourselves. Small, local businesses—one, national chain stores—zero!"

"Hear hear!" Jean-Marc shouts, raising his glass. Everyone joins in the toast with shouts and cheers.

"What an incredible night." I shake my head, still amazed we pulled it off. My gaze flashes over to Jason. "But the fire here was fake, right?"

"Oh, yeah, totally fake," Drew pipes up. "I'm not gonna let my place burn down. That was fake smoke, fake alarms...the whole nine yards. A little theatre magic, as we like to say in the biz. A friend at the fire department doesn't hurt either." He gives us a wink as his wife wraps her arm around his waist with a proud smile.

Lindy and Meric jump up from their spots at the table. Lindy is still looking completely radiant in her sparkly ball gown, but Meric has loosened his bowtie. "You know what wasn't fake?" Lindy shouts, stretching out her hand to show off a glittering diamond and a matching band. Meric lifts his hand in the air. "Nope, not fake at all."

"What?!" I turn to Jason. "Did you know about this?"

"No, of course not!" he fires back.

"Oh my gosh, guys, you actually got married?" Sonnet gushes. "It's almost as crazy as our wedding, honey!" With her arm still around her husband's waist, she smiles up at him after he bends down to plant a kiss on the top of her head.

"Well, not this afternoon at the fake ceremony,"

Lindy explains with a giggle, "not with those stupid vows. But after everyone dispersed, Mr. Robinson took us back out to the beach in the moonlight, and we exchanged real vows...the traditional ones."

"Oh my god, that's fantastic!" Claire's face is beaming as she sweeps her gaze over two of her best friends. "Were your parents able to stay for it?"

"Yes," Lindy confirms. "Then Jason's brother Russ took them home because it was getting too late for them, and my dad needed to take his medication. Russ'll be back in a few minutes."

Oh, I'd wondered what had happened to him. Everyone laughs and offers their congratulations to the happy couple. A few people complained that they were sorry to miss it, but Meric and Lindy assured us that after all the public attention today, they were more than happy to have a private ceremony. And that they'd be having a huge reception in the coming weeks.

I walk over to my father and wrap my arms around his neck. "That was really sweet of you to do, Daddy."

"Well, I know true love when I see it," he tells me. "I've been in the wedding biz for a long time."

"Morris, Liz, it's been a pleasure catching up with you after all this time," Jason's dad says as he stands up from the table. "I probably better get home. I'm pretty sure my cardiologist would frown upon all the excitement I've had today!"

"Wait, there's just one more surprise before you go," Jason pipes up. "Hopefully your heart can handle this, Dad!"

I hear a high-pitched bark from the back of the room and turn to see Russ and his wife Jen, who is carrying their adorable-but-very-sound-asleep daughter in her arms. I notice Russ is holding something, and after he bends down for a moment, a streak of coppery brown floof rushes toward me.

"Dolly!" I exclaim, patting the little dog Jason erroneously calls Tank on the head. That's when I notice something attached to her collar. I turn around to see Jason pace toward me with the biggest grin I've ever seen on his face.

He kept telling me he had tricks up his sleeve, so who knows what else he could possibly have up there at this point. He's already blown me away and then some. As soon as I reach him, he drops down to one knee, removes the box I spotted from Dolly's collar, and every single nerve in my body freezes. The only reaction I can make is a breathy gasp as my hands fly to cover my mouth.

He unfurls his fist and opens up the tiny box, revealing a beautiful round diamond ring with a halo of twinkling diamonds encircling it. "Hannah," he says, his eyes bluer than I've ever seen them.

I don't glance around because my gaze is completely locked on him, but as quiet as it is, I imagine everyone is as frozen and shocked as I am. Even Dolly, apparently. I tune them out, and all the mess, and all the crazy chaos of the day. The only thing breaking through my impenetrable bubble is the sound of his voice.

"I know it's only been six weeks since you came back into my life, but I feel like I've known you forever. I very nearly have, and if not you exactly, then the idea of you. I could have never imagined all those years when I was growing up when I heard my family members grumble about the Robinsons that they were talking about my—I hope—future bride and in-laws."

A soft, stunned giggle rises up from the crowd around us, but I barely notice.

"It only took spending a couple hours with you to know that everything I'd heard about the Robinsons was wrong. There was no way your family could be bad, not if they produced you. You are the most beautiful, smartest, amazing woman on the entire planet, and the only thing I want to do in this world right now is plan a real wedding with you as my bride."

Tears are streaming down my face as I hear Daddy shout, "Well, Sugarbunz, whatcha gonna say?"

I stretch out my hand so he can place the dazzling engagement ring on my finger. "I've never been more certain of anything in my entire life, Jason Friday. My answer is yes."

He sweeps me up in his arms and twirls me around while the rest of the crowd around us bursts into applause and Dolly barks her approval. I was just thinking that I was sad our wedding war was already over. Even though we came out victorious, it is still a little bit of a letdown to know all of our planning and scheming is over.

Only it's not. The war might be over...but our wedding season has just begun.

THE END

See all the Romance in Rehoboth books at www.klmontgomery.com.

The series will continue with Book #6, Stage Mom.

ACKNOWLEDGMENTS

Thank you to my very patient husband, who first heard my idea for this book around two years ago when we were coming back home after a concert (I think?) Since then, I have rambled on and on about it a lot, and he has always offered me great ideas, some of which I actually used! (hehe) It seemed like I was never going to get to this book on my list of books to write, and then once I did, I wasn't sure I could do my original idea justice. But now that I've just finished my first edit, I'm sitting here crying because I think maybe I did do it justice. I hope you will think so too.

I'm also so grateful for my proofreader, Tina Kissinger, and my personal assistant, Jared Gallant, who are always cheering me on and sticking to crazy deadlines to help me achieve my dreams. A big thank you to my Angels, especially those of you waiting on pins and needles for this book. You know who you are!

As you know, I never hesitate to make personal statements in my books, whether it's advocating for body positivity or just reminding people to be decent human beings about polarizing political issues (I'm speaking, of course, about my book *The Light at Dawn*.) *Wedding War* is my attempt to remind you how important it is to support local and small businesses.

I am the owner of my own small business, Mountains Wanted Indie Author Services & Publishing. I'm not sure that non-business owners really understand the blood, sweat, and tears that go into running your own business. I have not, in the past, been as good as I should be about supporting my friends' businesses or local businesses in general, but writing this book symbolizes my new and ongoing commitment to do so. I hope that after reading Jason and Hannah's story, you'll make a commitment to support small and local businesses as well. You just did by buying this book, so you're already well on your way!

Thank you to all my readers for helping me keep my dream alive.

XO,

Krista

ABOUT THE AUTHOR

K.L. Montgomery grew up in Greencastle, Indiana, and studied psychology and library science at Indiana University. After a career as a librarian, she now writes novels and wrangles three sons and four cats at her home in rural Delaware, which she shares with her husband and the aforementioned creatures. She has an undying love of Broadway musicals, the beach, the color teal, IU basketball, paisleys, and dark chocolate.

Visit K.L.'s website at http://www.klmontgomery.com and sign up for her newsletter.

You can also follow her in these locations:

Facebook: www.facebook.com/greencastles

Facebook reader group (shared with Phoebe Alexander pen name): www.facebook.com/groups/PhoebesAngels

Twitter: www.twitter.com/klmontgomery8

Instagram: www.instagram.com/k.l.montgomery

Bookbub: www.bookbub.com/authors/k-l-montgomery

ALSO BY
K.L. MONTGOMERY

The Light at Dawn

No matter how dark the night, hope is reborn at dawn.

It wasn't just her marriage that crumbled in the wake of unspeakable tragedy, it was her entire life. Even though five years had passed since she lost Evan, Angelia White was still picking up the pieces. Getting involved in a cause she could pour her broken heart into was just another part of the healing process.

The wounds were too fresh for Mark Lyon to keep his grip on reality. Everything he thought he knew and believed was obliterated when he lost Ashleigh, along with his heart. The only way he could pick up the pieces was to fight for a way to prevent any other parent from ever suffering such merciless pain.

Two heartbroken parents enduring the darkest of nights.
Two wounded souls waiting for the light at dawn.

Given to Fly

Can you break your vow if it's the only way to save yourself?

Annelise thought her purpose in life was to get married

and have babies. That's what her family and church have been telling her since she was a little girl. But when her marriage turns rocky, and she struggles with her weight and infertility, she fears the childhood dream thrust upon her will never come true.

Then she meets Trek Blue, the father of a little girl in her preschool class. After losing his wife to cancer, he's moved to Indiana with his two young children to seek a fresh start. In need of a friend, Trek is immediately drawn to Annelise, who begins to think of him as a confidant and bright spot in her otherwise dreary life.

But when the two grow close enough to raise eyebrows, she is forced to make a choice. Will Annelise honor her faith, family, and wedding vows? Or will she spread her wings and fly away?

Green Castles

Inspired by true events, Green Castles tells the story of three former high school best friends; Jennifer, Kat, and Michelle; who are reunited in their small Indiana hometown when Jennifer's daughter loses her battle with mitochondrial disease. Through a series of flashbacks to their teen days in the late 1980's/early 1990's, the three women learn about resilience, forgiveness, and just how strong the bonds of family and friendship truly are.

Fat Girl, Romance in Rehoboth #1

Fresh ink on her divorce papers.
A new job on the horizon.
40 is right around the corner...

The time is ripe for reinvention, and Claire Sterling is tired of being the Fat Girl. With the help of her gay best friend, therapist, a new fitness regime and lots of wine and snark, Claire sets out to find her happily ever after.

Will she get the body and the man of her dreams, or is she forever destined to be the Fat Girl?

The Flip, Romance in Rehoboth #2

Aunt Penny's beach house isn't the only thing getting flipped in this hilarious romantic comedy!

Andrew and Sonnet hated each other in high school. Always rivals for the best grades and top academic honors, there was no love lost between these two nerds after graduation.

Ten years later, they're both named heirs to property in coastal Delaware after the passing of its owner, Penelope Vaughn, who was Andrew's great aunt and Sonnet's beloved next door neighbor growing up. The quaint beach cottage needs serious work before going on the market.

Andrew and Sonnet are both willing to bury the hatchet in exchange for drills and saws, especially since they stand to make a pretty penny with the beachfront property, which will finance Drew's dream of opening a business and Sonnet's plan to earn her doctorate in astrophysics. But when they face a multitude of home improvement obstacles, will these two former adversaries be able to pull off a successful flip?

Or did Great Aunt Penny have something else in mind

all along?

Plot Twist, Romance in Rehoboth #3

If you think what's happening on stage is entertaining...you should see what's happening BACKSTAGE!

A brand new show is coming to Rehoboth Beach! Jack and Claire (yes, THAT Claire) Reilly have written an original musical, and they have the perfect cast. Plus, there's pirates. Who doesn't love pirates?

Meric Chandler is a neurotic, introverted accountant by day, but at night he transforms into a magnetic leading man whose voice makes all the girls swoon. Just getting over a divorce, he has sworn off backstage romances. After all, that's how he met his EX wife.

Lindy Larson prefers to stay behind the scenes, but her girlfriends convince her to audition for a new local theater production. She has a stunning voice but plans to blend in as much as possible, which isn't easy to do when you're the awkward plus-size girl with two left feet.

While backstage romances are to be expected, they don't usually shut down the entire production. But you know what they say: the show must go on!

Badge Bunny, Romance in Rehoboth #4

Looks can be deceiving in this hilarious enemies-to-lovers romcom complete with a shocking secret hobby, a heavy metal playlist, and an uninvited wedding guest!

Chris Everson has a pretty sweet life: a great job as a state trooper, lots of buddies to hang out with, and he lives at the beach. What could be better? But he's harboring a secret--a secret that doesn't fit with his whole tough guy cop persona. He's gone to great lengths to keep his secret from his guy friends AND the women he dates.

Brynne Miller's job as an ER doctor means she's always meeting cops. In fact, she's dated so many that her friends call her "Badge Bunny." But she will never date Chris Everson. Nope. Not a chance. He managed to piss her off within two seconds of meeting him...and first impressions are everything.

Aren't they?

WEDDING WAR

43628308R00176